State

A BDSM Mé

By Lucy Felthouse

This book is a work of fiction and any resemblance to persons, living or dead is purely coincidental. The characters are productions of the author's imagination and used fictitiously.

Cover art by **Studioenp**.

Chapter One

Alice took a deep breath, in through her nose, and out through her mouth. Repeated the process once more. Then, realising she could sit there all day doing it and not feel any calmer, she forced herself to step out of the car and close and lock the door.

She bent to peer into the wing mirror of the vehicle and checked her hair and make-up. Satisfied, she straightened, then turned on her heel and walked quickly across the driveway to the great house before her nerve failed her.

Davenport Manor was currently open for visitors, so she walked in through the front door and was met by a smiling elderly lady.

"Can I help you?" the woman asked kindly.

"Yes, please." Alice twisted her hands together nervously. "I'm here to see Mr Davenport. I'm here for an interview for the property manager's role."

"Yes, of course," the woman replied, "that's today, isn't it? Follow me; I'll take you to Mr Davenport's office. But just hang on one second."

She ducked through the doorway into the next room and spoke with her colleague. Alice guessed she was letting her co-worker know she'd be gone for a few minutes. A few seconds later, she was back. "Okay, follow me, Miss…"

"Brown," Alice said, then fell in behind the other woman as she led her to Mr Davenport's office, and the interview that could change her life forever. It was hardly surprising that she was shaking like a leaf.

Alice quickly became disorientated as their journey took several twists and turns along dim corridors—their blinds drawn to protect paintings, tapestries, and furniture from the sunlight—and up a flight of stairs. She had a few seconds to worry about finding her way if she was lucky enough to get the job, then her guide stopped outside a door and turned around.

"Here you go, Miss Brown. Mr Davenport's office. Good luck with your interview."

Alice smiled and thanked the elderly woman, then smoothed down her skirt, which also conveniently wiped the nervous sweat off her hands. She stood up straight, gave herself a mental pep talk about being more than qualified for the role, and knocked on the door.

"Enter."

Alice knew that voice could only belong to Jeremy Davenport. The posh accent, and the fact he'd said "enter" instead of "come in", screamed money and an upper-class upbringing. Alice was suddenly desperately aware of her broad Midlands accent and lowly background, despite the fact she'd worked her backside off to get into a decent university in order to gain a Bachelor of Arts degree and then a Master's degree. No matter what she sounded like, or what her past was, she had all the skills necessary to do the job she was about to be interviewed for.

She realised she'd left rather a long pause before opening the door, and turned the handle before the occupants of the room thought they were about to interview some kind of simpleton who couldn't follow a simple instruction.

Fixing a polite—but hopefully not inane—smile onto her

face, Alice stepped into Jeremy Davenport's office. Her first thought—which certainly did nothing to help her nerves—was *good God, he's hot*.

Jeremy sat behind a desk, with a heavily pregnant woman sitting beside it. Alice barely noticed the woman. All she saw was him. A man with cropped dark brown hair, hazel/green eyes, a jawline you could cut bread with, and lips that looked capable of doing incredibly wicked, sexual things to a woman. Or a man. Alice had no idea what his sexuality was, but she found herself hoping he liked women.

She chastised herself. Even if he did like women, he wouldn't go for someone like her. A Plain Jane, with mousy brown shoulder-length hair, blue eyes, average height and above average weight. Alice had always known she'd never be a supermodel, so she'd worked extra hard academically, and here she was. About to be interviewed for her dream job.

The sinful lips she'd been so admiring twisted into a grin, and Davenport stood and made his way around the desk with his hand held out. She pushed her inappropriate thoughts to the back of her mind and made herself focus on the present, and the two people in the room that she had to try her best to impress. Her smile was still in place, and it widened as she took the hand that was offered to her, and shook it.

"Jeremy Davenport," he said, the posh accent even more obvious now. He indicated the pregnant woman, and said, "This is Erin Clarke, our property manager, who's due to go on maternity leave very soon." He let out a small laugh. "But I guess you've already worked that one out for yourself."

"Alice Brown. Thank you so much for seeing me." She nodded politely, then moved over to the woman, who was awkwardly attempting to manoeuvre herself out of her chair. "No, no, don't get up," Alice said, holding out her hand. The other woman sank back down with a sigh of relief, and gave Alice a wry grin.

"Sorry, I'm not so light on my feet as I once was." She took Alice's hand and shook it, then dropped her hand to her swollen belly. "It's lovely to meet you, Alice."

"Likewise."

Davenport indicated the chair that had been placed in front of the desk. "Please, sit. Would you like something to drink? Tea, coffee, hot chocolate, juice, water?"

She thought how strange it was to be offered such a variety of beverages. Usually it was tea or coffee, and that was pretty much it. It pissed Alice off no end because she didn't like either of them, and she usually felt like a nuisance for asking for something else. She decided to make the most of it.

"Um, juice would be great, thanks." She crossed her fingers it wasn't grapefruit. Anything but bloody grapefruit. Horrible stuff.

Davenport nodded, then asked Erin what she wanted before picking up the telephone on his desk and calling through their requirements. He thanked whoever was on the line before putting the receiver down.

"Okay," he said, sliding a manila folder from the edge of the desk to the space in front of him. He opened it and spread some of the contents out so he could see them all at once. "Let's get started, shall we? As you know, the role is a nine-month contract to cover Erin's maternity leave. So the successful candidate will be taking on of all her responsibilities, but we've deliberately timed the appointment of the temporary staff member to cross over with Erin's time off, so they will have a couple of weeks working alongside her, in order to learn the ropes. And of course, when Erin goes to have her baby, they'll always have me around to answer any questions."

He smiled, and Alice's heart rate increased. God, but the man was arresting. And it was more than just being easy on the eye. He had a way about him, a charisma, that made her want to listen to him talk all day. He could recite the telephone book and she'd probably still find it interesting. Or perhaps it was just his sexy accent that was doing funny things to her. Either way, she wished that Erin wasn't in the room so she could crawl into Jeremy's lap and beg him to do naughty things to her.

Alice could scarcely believe her own salacious thoughts. When did she become a sex addict? Oh yes, that would be when she'd walked into the room and laid eyes on Jeremy Davenport for the first time. Damn it, what was he doing to her? Up until now, she'd gone without sex for so long that she'd forgotten what it was like—and didn't really miss it. Now, what she wanted most in the world was to get this job so she could work alongside the delectable Mr Davenport for nine months. And get into his bed. Maybe.

It was only when she became aware that Jeremy and Erin were looking at her strangely she realised she hadn't responded to his last comment. For fuck's sake! The man was melting her brain. Normally she was the epitome of professionalism and a very desirable potential employee, but something about Jeremy Davenport was making her crazy. If she didn't pull herself together, they'd think she was some kind of useless ditz and she'd have absolutely no chance of getting the position—the step up she so badly needed to become a full-time, permanent property manager somewhere after she'd completed her contract at Davenport Manor.

"Yes, understood," she forced out, trying hard to shove her wayward thoughts somewhere where they couldn't distract her and make her look like a total fool in front of these people. "If I'm lucky enough to be chosen, I'd definitely make the most of the time with Erin. And I'm a fast learner. Plus I've been researching this type of role, so I know quite a bit about what's involved, anyway."

Now she was babbling. And sounding like she was showing off. Bugger. She needed to hit the right balance of knowledgeable without coming across as a know-it-all.

"Yes..." Davenport looked down at the pieces of paper in front of him. "It says here that this is the type of role you've been aiming at throughout your education and subsequent employment. You're very enthusiastic in your covering letter. And, unless I'm much mistaken, this is genuine enthusiasm, as opposed to the gushing missives people often send when they just want a job, any old job."

Alice nodded frantically. "Yes, no—no, you're not mistaken. My parents always called me a history buff. When I was younger, I liked things and places with a history, and as I got older it grew into a particular passion for old houses and their grounds. Now all I want to do is take an historical property, make it shine—figuratively, of course—and get as many members of the public in as possible and show it off. People need to see these places, or they're missing out on a vital part of British history."

She looked, wide-eyed, at Davenport to watch his reaction to her outburst. She couldn't help it—she genuinely was being interviewed for the job of a lifetime that could make her career, and she needed Davenport to know how badly she wanted it, and how determined she was to succeed. She thought she saw a smirk tugging at the corners of his lips, then he covered his mouth with his hand for a moment and cleared his throat.

"Yes, Miss Brown," he said, assessing her with a sober expression, "it's obvious how much you want this role, but you have to remember that this property isn't just history. I still live here, and I'm in the present."

The response was on the tip of her tongue. "And that's what makes this place so fascinating! Its history goes back hundreds of years, and by now things have often gone wrong—families dying out or losing all their money, and the properties end up going derelict, being made into private hotels, or get taken over by The National Trust. But you're still here. Davenport Manor has a past, a present, *and* a future, and they're all connected."

"Quite," Davenport said, dryly. There was no sign of a smirk on his face this time. "But I haven't lost the family money yet."

Alice's cheeks flamed. "Oh—oh! I didn't mean… that is, I'm not implying—"

Davenport held up a hand. "I know what you meant, Miss Brown. Your enthusiasm for this role is unquestionable. But Erin and I have some questions, if that's quite all right with you?"

She nodded again, and before she had chance to think up a suitable response, a knock came at the door. Their refreshments had arrived. By the time the member of staff had passed the drinks out to the three of them, then carried her tray back out of the room, Alice's heart was in her shoes. She'd fucked this up, royally. First she'd raved like a lunatic, then she'd made a stupid comment about aristocratic families going broke. Talk about insulting the boss. Potential boss. Well, ex-potential boss.

Erin hadn't said a word beyond her greeting, and yet Alice was convinced that the older woman also thought she was a lost cause. She was so screwed, it was all she could do not to put her head in her hands and rock back and forth like the crazy person her interviewers clearly thought she was. It was the job opportunity of a lifetime, and she'd blown her chance.

It didn't matter what her answers were to any of the questions. Pigs would fly before they gave her the damn job.

What a prize idiot she was.

Chapter Two

The second time Alice arrived at Davenport Manor, she wasn't nervous. She was stunned, almost into numbness. After the absolute shocker of an interview where she'd come across as a bumbling buffoon, she'd been convinced she was out of the running for the role. After all, who would employ someone to do such a pressurised, important job if they couldn't handle a simple interview?

And yet, they'd taken her on. She was so surprised she'd actually thought she was asleep and dreaming the whole thing when she received the phone call. But after a pinch hard enough to make her yelp and leave a bruise, she came to her senses. And rejoiced. She'd done it. Alice was temporary property manager of Davenport Manor. She'd be working alongside Erin for a couple of weeks, but then the place was hers. Sort of. As far as she was concerned, baby Clarke couldn't arrive soon enough.

Alice walked through the front entrance, beaming as she realised it would be the last time she did that. After today, she'd arrive earlier—today she'd been required to turn up at ten, as the doors opened to the public, giving Erin time to brief the staff beforehand—and use the side door that all the other staff members and volunteers did.

Thankfully, Erin was waiting inside the entrance hall for her. She'd doubted she'd be able to find Davenport's office again, but she didn't want to come across as stupid by having to ask, so Erin's presence was a lifesaver.

The older woman smiled as she caught sight of her, and

waddled forward with her hand stuck out. “Hi, Alice.” They shook hands, then parted.

“Morning, Erin. How you doing?” She nodded at the other woman’s belly.

“Oh, you know,” Erin replied, spreading her hands across the stretched expanse of skin and stroking it through her loose dress, “Okay. Not brilliant. Ready to have him or her out, so I can feel like myself again. But then I guess that won’t happen for a while either, because I’ll be suffering sleepless nights, sore and leaky nipples… you know the drill.”

She laughed, and Alice nodded because it was what was expected. But really, she didn’t know, and she now knew more about pregnancy and motherhood than she cared to. Ugh. She was a career girl through and through, and babies weren’t on her agenda for the foreseeable future, maybe never. If a maternal streak suddenly appeared, perhaps she’d reconsider. But at thirty, she doubted it would now. Not to mention the fact that she was missing a vital ingredient required for baby-making in the first place—a man.

As if by magic, a man appeared. Jeremy stepped from the gloomy hallway to their left and smiled at them. “Hello, ladies. Glad to see you here, Alice. I’m looking forward to working with you. I’m sure you’re going to be a valuable asset, more than capable of running the place when Erin here embraces motherhood.”

“Th-thank you, Mr Davenport. I can’t wait to get stuck in. I’m going to be like a sponge for the next couple of weeks, soaking up all the information Erin gives me.”

As soon as the words were out of her mouth, Alice’s face

grew hot. What a stupid thing to say; she sounded like a child! It was just as well she'd signed the contract they'd biked over to her the previous week—at least they couldn't sack her for saying something daft. Why on earth did the man have such an effect on her? His proximity meant she could smell his no doubt very expensive aftershave, and fuck, was it intoxicating. It certainly didn't help her state of mind.

"Please," he said, seemingly unaware of what a prat she was being, "call me Jeremy. Now, if you'll both excuse me, I've got some errands to run, but I'll catch up with you later. Have a great day, ladies." He gave a little bow and swept out of the front door, leaving Alice wondering how a man could still look so aristocratic when wearing jeans and a T-shirt. Designer labels, she guessed. They had a way of making someone look loaded even if they were on the breadline.

Both women watched him go, then Erin turned to Alice and indicated she should precede her. They walked down a beautiful wood-panelled corridor, their shoes tapping loudly on the floorboards, then out of the open door at the end of it and into the gardens, which Alice could immediately see were glorious, the plants and flowers all in their summer splendour.

"I brought us here so we can look around before the visitors come out. The first lot will be in the house for at least an hour—though realistically most people are in there around two—then they'll head into the gardens. So we've got a bit of alone time."

Alice couldn't help but wonder why on earth they needed alone time. But before she could dwell on the question, Erin answered it.

"I'm glad Jeremy's headed out for a bit, because I want to fill you in on some insider knowledge that you won't get from him. Not verbally, anyway." She fixed Alice with a serious look.

Alice frowned, then nodded. "Go on."

"I just want to make you aware of Jeremy's, er—habits, that's all. As you've no doubt noticed, he's a good-looking, charming, clever man with a healthy bank balance. And let's just say he uses that particular arsenal to his full advantage."

Alice remained silent, so Erin continued. "I'm not sure how to put it politely. What I'm trying to say is that he has his fair share of women. He's a bit of a playboy. He and Ethan, who's the head of security here, are best friends—have been since university days—and they've left quite the trail of broken hearts behind them. The two of them are very close."

Alice nodded. "Okay, thanks for the information, but I'm not quite sure how this affects me." She widened her eyes and gasped as a thought occurred to her. "You haven't…"

Erin waved her hands hastily. "No, no! God, no. I'm 100 per cent faithful to my husband, and I plan to stay that way. Now if I were single," she wiggled her eyebrows saucily, "then that would be a completely different matter!"

Alice giggled along with Erin, whose face then took on a serious expression. She said, "I'm just pre-warning you, is all. It might not affect you at all. But you know the saying, forewarned is forearmed."

Alice nodded thoughtfully. "Thanks. But I doubt he'd even

look at me that way, never mind anything else."

Just as Erin opened her mouth to respond, a group of visitors came out into the gardens, halting their private conversation. They turned their talk to work as they explored the remainder of the beautiful and perfectly-manicured grounds and then headed back indoors.

Room guides and visitors were in plentiful supply as Erin gave Alice a guided tour of Davenport Manor, so they never got chance to reconvene their delicate conversation.

Towards the end of their tour, a handheld radio that Erin had been carrying crackled to life.

"Erin?" Jeremy's voice came over the radio waves.

Erin held the receiver to her mouth and pressed the button. "Yes, Jeremy?"

"Is Alice still with you?"

"She sure is."

"Great. Could you ask her to come and see me in my office in ten minutes?"

"Absolutely. That will just give us time to check out the last room."

"Thank you. Over and out."

Alice looked incredulously at Erin. "Over and out? People really say that? I thought it was just in films."

Erin smirked. "It's his idea of a joke. Comes in pretty handy, though, because at least I know he's done talking."

Ten minutes later, Alice was walking along the landing which led to Jeremy's office. As she grew closer, she saw the door was ajar, and heard that someone was in there. More than one person, in fact. She frowned. Surely he wasn't in a meeting with someone else, having asked her to come and see him? Or maybe someone else was there to talk to her? She shrugged and stepped up to the door.

Just as she raised her hand to knock, a sound came from within the room that sounded distinctly un-meeting-like. A feminine moan, followed by a giggle, then the murmur of a masculine voice. Skin slapping against skin. More moans.

He couldn't be…? Alice refused to believe it. There was no way he could have summoned her to his office then managed to squeeze in a quickie before she got there. Yet the noises coming from the room continued, growing ever more frantic, building into a crescendo.

She stood, motionless, outside the door. More voices, urgent and breathless. Alice had no idea what to do. Should she leave and come back later, running the risk of Jeremy thinking she couldn't be punctual? Or should she knock and act as if she hadn't heard anything? They'd have to pull themselves together, and quickly, if they wanted to avoid her seeing them in the act.

Alice could scarcely believe she was having to make the decision in the first place. Despite Erin's warning, she hadn't expected her playboy boss to be screwing someone in his office in the middle of the day. Especially with the door open! It was terribly unprofessional, and anyone could have caught them. Fucking.

As the word flitted through her mind, Alice fell to thinking of Jeremy, fucking. Naked—or possibly semi-naked—and glorious, thrusting into… who? Alice had no idea. Was it one of the staff? Doubtful, unless Jeremy had a thing for the over-sixties.

What did his cock look like? Was it big? Thick? Long? There was no doubt in Alice's mind that he knew what to do with it—otherwise how would he be such a successful and notorious ladies' man? Women talk, and if he was crap in the sack word would soon get around, and Jeremy would have to look further afield to get his rocks off.

She'd remained stationary as her mind wandered, gazing unseeing at the door. So when an exaggerated cough, clearly designed to gain her attention, came from behind her, she let out a little squeal and clutched her chest in fright before spinning around to see who'd crept up so stealthily on her.

Chapter Three

Her assailant was an extremely tall man—he had a good few inches on Jeremy—and stood with his arms folded, looking at her very sternly. He wore black trousers and a white short-sleeved shirt, and a black tie. His attire, and the fact he had a radio clipped to his belt, led Alice to draw the conclusion that this was the infamous Ethan Hayes—Head of Security. He certainly had the perfect physique for someone working in that area. His height, coupled with the bulging muscles she saw peeking from his shirt sleeves, were intimidating enough to scare away any potential thieves. His biceps looked damn good, but she was sure they weren't just there for show.

His intense gaze made her want to run for the hills. After a few seconds of staring at each other in silence—a silence even more deafening since the office's occupants had now gone quiet—Alice finally plucked up the courage to speak. "C-can I help you?"

The giant of a man unfolded his arms and took two strides towards her, which brought him very close, almost invading her personal space. She resisted the temptation to shrink away from him, then quickly regretted it when her nostrils caught his masculine scent. The sexy smell did funny things to her already-heightened libido, and she began to realise something. Not only was Ethan Hayes tall and well-built, he was bloody gorgeous too. She now understood how the Terrible Twosome of Jeremy and Ethan had left such a trail of broken hearts behind them. No sane woman would get either of those two into bed and then let them go willingly.

His words interrupted her reverie. "I could ask you the same thing. Is there any particular reason you are loitering outside Mr Davenport's office?"

She didn't yet have a name badge pinned to her top like all the other staff, therefore Ethan clearly thought she was a member of the public snooping somewhere she shouldn't. Before she had chance to deny it, he turned and pointed down the corridor, away from Jeremy's office. "Come with me please, miss. I think we should talk in my office."

Alice remained rooted to the spot, her mind in a whirl. She was torn between doing what the six-foot-something giant was commanding her to do, and going to see her boss, like she'd been asked to do around twenty minutes ago now. She'd barely been in the place half a day, and she'd screwed up, which never usually happened. Throughout her education she'd been a straight-A student, never in trouble, and once she'd entered the workplace, she'd been the model employee.

How had she ended up in this crazy situation? The way Ethan was looking at her made her feel like a naughty child being sent to the head's office—and of course, she'd never experienced that. Except to receive praise and certificates for her academic achievements and impeccable attendance records, that was.

It entered her head that Jeremy should have heard the exchange between her and Ethan, given they were standing right outside his door. Perhaps he was still "busy", albeit much more quietly, and hadn't even noticed they were there. Therefore, he was probably also too distracted to realise more than ten minutes had passed and she was meant to be in his office right there and then.

She made her decision, and followed Ethan as he strode purposefully down the landing. Minutes later, they entered the staff corridor. Ethan stopped in front of a door. He pulled a key from the loop hanging from his belt, then unlocked the door. He pushed it open and gestured Alice inside, his expression stony.

She gave a nervous smile and walked into the room, her eyes immediately drawn to the bank of monitors on one wall, which kept flicking through a rotation of images from each room and corridor in the house. A thought started to form in her mind, but before she could pursue it, Ethan spoke. "If you'll take a seat please, miss, I'll be back in a few minutes."

Without giving her a chance to respond, he pulled the door shut. Alice heard the unmistakable sound of a key twisting in a lock, followed by retreating footsteps. Her mouth dropped open. He'd locked her in! For God's sake, he obviously thought she was some kind of criminal. Was he going to call the police? She hoped not. Despite the fact that she hadn't done anything wrong, it would be incredibly embarrassing for everyone concerned. Already was, actually.

A little smile tweaked at the corners of Alice's lips. Ethan had probably gone to fetch Jeremy. He'd soon realise his mistake—and would get a severe telling-off when it became apparent that he'd locked the new property manager in his office. She wondered if she'd be allowed to stay for the no doubt heated discussion, or if she'd be sent away. She crossed her fingers for the former, though she knew it was unlikely. A professional would never discipline his staff in front of others. But Jeremy had just proven that he wasn't overly professional by having sex with someone in his office while someone else waited outside for a meeting he'd bloody well called! Then there was the fact that the two men were good friends. So perhaps the telling-off would never happen.

Alice shrugged. There was no point trying to guess what would happen next. She'd just have to wait and see.

The low electrical buzzing sound emanating from the monitors drew her attention, and the thought that had begun to form in her head before Ethan had locked her in came to fruition.

Surely, if Ethan had been sitting in here since the house opened this morning he'd been looking at the monitors? It was his job, after all. And if so, he must have caught at least a glimpse of her and Erin making their way through the house together? He wouldn't have been able to hear what they were saying—it seemed the cameras were capturing images only, not sound—but it would have been pretty obvious that Erin was showing her around. As Head of Security, Ethan must have information on all of the staff and volunteers on the books at Davenport Manor. Plus he was Jeremy's best friend. Surely he must have known she was starting today? It was a pretty vital piece of information; one Alice thought would be of the utmost importance for the man in charge of security.

Her eyes narrowed. If that were indeed the case, then why on earth had Ethan claimed not to know who she was and locked her in his office?

The sound of two lots of footsteps approaching shook Alice from her thought process and she knew she'd have the answer to her questions very soon. This had to be Ethan returning with Jeremy.

A click came from the door, then the handle turned and the men entered. Alice's heart sank when she saw that Jeremy looked just as stern as Ethan, if not more so.

"Miss Brown," he said, before taking a seat across the table from her. Ethan sat next to him.

Alice nodded in response, all the while worrying about how serious he sounded, and how they'd reverted to last name terms again. He was obviously seriously pissed off, but she wasn't quite sure why. She'd had a legitimate reason for being outside his office, and an even more legitimate one for not going in—she wasn't some kind of voyeuristic pervert, after all.

"I'll cut straight to the chase. Ethan—Mr Hayes—tells me that he found you loitering outside my office."

"Bu—"

He didn't let her speak. "Outside my office," he continued, "listening at the door when I was in there with an… acquaintance."

It wasn't one of the staff then, she thought with relief. She only had to be embarrassed around him then, not any of her other colleagues. But he thought she'd been listening. Her expression turned indignant and she opened her mouth to deny it, but Jeremy held up a hand.

"I'm not done. What you did was unprofessional and a serious encroachment on my privacy. I thought better of you, Miss Brown."

Surely he had to realise the reason she was there was because he'd summoned her? Or did he have short-term memory loss? Early onset Alzheimer's? Very early in his case.

His tirade—for it was a tirade, despite the fact he wasn't shouting—continued. "Your behaviour was immoral and unacceptable. I should fire you right now—and on your first day, too!"

Finally, he fell silent and raised an eyebrow, as if waiting for her to speak. Alice immediately broke the silence, before he changed his mind. "But Je—Mr Davenport, I was only there because you asked me to come and see you. I didn't—I wasn't… Please don't fire me. I'll do anything."

She stopped short of sliding to the floor and begging on her knees. She was desperate to keep this job, but somehow she sensed that Jeremy wanted her to be apologetic, not pathetic.

It seemed she was right. He gave a thin smile. "*Anything*?"

Alice nodded eagerly, her enthusiasm waning as Jeremy's smile grew wider and wider, until she thought it would touch his ears. He obviously had something in mind. Her imagination took flight. God, what was he going to make her do? Hold a spider, or a snake? Run naked through the gardens? Each possibility she conjured up was worse than the last, and she shut down the train of thought before she drove herself completely crazy.

He slid one of his hands from where it had been resting on the table and it disappeared from view. The angle of his arm and the fact he leant forward a little showed that he was getting something from the back pocket of his jeans. Sure enough, a second later he slapped a folded piece of paper onto the table and began to open it up. Once done, he flattened it out with his palms and flashed another smile at Alice before turning towards Ethan, who grinned back at him.

Alice frowned. Ethan hadn't looked at the piece of paper and yet he was returning his friend's smile, so he obviously already knew what the contents were. A trick they always played on new staff, perhaps?

She didn't quite buy that idea. She couldn't see the men joking around with most of the people who worked or volunteered at Davenport Manor. From what she'd seen of them so far, they were stoic, old, or both. Somehow, she didn't think that Jeremy and Ethan would expect Mrs Jenkins to run across the garden naked. Not that anyone would want her to. Alice suppressed a shudder.

Mind you, why the hell would anyone want *her* to run across the garden naked? Granted, she had nice big tits that didn't swing around her knees, but the rest of her was certainly nothing to write home about. If someone was being polite, they'd call her curvy, or Rubenesque. Otherwise, they'd just say fat, plump, chubby, or overweight. Or chunky. She'd heard them all.

The sound of Jeremy clearing his throat brought her back to the present, and he picked up the piece of paper and held it in front of him as if he were about to start reading. He caught her gaze, and there was something dancing behind his eyes that she felt like he was trying to hide from her. Excitement? Whatever it was, it was *intense.*

"This," he said in his Queen's English accent, "is a list I made not long after my father died and left me Davenport Manor. Sadly, it's been neglected for the eighteen months since then. But now, Miss Brown, I think it's time to give the list an airing, and start checking things off of it."

"W-why's that?" What she really meant was *why now?*—but she didn't want to say that in case this whole thing was nothing to do with her and she put the idea in his head that it could be.

"Because, my dear, of you."

Bugger. So much for her not being involved.

"You see, in case you didn't know, Ethan and I are best friends. We've known each other since we were at university, and have shared all sorts of experiences. This list holds some of the plans I have for Davenport Manor, plans that Ethan and I would like to execute sooner rather than later."

Ethan and I? He kept saying that. Was he trying to tell her they were a couple or something? And they needed help making the manor into more of a home? But why her? And why now? Surely Erin could have helped out with that. She hadn't been pregnant for eighteen months, after all. And then there was the fact that Jeremy had been with a woman in his office. No, she was pretty certain neither of them was gay. Or even bisexual—she just didn't get that vibe from them.

"Okay…" she said warily, wondering what on earth he was going to come out with next.

"Well, I've been thinking about it, and after talking it over with Ethan just now, we've decided you're the perfect person to help us."

Alice waited. Raised her eyebrows expectantly. Why couldn't he just say it?

"This list," he continued, putting it back on the table and spinning it around so the writing was the right way up for her, then sliding it in her direction, "is a collection of, how should I put it, challenges that I'd like to complete. Challenges set in and around Davenport Manor. My way of enjoying the house to the best of my ability, and thoroughly putting my stamp of ownership on it. After all, it's mine, so I can do whatever I like."

He jerked his head in the direction of the list, and Alice dropped her gaze to the piece of paper, pulled it in front of her, and began studying the sentences that were printed on it. She'd barely finished the first bullet point before she let out a gasp. She scanned a couple more bullet points to be sure she hadn't misunderstood, then snapped her head up and looked at Jeremy, wide-eyed and open-mouthed.

He gave a casual smile and nodded towards Ethan. "I told you, we've shared all sorts of experiences, many of which included women. Especially women. We like to take them to bed—or wherever—and pleasure them until they can't take any more. Then do it again anyway. The thing is, up until I owned the manor, we couldn't possibly bring ladies back here. My father would never have approved. So we weren't able to act out some of our most potent fantasies. Now, though, we have this huge brick and timber playground at our disposal, and we plan to make the most of it."

The twinkle in his eyes told her that the emotion she'd suspected earlier was, in fact, excitement. He was incredibly excited about this challenge thing—which, having looked at the first part of the list, was basically kinky sex in multiple locations—and a glance at Ethan told her that he was too. They were both gazing at her intently, and looked not unlike two little boys begging for sweeties.

Except it wasn't sweeties they wanted. It was *her*.

Clearly unable to stand the lack of response any longer, Jeremy spoke again. "Look, you said you'd do anything to keep your job. You do this thing for us, and I'll forget all about your little indiscretion, and when you leave here after your contract is up, you'll have the best reference anyone could ever ask for. I've also got some friends in high places, so I'll do what I can to assist your next career move too."

Alice was speechless. First she'd been railroaded by the challenge thing, and now he was attempting to blackmail her! If she didn't do it, he'd sack her, and any future career prospects would be screwed, to say the least. She had no doubt that his friends in high places could also scupper her next career move, as well as assist it. But if she did as he asked, he'd do everything he could to ease her climb up to the next rung on the career ladder. All she had to do was, basically, fuck and be fucked by Jeremy and Ethan in a variety of locations throughout Davenport Manor and its gardens.

She looked at each of the men in turn. It couldn't be that bad, could it?

She wouldn't be the first woman to shag her way to the top, and she wouldn't be the last. There were certainly worse things a girl could do to advance her career. Or worse men, anyway.

Chapter Four

Alice twisted the controls on the shower, waited until the temperature was right, and stepped in. The spray pounded down on her, and yet she still turned around and upped the water pressure until it was almost like having a deep tissue massage. She wanted it—no, *needed* it—to send her into the usual state she reached while in the shower. Which was supremely relaxed and prone to good ideas.

A good idea would be gratefully appreciated right now. Anything that could help her work out this situation she'd got herself into. And preferably find a way out of it without wrecking her chances at career advancement.

She closed her eyes and tilted her head back, enjoying the feel of the spray against her scalp and face. If she stood there long enough, she wondered, would all the crap inside her brain be washed away? Unfortunately, the more she tried to forget about it and empty her mind, the more it plagued her, which was annoying, as her "eureka" moments usually came out of the blue, rather than when she actively thought about them.

So many things didn't add up about the Jeremy and Ethan situation. Now she was away from the two men—who, combined, made her even more tongue-tied than Jeremy by himself—she could think through the sequence of events. And no matter how she tried, she could not make sense of it. How on earth had a simple summons to her boss's office turned into a telling-off and an attempt to blackmail her into some outlandish kinky sex challenges? It didn't compute—she hadn't done anything wrong! Even if she *had* been loitering at the door, it was hardly a sackable offence.

The more Alice thought about it, the more she became convinced there was some kind of conspiracy going on. The pair of them had set her up, and now she was being forced to play their depraved games. Not that she actually knew what most of those games were. After the conversation in Ethan's office, where she'd remained shocked and silent, Jeremy had given her the list and sent her home.

She'd left the room without a word and driven back to her rented flat in a daze. Once there, she'd stripped and headed straight into the shower. Now she was cleaner than clean and starting to turn all wrinkly, and she was still in a state of shock and confusion.

Alice turned the taps off, then stepped out of the shower, grabbed a towel and wrapped her hair up in it. She slipped into the dressing gown that she'd retrieved from the hook on the bathroom door, then headed for her bedroom and the pile of stuff she'd dropped on the floor when she undressed. She retrieved the slightly creased sheet of paper from the depths of her handbag and sat down on her bed to read it.

When she reached the end of the list, she felt much worse. She'd only read the first few items at Davenport Manor, and they were bad enough. But the tasks grew steadily more depraved. There was nothing illegal—she didn't think—but there were things she'd never have dreamed of doing, or trying. Not that she had anyone to try them with, of course. There hadn't been anyone for a long time. And now two extremely sexy men had come along and declared that they wanted to do those things with her. She scarcely believed it—

both that Jeremy and Ethan wanted to have sex with her, and that they had all those kinky scenarios in their fantasy bank. For Alice was certain it wasn't just Jeremy's list. Ethan must have had a hand in it too, as he appeared as eager as Jeremy to start checking things off it.

It wasn't the sex that bothered Alice so much. She wasn't a virgin, for heaven's sake; just someone who hadn't had a lot of experience. Or orgasms, for that matter. It was the stuff that went with it. Some of it was quite extreme, and she just didn't know if she could handle it.

After much soul-searching, Alice concluded that she would *have* to handle it. It was only nine months—if the games lasted that long—and then she could leave and move on to bigger, better things, things she'd been working her arse off for years to achieve, and forget all about the debauchery at Davenport Manor.

It wouldn't be all bad, she supposed. She'd had sex with worse-looking, less charming men, after all. Many of them hadn't really known what they were doing, either. So great sex with two supremely attractive men was most welcome. Particularly the part about sharing her. Now that sounded really rather good. Two pairs of hands on her body, two mouths, two hard cocks…

Though she wasn't sure about taking them both… inside her at the same time. Whether it was the more traditional way, or back… *there*, she was pretty sure it would hurt and be altogether unpleasant. Maybe she could talk them out of it, or suggest using her mouth on one of them instead? She shook her head. She was getting rather ahead of herself now. Crossing that particular bridge when she came to it was the best plan of action, she surmised. No need to worry about all that now.

With a sigh, she put the list on her bedside table. Then she dried herself, pulled on her pyjamas, and brushed her hair before climbing into bed. It was still early, but the shock had quashed her appetite and she didn't feel like doing much, especially not making dinner. And she definitely didn't want to tidy her flat or do the laundry. She'd just curl up with a good book for a while instead, and then catch up on some sleep. Everything would look better in the morning—wasn't that the saying?

Alice was a couple of chapters into a riveting thriller when her mobile rang. She heaved herself reluctantly out of bed and retrieved the phone from her bag.

Fuck. It was Jeremy. She rolled her eyes. What the hell did he want? She guessed there was only one way to find out. Mentally reminding herself that he was her boss and, therefore, "What the hell do you want?" would not be an appropriate way to greet him, she pressed the green button and lifted the device to her ear.

Thinking of her career, and Jeremy's influential friends, she smiled, knowing it would be evident in her voice, and said, "Hello?"

"Alice?" They were back on first name terms, apparently. Something in his tone piqued her interest—was he flustered? "It's Jeremy. I'm sorry to bother you so late, but I didn't want to spring this on you in the morning. I just had a call from Erin's husband. She's gone into labour and they're on their way to the hospital. So, basically, what I'm calling you to say is, as of now, you're in charge. You're acting property manager of Davenport Manor."

Alice didn't know whether to laugh or cry. Naturally it was brilliant that Erin's baby was on the way, and that she was now in her dream job, albeit temporarily. But she'd lost out on Erin's tutelage, even though she'd admitted to herself she didn't really need it. More worryingly, there was now no buffer between her and the two men. She knew they'd never speak of their proposition in front of the other woman, so she was hoping to have her around a little longer in order to avoid the no doubt very awkward conversations that were looming in her future.

Perhaps, though, the fact she'd been thrown in the deep end meant there'd be no time to talk about this challenge thing? She'd be so busy doing her job that having unrelated meetings would be a terrible waste of resources. And she couldn't see Jeremy letting that happen. It was obvious that Davenport Manor meant everything to him and he wouldn't see it run into trouble, not for anything.

"Excellent," she said, aware of the fact she'd been silent for a few seconds as her mind raced. "A little sooner than we all expected, but I'm confident that I'll manage. I look forward to the challenge."

As soon as the words were out of her mouth, she wanted to grab them and stuff them back in. Why on earth did she have to pick that particular phrase? Maybe he wouldn't notice.

His soft laugh told her otherwise. "Do you now? Well, you're not alone there. The next few months are going to be quite the wild ride. Hopefully in more ways than one."

So he hadn't taken that as a yes, thankfully. She was pretty much there in terms of decision making, but it couldn't hurt to make them wait a little longer. Couldn't hurt her, anyway. With any luck it would drive the men crazy. And it would make her feel a tiny bit better, given what she'd be subjected to if she did say yes.

Who was she kidding? She was going to say yes. Just not tonight.

As coolly as she could, she replied, "Thank you for calling to let me know, Jeremy. I'll come in early in the morning to get started on things. I don't have a key yet, though, so would you arrange for someone to be there to let me in? At around 7.30?"

Hell, it would kill her to get up so ridiculously early, but she genuinely wanted to try to get her head around everything, and that meant starting as soon as she could. And if it inconvenienced Jeremy or Ethan, or both, all the better. She was determined to get her digs in now, although admittedly her tiny jibes were the equivalent of cutting a lawn with a pair of nail scissors.

Equally coolly, Jeremy replied, "That's fine. I appreciate your enthusiasm and work ethic. Either Ethan or I will be there to let you in. And we'll make it a priority to sort you out with your own set of keys and a name badge. Then we'll get the staff and volunteers briefed on the situation. But there's nothing to worry about. Everyone's really helpful and will give you all the support you need. That includes Ethan and me."

She frowned, wondering at the swift change from playful and flirtatious to consummate professional. Perhaps he'd realised that whatever happened with their kinky games, he still needed someone to do her job; otherwise he'd see his inherited empire come tumbling down around him. Alice concluded that, despite his occasional misdemeanours and his fixation on the damn challenges, he was actually a very nice guy, and genuinely wanted her to succeed.

"Thank you. That means a lot. Will that be all?" She spoke as warmly as possible, not wanting him to get the wrong idea and think she was being sarcastic.

"U-uh, yes, thank you." He seemed taken aback by her sudden friendliness. "I just wanted to give you a heads up. I'll see you tomorrow then."

"Yes, see you tomorrow. Thanks again, Jeremy. Goodnight."

"Goodnight."

She hung up before he had chance to say anything else. There was no way she was discussing anything that was not related to work tonight.

Though, she thought a little glumly as she set her phone down on top of the list and crawled back into bed, everything was intrinsically linked, wasn't it? The challenges themselves weren't work-related, but the reason she would be doing them certainly was.

She fell asleep wondering just how far most people would go to secure their careers, and how many of them were subjected to such indecent proposals.

Chapter Five

At 7.28 a.m. the next morning she rapped on the side door of Davenport Manor, and almost fell through it when it was pulled open suddenly. Righting herself, she glared up at Ethan, who was grinning like the Cheshire Cat.

"Good morning, Alice," he said brightly—far too brightly for this time of the morning, Alice thought—and moved his huge frame to one side so she could enter the building.

"Morning," she grumbled, before marching past him and heading for the staff room. She'd been in such a rush to leave for work that she'd gulped down a bowl of cereal and a glass of apple juice before dashing around to get washed and dressed. Now she was regretting it. The last thing she wanted to do was face Jeremy and Ethan in her still rather sleepy state. She'd indulge in some alone time in the staff room and hope it woke her up.

A little while later she was settled into the comfiest chair in the staff room, cradling a mug of hot chocolate and slowly starting to liven up. She wasn't particularly relaxed as she knew Jeremy and Ethan were around somewhere, but no other staff would be here for at least another hour, so she had time to enjoy the peace and quiet. And enjoy she did, because she knew it would be the only opportunity she'd have all day. Especially given what she was going to do next.

When she finished her drink, she washed and dried her mug and put it back in the cupboard, then grabbed her handbag and made her way to Jeremy's office. She didn't bother knocking on Ethan's office door as she passed it. Somehow she knew he wouldn't be there.

Her suspicions were confirmed when she walked up the corridor towards Jeremy's office. The door was wide open and both men were studying something laid flat on the desk. They were facing her, and when she grew closer they seemed to sense her at the same time and snapped their heads up to look at her. It was unnerving.

She pasted on the most convincing smile she could and walked into the room. "Morning, gentlemen."

Ethan gave a nod, obviously of the mind that one "good morning" was quite enough. Jeremy, on the other hand, gave a smile that put her in serious danger of melting into a puddle of lust on his antique rug, and said, "Good morning, Alice. Thanks again for coming in so early. We have lots to discuss and sort out. Baby Clarke's early arrival has put us at a bit of a disadvantage, hasn't he?"

"He?"

"Yes," Jeremy said with a frown. "Didn't you get my text message?"

Alice shook her head, and dug her hand into her bag to retrieve her phone.

"I sent it at about 1 a.m. Erin's husband sent me the vital information. A baby boy, seven pounds, dark hair, blue eyes. They're calling him Arthur, and both mother and baby are doing great."

Glancing at the phone screen, Alice saw that Jeremy had indeed texted her in the middle of the night. She must have been so fast asleep she didn't hear it, and this morning she hadn't even thought to check—she'd just tossed the device into her handbag in her haste to get to the manor.

"Sorry," she said, "I didn't hear the text arriving. And I didn't check this morning."

Jeremy shrugged. "It's okay. It's hardly part of your job description. I just thought you'd want to know, that's all."

"I did—I mean, I do want to know. I was just in a rush to get here this morning. Of course I'm happy for her and her husband, and glad everything went okay. I'll do a collection amongst the staff, if that's all right? Send a card, some flowers and a gift?"

He smiled and gave a nod. "That would be wonderful. I'll happily chip in. Now, are you ready to get down to business?"

Her jaw dropped at his forward phraseology, then she caught herself. He meant business as in *her job*. She'd thought the two men were dirty-minded, but it seemed the longer she spent around them, the more perverted she herself became. That didn't bode well for the next nine months.

She nodded and took a seat in front of the desk. Ethan came around and settled into the chair beside her, and Jeremy sat in his usual place.

"Now," she began before they discussed anything else and, more importantly, before her nerve failed her, "I just want to say this before I start. I accept the challenge, okay? Providing you're still willing to keep your part of the bargain, of course."

Jeremy quirked an eyebrow, and Ethan's gaze burned into the side of her head. She wriggled restlessly in her chair.

"Of course I'll keep my side of the bargain, Alice. I'm a man of my word. I take it you've had time to study the list thoroughly?"

She inclined her head.

"Good. Now I'm glad you brought that up because I was going to ask. Ethan and I have been discussing something else we believe will be beneficial all round."

"What's that?"

"Your flat. You're renting on a temporary basis to coincide with your employment here, correct?"

Alice nodded again.

"Well, I'm not sure if you're aware, but there's plenty of room in Davenport Manor's private wing. I wondered if you'd be interested in moving into one of the spare rooms? Rent-free, of course, which will save you money, and it will mean you'll be amongst friends. Plus you'll only have to cook one out of three nights."

She frowned. He wanted her to move into the manor? She could see the logic in terms of saving money, and she wouldn't have to commute—not that her rented flat was far; that's why she'd chosen it—but did he just want her to be at his beck and call twenty-four hours a day, seven days a week? Was that his ulterior motive?

"I'll settle up with your existing landlord, so you're not out of pocket."

Alice had to stifle a laugh. Did he seriously think her only misgivings were to do with money? She supposed any other woman, given the chance to be with the two men and to live in the manor, would snatch his hand off, so her reticence must be giving him cause for confusion. Clearly he needed a little education. "Thank you. But

I can't help but wonder if your offer is simply work-related, or whether it is linked to your… games. You think I'll be available for your convenience whenever you like?"

Jeremy gaped, looking like she'd slapped him in the face. After a few seconds, he regained his composure. "No. That's not what it's about at all. I thought it would help you out and make your life easier. Our *games*, as you call them, are purely voluntary for all concerned, and will only take place when they are convenient for the three of us."

A blush heated Alice's cheeks, and she looked at her lap. He hadn't sounded angry, as such, but he was certainly disappointed.

"I'm sorry. But given all that's happened, I'm sure you can understand why I might think that."

Now it was his turn to nod. "Yes, I suppose I can. But rest assured that is not what my offer is about. I'm not saying it won't be easier with you living here, but it's not my intention to make you into some kind of live-in sex slave."

She remained quiet, her mind racing. The kinky sex games aside, it was a generous offer. He was going to let her live in his house for free. And what an incredible house. It was her ultimate fantasy come true—she didn't just get to run the place, she got to live in it! She could pretend she was lady of the manor.

"Okay, yes. Thank you. It's very generous of you. But perhaps you could just clarify something for me?"

A slight incline of his head indicated that she should go ahead.

"What did you mean about only cooking one night out of

three? Do you have a cook or something?"

She trusted he'd be smart enough to realise she didn't mean the one who ran the kitchens for the public restaurant.

Jeremy shook his head. "No, of course not. I may be well off, but I'm just a normal man, not a member of the Royal Family. Ethan and I take it in turns."

"E-Ethan lives here too?"

She felt the weight of both their gazes on her. Then Ethan spoke. "Yes. The place doesn't just need security in the day, you know. If an alarm goes off or a window gets smashed, there's got to be someone around to deal with it."

Turning to him, she said, "Yes, that makes sense. I just didn't really think about it. About both of you living here."

"It's not a problem, is it?" Jeremy said coolly.

She twisted back to face him. "No, not at all. It's just this is a bit overwhelming, is all."

"You're right." He smiled gently. "I'm sorry. You really have been thrown in at the deep end, and we're giving you even more to deal with. Let's make it easier for you. You agree to the challenges, you agree to move in. Everything else that's not strictly work related can wait. Let's get you sorted out with a set of keys, your name badge, and everything else you need to greet your visitors when the doors open at ten. Yes?"

Flashing him a grateful smile, she thanked him. Immediately, he and Ethan set about getting her ready and prepared, and by the time 8.30 rolled around, she was ready to give her first staff briefing. She couldn't help but feel nervous.

"Don't worry," Jeremy said. He stood beside her at the staff door, ready to let everyone in. Squeezing her shoulder, he continued, "You'll do great. Everyone will love you, and as I said, we'll all do as much as we can to help. Within a week, you'll think you've been here forever."

Within a week, she thought, *everything could have changed. We could have started on the list of kinky challenges and I could be ready to run screaming for the hills, reference or no reference.*

As it happened, by the end of the day, her nerves had evaporated. Everyone had indeed been very kind, helpful, and informative, and already she felt much more equipped for the next day. But of course, there was the evening and night to get through first. Jeremy and Ethan wouldn't expect her to jump into the games right away, would they? She doubted it. Despite their eagerness to get her to agree, they'd also been very eager to make sure she was settled in, and happy. They didn't seem the type of guys to force her into anything. Physically, anyway. The blackmail was a different matter altogether. And one she'd condoned by going along with it. So anything that happened now, she'd essentially agreed to. What woman wouldn't, anyway? Sex with two gorgeous men in return for career advancement? It was a pretty good deal, really.

Chapter Six

Ethan came to her as she was closing the house for the evening. The staff were excellent when it came to matters of security, but she couldn't help but double-check that all windows and doors were closed and locked, blinds and curtains were drawn, and so on. She didn't find a thing wrong, and she turned to Ethan with a genuine smile.

"Okay?" he asked.

"Okay."

"I've just come to see if you need some help moving your stuff? I don't know how much you've got, but I'm pretty good with heavy lifting."

I bet you are, she thought. *But you'd struggle to lift me, I'd wager.*

"Um, all right." She hadn't been betting on moving that day, but she came to the conclusion she might as well get it over and done with. She was currently running on the adrenaline of a successful first day and figured tiredness might hit her at a later date. So now was as good a time as any.

"Great, thank you. Is Jeremy coming? All hands on deck and all that?"

"No, he's gone grocery shopping."

Alice scrutinised Ethan, expecting him to confess that he was pulling her leg. But he appeared to be deadly serious. She couldn't believe it. She knew Jeremy had said he was just a normal guy—who cooked, even—but she just couldn't reconcile the image of him walking around a supermarket pushing a trolley. Packing carrier bags, loading the car. It was just awfully domestic, and seemed like something the owner of a manor house would leave to someone else. Or at the very least, get it ordered in.

"Hasn't he heard of internet shopping?"

Ethan shook his head. "He won't do it. He likes to choose the vegetables and meat for himself. Well, what veg doesn't come out of the kitchen gardens, anyway. He's a fussy bugger, that's for sure. He only likes the best."

So what on earth is he doing with me, then? she thought. *What is either of them doing with me?*

"Ready?" he asked. "Got your keys? Or would you prefer to go in my car?"

"No, it's fine. We'll go in mine. I don't want to put you out any more than I already am."

"You're not putting me out. I offered to help, didn't I?"

He took her arm and they headed to the private exit. Ethan set the alarm, then closed and locked the door, and they heard a couple of reassuring beeps before they moved to Alice's car. He dashed in front of her, stood by the driver's side door, and grasped the handle.

"What?" she said, confused. "You want to drive?"

"No," he replied solemnly. "I'm waiting to open the door for you."

Alice bit the insides of her cheeks to avoid either laughing or gaping. Was this guy for real? He wanted to hold the door open for her?

"Um, thanks." She pressed the relevant button on her key

fob; the doors unlocked, the lights flashing in the approaching darkness. She smiled as Ethan did as he'd promised. Sliding past him and into the seat, she glanced up and observed him as he watched her tuck her legs into the footwell before closing the door carefully behind her. By the time he got around the back of the car and folded his huge frame into the passenger side, she'd started the engine and selected reverse gear.

"Ready?" she said.

He pulled his seatbelt across his chest and clipped it in to place, then gave a nod.

She gave him a hard stare. "Are you mocking my driving before I've even started?"

He held his hands up. "No! It's just routine. I always put my seatbelt on before I go anywhere, whether it's me driving or someone else."

She narrowed her eyes, but his innocent expression remained. "Okay. I'll have you know I'm a very good driver. Not a single accident or speeding ticket in the whole time since I passed my test."

"You shouldn't say that. You might jinx it."

"God, you don't believe in all that crap, do you?"

"I dunno, really. I'm yet to be proven either way. It's like ghosts, isn't it? If I see one, I'll believe in them. If someone can prove categorically that they don't exist, then I won't believe. But for now, I kind of think that maybe there's no smoke without fire, you know? So many people believe and claim to have seen them. They can't all be crazy, can they?"

Alice drove neatly out of her parking spot and turned the car around so it was facing the exit, dropped it into first, then second gear as she drove down the driveway. Out of habit, she glanced across to the junction which led out of the visitor car park, despite knowing all the visitors had gone home long ago. She hoped. It was rumoured that someone had got incredibly lost in the maze once upon a time. The worst part was they'd come on the bus, so there was no tell-tale vehicle remaining in the car park to let them know that someone was still in the grounds. The fact that Mrs Jenkins had chosen to tell Alice the story on her first day made her think perhaps it was a joke. If anyone else had imparted the information, she would have been absolutely convinced of it—but Mrs Jenkins was adamant, so Alice didn't bother to argue.

If she was honest with herself, the woman was so stern that Alice was a little afraid of her. She certainly wouldn't dare to upset her.

She and Ethan shared a companionable silence for a while as she drove to her flat. It meant Alice had time to be affected by the proximity they shared. She imagined she could feel the heat from his body down her left-hand side. But that was ridiculous. Wasn't it? Real or imagined, he was making her hot. She was relieved when they reached their destination and she could put some distance between them.

"So," he said, following her dutifully to the door of her ground-floor flat and gesturing her in front of him when she opened the door, "how many trips do you think we'll have to make?"

"Honestly? One, I suspect. None of the furniture is mine, and as it's a temporary role, the vast majority of my stuff is in storage.

It’s mainly clothes, books, and essentials.”

“Essentials?”

They were in the hallway. Alice had turned to answer his question, which meant he could now see the blush that crept across her face. “Yes. You know, toiletries and stuff. Girly things.”

“Oh, I see. Girly things. You mean teddy bears?”

She took a playful swipe at him. “No. Not bloody teddy bears. Right…” She went to the hall cupboard and pulled out a stack of collapsed cardboard boxes, then crossed the room to the dresser and retrieved a roll of brown tape. “You’re on box-building duty. You build ’em, I’ll fill ’em. Then you lug ’em to the car. Put those muscles of yours to good use.”

He looked down, twisting his arms at the elbow so his muscles flexed. Then he peered back up at her with a wicked smile. “Oh, don’t worry. I intend to put them to *very* good use.”

Alice threw the roll of tape at him, forcing him to break eye contact as he scrabbled to catch it, and disappeared into the kitchen. She stood where he couldn’t see her through the open door and sucked in a breath. Was he flirting with her? She chastised herself for being surprised. It was obvious he fancied her—though she had no idea why—otherwise he wouldn’t have been into the whole challenge thing. But she’d thought the arrangement was strictly a three-way thing, whether both men were actively playing, or one was playing and one was watching. Either way, she hadn’t expected any sexual advances from either man while she was alone with him.

She sucked in another breath in an attempt to steady her nerves, then moved over to the fridge.

"Do you want a drink?" she called.

"What do you have?"

Alice noticed the tone of surprise in his voice. Surely it wasn't because she'd offered him a drink? No, it'd be because she sounded so cool and collected after dashing away from him, she wagered.

"Not much, actually. I don't drink tea or coffee so you'll have to make do with juice, squash, or water."

"That's fine," he replied. "Squash would be great, thanks."

His voice sounded closer, and Alice turned to see him standing in the doorway. He hadn't changed his clothes before leaving the manor, so he looked every inch the security guard. Big, fast, and mean. Except Alice knew he wasn't really that mean at all. Not to her, anyway. Teasing, perhaps, but definitely not mean.

As though he'd read her mind, he smiled—which transformed his face and made him look very un-scary—and stepped into the kitchen. Crossing the floor in a couple of strides, he stood right in front of her, effectively trapping her between his bulk and the cupboards behind her. The heat she had imagined coming from his body when they were in the car was absolutely for real now. He inched forward until a drawer handle dug into her back.

She had to tilt her head to look up at his handsome face—now complete with the intense expression she was becoming so used to. She actually gulped. She wanted to say something, ask what he was doing. But her mouth was dry, and she couldn't seem to get her voice-box to respond either. Besides, it was pretty obvious what he was doing, wasn't it?

Seducing her. Perhaps he'd planned it all along, since before he'd offered to help her move her stuff from the flat to the manor.

Before she could linger on the thought, Ethan did something that abruptly chased it, and all other thoughts, clean out of her head.

He leant down and kissed her. She saw it coming, as he had to lean quite a way to bring his towering frame down to her level. He slanted his lips over hers. They'd barely touched when Alice's hormones started racing around her body at a million miles an hour and a trickle of pussy juice soaked into the gusset of her knickers. The action suddenly made her very glad she'd worn nice underwear that day, as it seemed Ethan would be seeing it—and soon.

Ethan's mouth against hers was sexy and sublime, but she still couldn't help wondering why he hadn't yet deepened the kiss.

She didn't have to wonder for long. Ethan pulled away from her with a guttural groan, gave her a look that made her feel like a juicy slab of meat to a starving predator, then put his large, strong hands on her hips. Alice frowned, then let out an involuntary squeal as he hoisted her onto the work surface. She threw her arms around his neck to steady herself as he shifted her, and once she was safely settled, she couldn't see any reason to move them.

Tangling her hands in the chin-length hair she'd been dying to touch since she met him, Alice drew in a deep breath. The scent that hit her nostrils was a combination of shampoo and a delicious aftershave. She pulled in another breath, savouring the smell of him. Then she moved in to kiss him.

He accepted her kiss eagerly, his hands on her arse sliding her to the edge of the work surface so their groins pressed together.

A powerful zing of lust rushed through her body as his impressive erection crushed against her vulva, albeit through her thong—her skirt was up around her waist by now, pushed there by the necessary spread of her legs to accommodate Ethan's hips—and whatever he was wearing. Tight-fitting boxers beneath his trousers, she hoped. Or nothing at all.

Suddenly, nothing at all was her preferred option as Ethan slipped his tongue between her lips and sent her libido climbing to oh-my-God-I'm-so-horny-fuck-me-right-now heights. The touch of his tongue against hers sent searing heat scorching through her body before centring in her pussy. God, she wanted him. She couldn't remember the last time she'd been so fired up, or craved a man so much. Because it was him she wanted, not just sex. The tall, handsome Head of Security, who was on the verge of reducing her to a teeming mass of female hormones with his tongue in her mouth and his hands on her arse, massaging and squeezing her buttocks.

She pulled away and gasped, sucking in a lungful of air.

A tiny line appeared between Ethan's brows. "You all right?"

Alice nodded, not quite up to speaking. Instead of attempting to find the words to tell him how she was feeling, she decided to show him. She grasped his left wrist and guided him between her legs, using her other hand to pull the gusset of her thong to one side.

A glint appeared in Ethan's eyes, and without hesitation he took the elaborate hint. His long fingers slipped past her already-swollen nether lips and touched the sensitive skin there. He gasped, and Alice looked down in alarm, then back up to Ethan, a question in her eyes.

His eyes were dark with desire. "You're just so wet, is all. I didn't think it was possible, but you're making me even harder." He grabbed her free hand and pressed it to the stiff length which threatened to burst from his trousers.

Now it was Alice's turn to exclaim. And because her mind and body were befuddled with lust, she said something she'd never have said otherwise. "Hmm. I'm very wet and you're extremely hard. Perhaps we should do something about it."

Ethan raised his eyebrows, then gave a wicked smile. "You know, I think you're absolutely right. Bedroom?"

Alice shook her head. "Bollocks to the bedroom. I want you right now, here." She swallowed hard—had she really said that? Where the hell was this bravery, this outspokenness, coming from? But he'd already looked away and was in the process of retrieving a condom from his wallet. She silently willed him to rubber up quickly.

Mercifully, he did. She barely had time to glance at his cock before he was rubbing it up and down her slick pout, knocking against her clit with each stroke. He grasped his shaft with his index finger and thumb, bringing the head up against her entrance, and was just about to push inside when Alice choked out a hasty, "Wait!"

He looked incredibly confused until she grabbed the waistband of her thong and began to wriggle madly. After a beat, he lifted her thighs, helping her as she pulled the material past her ample bottom, then placed her gently back down on the worktop before batting her hands away and dragging the underwear down her legs and dropping them on the floor.

Alice gave a bashful giggle. "Thanks. They were in the way. Now, where were we?"

Ethan said nothing. Instead, he captured her mouth in a soul-searing kiss, meaning she couldn't see what else he was doing. And that happened to be pushing his long, thick cock between her fattened pussy lips, seeking her entrance and inching inside. She moaned into his mouth. The sound seemed to spur him on—suddenly he went from sliding gradually into her slick cunt to gripping her hips and burying himself balls-deep inside her in one desperate movement.

Alice let loose with a prolonged moan. *Fuck the neighbours—I'm moving out anyway.* She was plenty lubricated, so the sudden invasion of Ethan's cock hadn't hurt, but it had sure surprised her. Her inner walls stretched to accommodate him, and she squeezed her pelvic floor muscles almost violently, savouring the feeling of his hardness, and smirking against his lips when he groaned.

Jerking her hips impatiently, Alice was delighted when Ethan started to move inside her. He shifted deliberately, rolling his pelvis so his pubic bone stimulated her clit with each movement. She showed her pleasure at his efforts by sucking his bottom lip into her mouth, then nibbling it gently as his tongue flicked around her top lip, tickling the sensitive skin. She giggled and reached around to get a handful of Ethan's arse. Just because she couldn't see the goods right now didn't mean she shouldn't enjoy them.

And enjoy them she did. As she'd expected of a man with his physique, his bum was firm and strong, and the way the muscles flexed powerfully as he thrust into her felt totally divine beneath her fingers. She tugged at him, urging him deeper, harder, and pulled away from his mouth with a gasp as he complied, holding on to her tightly so she wouldn't slip away as he fucked her ferociously on her kitchen counter. Soon to be ex-kitchen counter.

The fact she'd been celibate for heaven knew how long, combined with her not-inconsiderable attraction to him, and his obvious skills in the bedroom—well, kitchen—department meant her orgasm approached quickly. Digging her fingernails into his buttocks in the dizzy heights of lust, she yelped as he increased the speed and depth of his thrusts. She hadn't thought that was even possible, and half wondered if the room would soon be filled with the scent of burning rubber. A laugh bubbled from her lips.

"Something funny, Alice?"

He looked serious, so she shook her head rapidly, then rested it in the crook between his neck and shoulder, and hung on for dear life as he screwed her. As her climax grew closer, she had to resist the temptation to sink her teeth into his shoulder. He was a big, tough guy and she was sure he could take it, but she didn't know him well enough for that yet. It might put him off his stride, and she definitely didn't want that.

Ethan's breathing became increasingly laboured—was he getting close to coming himself? There was no way she wanted him to finish before she did, so she moved her hand from his arse cheek to between her legs. Her clit didn't take much finding. It stood out from her body like a tiny marble, and when she touched it she yelped, it was so sensitive. She was closer than she thought.

Tilting her head back a little so her lips were close to Ethan's ear, she whispered, "I'm going to come soon. My clit feels like it's going to explode."

"Fuck," he replied, "that's so hot. But I'm glad you told me because I'm getting there too. I normally last much longer, but there's just something about you…"

Alice gave a wry laugh. "That's what they all say. Now—"

Her words were cut off abruptly as Ethan pulled her off the worktop and seated her even more deeply onto his cock. Then, in a display of what Alice thought must be superhuman ability, he started to thrust up into her. She tightened her grip around the back of his neck with one arm, and used the other to continue to stroking and fiddling with her clit as she was bounced up and down on his shaft like a ragdoll.

Soon, the blissful waves of orgasm overtook her. Pleasure coursed through her veins, and her insides wound tighter and tighter, until suddenly, the dam broke. She yelled her satisfaction into the air, vaguely aware of Ethan grunting and groaning as her spasming core tightly gripped and released his cock.

The last ebbs of the wave flowed out of her, and she was just about to flop her head onto Ethan's shoulder once more when his orgasm hit. She looked into his eyes, thrilled by the raw sexuality she saw there as he emptied himself into the condom. His shaft twitched and leapt inside her for a while until he finally sucked in a huge breath and let it out, shakily, before shuffling back to the work surface and gently lowering her onto it.

He slumped against her chest, their ragged gasps for breath

combining and sounding very loud in the silence of the room. She stroked his soft hair, quashing the urge to tug it. She decided to save that for another time. Suddenly, she was very glad there would be other times. Hopefully many of them, and with Jeremy involved too.

Now, if she could only be as enthusiastic about the tasks as she was the men she'd be doing them with, then everything would be perfect.

After a few seconds, Ethan's voice intruded on her thoughts. "I guess we should start packing boxes, eh?"

Alice sighed and pressed a kiss to his hair. "Oh yeah. Guess we should. I almost forgot about that."

Chapter Seven

After doing most of the manual labour involved in getting Alice's belongings from the car up to her new room in the private wing of Davenport Manor, Ethan said he'd leave her to it. Disappointment dropped a stone into her gut—she'd enjoyed the sight of him lifting and bending, flexing those muscles; not to mention she was still feeling pretty hot from their earlier encounter.

Heaving a pleased sigh following the toe-curling kiss Ethan gave her as he headed out, Alice closed the door. She didn't bother locking it—both men had a key anyway, so what was the point? She made a mental note to discuss privacy with them at a later date to avoid any potential embarrassment. Then she began unpacking.

After a while she came to the conclusion that some of her things simply didn't belong in her bedroom, or the en suite. It was kitchen and living room stuff.

The thought of kitchen stuff reminded her she hadn't eaten since lunchtime. Packing all the items that didn't belong in her room into one large box, she struggled out of her new living quarters with it, and went in search of Jeremy and Ethan. Conveniently, she found them in the kitchen.

"Ah." Jeremy paused in his task of unpacking the grocery shopping. "There you are. I was just going to send Ethan up to ask what you wanted for dinner."

Alice smiled. She could hardly believe her ears. Lord of the manor, Jeremy Davenport, asking what she wanted for dinner. It would have been impressive enough had he then relayed her menu choices to a cook, but the fact he was going to cook it himself…

Well, it was incredibly impressive. She'd never lived with a man—excepting her father, of course—much less one that made her dinner, so the idea that she'd truly fallen on her feet here was not surprising.

A couple of hours later, after a delicious meal and delightful conversation, Alice was in heaven. She was sandwiched between the two men on the sofa in the sitting room as they relaxed after dinner. They chatted some more, and watched TV for a while. That was until Jeremy suddenly hit the "off" button on the remote control and stood up.

Alice frowned. Was he going to bed already? She doubted it, as that was no reason to turn the TV off—she and Ethan might have wanted to continue watching it. The way Ethan tensed up beside her reinforced her suspicion that it was something else altogether.

Jeremy fixed her with a stare that could only be described as expectant.

She gulped, her mouth having gone abruptly dry. Was this the beginning of her first challenge? So soon?

"Stand up, please," Jeremy said. The command—for it was definitely a command, not a request, despite his impeccable manners—was aimed at her, but Ethan stood too.

Jeremy moved over to a dresser at the edge of the room and beckoned them over. He didn't look happy. Alice's heart sunk. Had he found out what she and Ethan had done earlier and decided he wasn't pleased about it? She didn't see how he could have done, unless Ethan had told him, and she couldn't see that happening if Ethan thought his friend would be pissed off about it. He also hadn't asked her to keep quiet, so it clearly wasn't a secret.

"Bend over the dresser, please."

Looking at him with wide eyes, she was just about to ask why when he raised an eyebrow. Fearful of upsetting him and causing him to call time on their mutually beneficial agreement, she did as he asked.

"Alice," he said softly. He moved behind her. "Press your forehead to the dresser, and keep it there."

More confused than ever, she complied, feeling ridiculous. She couldn't stop her brain from working overtime. Surely this wasn't the first challenge? They weren't in the right room—if the challenges were listed in order, that was—and she hadn't seen any of the relevant props. But she supposed there were more than enough hiding places for them in this room. One of the reasons she'd always adored old houses like this was the number of cool hidey-holes scattered throughout. They appealed to her sense of adventure.

The hem of her skirt was grasped and lifted up over her waist, exposing her. She was bent far enough over that there was no risk of it slipping back down of its own accord. If she angled her head just right, she could make out glimpses of what was happening behind her.

"I'm glad you wore a skirt today, Alice," Jeremy said. "And I'm sure Ethan is too."

The two men sniggered, and her cheeks—the ones on her face—grew hot. Not only were they staring at her bare backside, they were making subtle references to what she and Ethan had done earlier. So he did know! And, apparently, didn't mind.

"I hope you have lots of skirts and dresses," Jeremy

continued. “Because you will be expected to wear them all the time, unless one of us tells you otherwise. And what’s more, you won’t need much underwear, as when you’re wearing skirts or dresses, you will be without knickers or thongs of any kind.”

He laughed, then reached beneath her to tweak a nipple through her clothes. “Of course, you won’t be required to go without a bra. Those big tits of yours can’t be expected to behave without one to keep them in line.”

Alice was embarrassed and relieved at the same time. Going without knickers would not be pleasant, but at least no one except the three of them would know. If she went without a bra, it would be obvious to everyone. Jeremy was right; her breasts would not behave without one.

“So, shall we get started?”

Jeremy clearly required an answer to his question, but Alice said nothing. She didn’t know what to say, because she didn’t know what he meant. Get what started? The challenges? Something else?

He sighed dramatically. “I suppose I’ll have to do it myself, won’t I?”

Hands dragged at the waistband of her thong—for the second time that day—and pulled them down until they hit the floor.

“Step out of them.”

She did as she was told. It was pointless delaying the inevitable. Whatever Jeremy and Ethan had planned was going to happen, and soon. The anticipation made her shiver with delight.

Jeremy bent down and scooped up the flimsy piece of material. Straining her eyes until it hurt allowed her to watch him hold the knickers up and inspect them.

A smile crept onto his face. "Well, these *have* seen an exciting day. They're much damper than you'd expect from a normal day, anyway. Ethan get you all turned on before he fucked you, did he?"

He's not the only one who got me hot. It's just he's the only one who did anything about it.

She heard the loud noise before the rest of her senses caught up. Then red-hot pain bloomed across her arse—he'd spanked her!

"Well," Jeremy said, haughtily. "Did he?"

She'd almost forgotten the question, but managed to bite back the scream she wanted to let rip and gave him what he wanted. "Yes," she said quickly, desperate to avoid another slap. "Ethan got me very excited."

"How?"

"W-what?" He couldn't seriously expect her to describe exactly what had happened in the kitchen, could he? Especially since he'd already heard it all from Ethan.

"You heard. I want to know how Ethan got you excited."

She wracked her brain, trying to recall the exact order of events so she could relate it back without a mistake. Getting it wrong would undoubtedly earn her another slap.

Once she figured it out, she recounted the story, trying hard not to stumble over the salacious details.

When she finished, there was silence for a few seconds, then Jeremy spoke. "Well, it seems there's nothing wrong with your memory. Shall we see if mentally reliving the experience has had an identical physical response to when it actually happened?"

Fingers probed deftly at her pussy. They parted her labia—which, she realised to her mortification, were swelling again—and dipped into the warm, wet crevice within. And she was *wet.* Not quite as much as she'd been before Ethan had screwed her on the worktop, but considerably more than the normal amount of natural lubricant a woman produces during day-to-day activity. But was it down to the fact they were both staring at her naked crack, because he'd spanked her, or because she was anticipating what was going to happen next? Or all of the above? Her inexperience made her somewhat clueless, so she had no choice but to go with the flow.

The fingers—she wasn't sure which man they belonged to—stroked up and down her vulva, stopping maddeningly short of her clit each time until she itched to grab the hand and guide it to where it was needed, humping it until she climaxed, if necessary.

She didn't, of course. That would get her nowhere, and would probably result in her having to wait even longer to be touched there, if at all. Instead, she gritted her teeth and waited.

Her clit and pussy lips engorged further as the teasing continued. As a fingertip brushed against the sensitive bud at the apex of her vulva, she let out an involuntary whimper.

The hand stopped moving, and Jeremy spoke. "Horny, are we? Do you want to come?"

She attempted to nod, then realised that was impossible with her forehead pressed against the top of the dresser. Jeremy hadn't given her permission to move either, so she simply murmured, "Yes, please."

"Polite, isn't she?" Jeremy said, obviously aiming his words at Ethan. "What a fast learner. She already knows she needs to wait for permission."

"She is *very* polite," the other man said. "And responsive, too. I mean, look at how wet she is. She'd never say so, but I bet inside she's absolutely screaming for you to let her come. Or to fuck her. I'm sure she'd be agreeable to either option."

Jeremy laughed. "You're right. If I didn't know better, I'd say she was a bit of a slut."

Alice barely stopped herself letting out an indignant retort. That was what he wanted—an excuse to tease her more, to punish her. He knew damn well she was no slut. Or did he? She had, after all, had sex with Ethan on a kitchen counter after knowing him for all of a couple of days. And they hadn't even been on a date. It hardly counted though, did it? Based on the things on that damn list, even if she hadn't had an impromptu fuck with Ethan, she'd have ended up having sex with him very soon, anyway. So what did it matter?

It didn't. Jeremy was just trying to get a rise out of her. And he was going to be severely disappointed. She was no sexual deviant, unlike the two of them, but she was tougher than she looked, and she'd put up with anything and everything they threw at her. Rather than lying back and thinking of England, she'd lie back—or kneel, or stand, or crouch doggy-style—and think of her career. All she needed to do was weather this smut storm and she'd be made for life.

The hand between her legs began to move again, and she

held in a sigh of relief. Maybe she *was* going to be allowed to come. But it'd take a while if those fingers kept moving at such a maddeningly slow pace. She'd have to do something to speed things up. She decided to utilise her most powerful sexual organ—her brain.

Closing her eyes—which immediately helped her focus on the sensations in her groin—she cast her mind back to what had happened with Ethan. She recalled how he'd looked—his trousers and underwear around his ankles; his face a picture of concentration and intensity. Then she remembered the way he'd made her feel. When he kissed her, lifted her onto the work surface, touched her pussy. Fucked her…

This time, the moan was out of her mouth before she could stop it. Her eyes flew open wide with panic. Even without being able to see the facial expressions of either man, she knew she was in trouble. The hand between her legs was snatched away, and she heard tutting.

"Really, Alice. You were doing so well, too. I was going to let you come in about a minute, but now you've gone and ruined it." There wasn't a hint of humour in Jeremy's voice, and Alice screwed her face up in frustration, but only because she knew they couldn't see it. "Stand up, please, Alice."

Slowly she straightened up. A smirk tugged at the corners of her lips as gravity pulled her skirt back down, covering her up. No more exhibitionism for her. She forced her mouth into a neutral position as a hand grabbed her wrist and moved her so she was facing into the room—and towards the two men.

The smirk threatened to re-emerge as she noticed Ethan shift uncomfortably and press a hand over his crotch. He clearly had a hard-on—for the second time that day that she knew of—pressing against the inside of his clothes. Using her peripheral vision, she sneaked a peek at Jeremy's crotch area. He either had an unusually large cock—she guessed she'd find out soon enough—or he too, had an erection.

Alice was dumbfounded. She, Miss Plain Jane, had two super-hot men standing in front of her with stiff dicks. They wanted her. She resisted the temptation to pull all her clothes off and sprawl on the floor like some kind of wanton woman and beg them to fuck her. Both of them. At once, if they liked.

God, how she'd changed in such a short time. She'd gone from someone so un-sexual—if that was even a word—that she hardly ever masturbated, to a person who was almost a nymphomaniac. She blamed Jeremy and Ethan.

Jeremy, with his dark, cropped hair, expressive blue eyes, sinfully plump lips and… Fuck, he even had beautiful hands. Long, graceful-looking fingers that she suspected had just been playing with her pussy. So they probably smelled of her. Words just couldn't describe how sexy he was. And she hadn't even seen any of his body yet. It was clear he looked after himself, but he wasn't as big as Ethan in the muscle department. Regardless, she'd probably still turn into a puddle of mush at his feet when she saw him naked for the first time.

Then there was Ethan, who certainly didn't play second fiddle to his friend in the looks department. He was attractive in a completely different way. His height and muscular frame would immediately draw the eye of any straight woman in a room. Even if her husband was Brad Pitt or George Clooney. But where Jeremy was handsome in a brooding and traditional sense, Ethan was much more approachable. His chin-length brown hair, green eyes, and smile to die for would have the ladies queuing up to talk to him, especially when he flashed his dimples. But he could also give off vibes designed to keep everyone away—particularly when he came over all intense. Dependent on the reason for the intensity, of course. He'd been pretty full on at her old flat earlier, and she couldn't remember the last time a man had got her quite this hot under the collar.

Until now. She was super-hot for both of them. Two fucking men, for God's sake! Two intelligent, gorgeous, sexy men.

Suddenly, Alice was worried. They hadn't even started playing their kinky games for real yet, and she was already shocked by the strength of her need. If they carried on like this, those feelings would grow stronger and maybe mutate into something emotional, as well as sexual. And that would never do.

She couldn't afford to fall in love with one of them. That would cost her much more than her career. It would cost her heart.

Chapter Eight

The next morning, Alice woke feeling incredibly well rested. After their encounter the previous evening, Jeremy had sent her to her room. She'd done as she was told, feeling every inch the child being sent to bed for bad behaviour. As it happened, she was happy to go. Her bizarre day had left her exhausted, and she showered, then pulled on a pair of pyjamas and crawled eagerly beneath her new sheets. Everything had been so crazy that she hadn't had time to think about how cool it was that she had a four-poster bed. It wasn't an original, like the ones in the rooms of the house open to the public, but it had been designed to look like one. Alice loved it regardless. She'd pulled the covers up over her body and masturbated herself to a desperately-needed climax before falling into a deep sleep.

Now she was ready to face the world and whatever it saw fit to throw at her. She washed and dressed, then made her way down to the kitchen. She found both men in there; Ethan waiting for the kettle to finish boiling, and Jeremy munching a bowl of cornflakes.

"Morning, Alice." Ethan pulled open a cupboard and retrieved another mug. "Great timing. Tea or coffee?"

Alice had to stop herself from rolling her eyes. Ethan had forgotten she didn't like either and was just making the same offer any polite person boiling a kettle would. She shook her head. "No thanks, I don't drink tea or coffee. I'll have a glass of juice if you let me know where the glasses are. Morning, by the way." She aimed the last at both men, and Jeremy swallowed a mouthful of cereal before responding.

"Good morning, Alice. Did you sleep well?"

"Yes, thank you." She deliberately didn't ask if he had—it was a little early for dirty talk and she suspected she wasn't the only one who'd masturbated after last night's encounter.

A clink pulled her attention back to Ethan. He'd grabbed her a glass and, when she turned to him, he pointed to the cupboard he'd got it from. Nodding her thanks, she walked over, picked it up, and moved to the fridge. She poured herself some apple juice, then settled herself at the kitchen table opposite Jeremy, and sipped the cold liquid.

"So," she said, looking at him, "what's the deal with breakfast? No cooking rotation?"

Jeremy finished crunching his mouthful, before swallowing. "No, not usually. Though the Monday we close—you know, the one in each month so the house can be thoroughly cleaned—we let the cleaners in to do their thing, then come back here for a fry up."

"Sounds good. And usually?"

He held up his spoon. "Cereal, or toast. Something quick. Whatever you fancy. Just help yourself."

"Okay, thanks." Alice took another sip of her juice and stood up to go and explore the kitchen. She needed to figure out where everything was.

By the time she'd grabbed everything she needed and made herself a couple of slices of toast, both men were done with their breakfast. They stood up almost simultaneously, and Jeremy picked up his and Ethan's dirty crockery and cutlery, which he loaded into the dishwasher.

"It's almost full. Alice, would you mind grabbing a tablet out of that cupboard," he pointed to it, "and switching the dishwasher on when you're done with your glass and plate?"

She hastily swallowed a mouthful of toast to avoid speaking with her mouth full. "Sure."

"Brilliant, thank you. Could you come to my office when you're ready? There's no rush."

Alice nodded. They left the room and she finished her toast and juice in peace, before loading and switching on the dishwasher as she'd been asked. She headed back upstairs to clean her teeth, then double checked her hair and makeup before making her way to Jeremy's office.

The door stood open when she got there, and she walked right in without knocking. Jeremy and Ethan were leafing through separate piles of paperwork, but they stopped when she entered the room.

"Alice," Jeremy said with a smile. "That didn't take long. I meant it when I said don't rush, you know."

Alice shrugged. "I didn't rush. It's okay, I'm here now. So what can I do for you?"

"Ah, the possibilities." He smirked, then quickly straightened his face. "No, I shouldn't joke. Ethan and I have something utterly serious to say."

"O-kay…"

"We just want to confirm you're absolutely sure you're happy to participate in the challenges. I realise I put you on the spot with this whole thing, but I'm not a complete brute. So I'm giving you a chance to back out."

Wow, she hadn't been expecting that! Though she'd already come to the conclusion that he wasn't, as he'd put it, a complete brute. And that was in spite of the things that had happened since they'd met. But she'd already made her decision, and she had no intention of going back on it. Her eyes were firmly on the prize. The fact she'd had more sexual pleasure in the past few days than she'd had in months—years, even—helped her to stick with it too. Excellent job prospects, with the bonus of two hot men to keep her entertained while she worked out her existing contract; it wasn't exactly a hardship.

She shook her head. "No, it's all right. It's good of you to check, but I'm more than happy to continue with our agreement."

The men exchanged a look. Jeremy nodded slowly. "Excellent. We were hoping you'd say that. Now," he glanced at his watch, "we still have an hour or so before the staff turn up for today's shift. I have an idea how we can make good use of that time. Let's go to the schoolroom."

Shit. Now? She thought they'd all go on their merry ways and begin their working day. But it seemed Jeremy wanted to start playing kinky games before work—which somehow made it all the more extreme, given there was a chance they could be interrupted by an early-arriving staff member requesting admittance to the building. As well as that, Jeremy had mentioned the schoolroom, which was the location of the first task on the list. If her memory served her correctly, they certainly weren't starting her off with an easy challenge. Far from it.

She fell into step behind Jeremy and Ethan as they left the room. Silently, she followed them through the house, psyching herself up for what would happen next. By the time they reached the schoolroom, Alice was calm and confident—she was sure she could handle the task, which would bring her one step closer to her goal.

Jeremy opened the door, and Ethan and Alice walked in before him. Jeremy pulled the door to, and gave Ethan a nod. They'd obviously discussed this beforehand, because Ethan knew exactly what to do.

"Alice," he said, firmly but softly. "Bend over a desk and pull your dress up around your waist."

Alice was extremely glad she'd obeyed her orders and not worn knickers that day. She'd have been caught out very early on otherwise. After walking to the nearest desk, she did as Ethan asked.

"Good," Ethan said, moving close behind her and caressing her bare buttocks. "These won't be nearly as pale when I'm finished."

Alice was surprised that Ethan was going to be the one doing it. She'd always thought of Jeremy as the ringleader and assumed it would be him. She was about to have her arse turned red, though, so it hardly mattered who was going to do it.

Alice became aware of Jeremy moving to the front of the classroom and retrieving something from the teacher's desk. He didn't bother to hide the item as it was an integral part of the task, and therefore she already knew what it was.

A wooden ruler. Watching Jeremy—and, more specifically, the ruler's journey—from the corner of her eye, her resolve slipped a little. It was *wood*, for goodness' sake! It would hurt if a weakling swung it at her bare cheeks, never mind a muscular giant of a man. *Fuck.*

Jeremy handed the ruler to Ethan, who stroked his big hand over her exposed skin once more. It took all of Alice's willpower not to clench her fleshy cheeks. She may be nervous, but she sure as hell wasn't going to let them know that.

Both men were right behind her now, and one of them let out a low whistle. From the words that were spoken next, she gathered it was Jeremy. "That's quite a sight, isn't it? Our Alice bent over, arse in the air, slit on display. She looks…" He seemed lost for words now; a rare occurrence.

"Beautiful," Ethan supplied. "She looks beautiful, mate. My cock is rock hard already, and all I've done is stroke her bum."

Her face grew hot. They were examining her, presumably in quite some detail and, far from finding her lacking, they thought she was beautiful. And Ethan had admitted to having a hard-on caused by the sight of her naked arse and pussy.

Jeremy laughed. "And you're not the only one. I'm tempted to stick my cock inside her right now. Never mind the spanking!"

"In that case, I'd better get on with it, hadn't I?"

"Probably wise."

Jeremy stepped back into Alice's peripheral vision, presumably to give Ethan room for manoeuvre. His expression was perfectly sober, but a glance down told her he hadn't been exaggerating about the erection—it tented his smart jeans and made her wish he had just stuck it inside her, like he'd threatened to.

She didn't have too much time to think about being fucked by Jeremy, though, as she heard a small whooping noise—the sound of the wooden ruler rushing through the air—then the slap of it hitting her arse. Just as the thought that it hadn't hurt entered her head, the pain hit. A powerful stinging sensation raced in a diagonal stripe across her right cheek. Much to her pride, she didn't yell or scream. She just pulled in a sharp breath and screwed her eyes shut, breathing in and out slowly and steadily, trying to work her way through the agony.

She'd just about dealt with it when the next blow came, this time on her left cheek. Gripping tightly to the desk she was bent over, she watched her knuckles turn white, determined to let nothing but the most negligible of noises pass her lips. Again, as the white-hot fire burned through her nerve endings, she sucked in a breath and bit her bottom lip. She would not cry out. She would *not*.

Given her relative silence, it seemed Ethan thought he wasn't hitting her hard enough. Or fast enough. After the searing agony of the second blow had dulled into a more manageable ache, he started to spank her more rapidly and with increased force. Alice was incredibly glad that neither of the men had asked her to count the strokes, because there was no way she'd have been able to. The pain was just too much.

Thwack! Thwack! Thwack!

By the time the blows ceased, Alice was collapsed onto the desk, her upper body crushed against it, with silent tears running down her face. But she hadn't screamed, or yelled. Granted, she'd almost clawed holes in the desk, and bitten her lip until it bled, but still, she'd kept quiet. And for that, she was incredibly proud of herself.

As she started to come back to herself, she noticed two things—one, her pussy was saturated and ached to be penetrated, and two, Jeremy was standing right in front of her, his stiff cock in his hand.

Arching her neck to look at him, she opened her mouth when he indicated he wanted to put his prick in it. It was long, thick, and warm. Stinging arse almost forgotten, Alice moved forward to pleasure him. It was the first time she'd seen or touched Jeremy's cock, and she was determined to make a good first impression. She stuck her tongue into the slit at the top, enjoying the salty taste of his arousal, then took as much of his shaft into her mouth as she could. She stopped only when his bell-end hit her gag reflex. Deep-throating was not something Alice had ever tried and although she wanted to impress Jeremy, she didn't want to rush things and end up vomiting. That would definitely not be a good look.

She made up for her relative lack of skill with plenty of enthusiasm. Using her hands to push and pull at the edge of the desk, she bobbed her head up and down, licking, sucking and slurping at him. Alice listened to the sounds Jeremy made and used those, the jerks of his hips, and the thickening of his cock to help her gauge her performance. She was no expert, but it seemed she was doing okay. Her hunch was confirmed when he grabbed her head, tangled his fingers into her hair and pushed forcefully between her lips before letting out a growl and spurting cum over her tongue and down her throat.

She continued to flick her tongue around the now-sticky shaft in her mouth until he disentangled his fingers and stepped back, pulling his cock out with an audible pop. Almost immediately, hands reached under her armpits from behind and Alice wondered if Ethan was going to fuck her. If he was, she hoped he'd be gentle—those marks on her arse still stung like mad.

But it appeared Ethan wasn't intending to fuck her—not then, anyway. He was helping her up. As she straightened, she was grateful for the help, as she doubted her shaky legs would hold her. Ethan turned her in his arms and held her tightly. Alice was surprised by the display of care and affection, but she still snuggled happily into his muscular chest, enjoying the warmth and strength of his body, and the mixed scent of washing powder and his body spray. The hard lump in the front of his trousers was flattering, too.

Seconds later, another warm body pressed in close behind her and a voice murmured into her ear. "You did brilliantly, my darling. We're very proud and pleased. Now I must go and wash up, but I'll leave you in Ethan's capable hands for a while until it's time to open the house." Jeremy kissed her cheek—the only portion of skin on her face that was exposed between her hair and Ethan's bulk. "Well done. I'll see you later."

As Jeremy's footsteps retreated, she stayed exactly where she was. It was a lovely place to be, after all. Not quite as nice as being snuggled up—preferably naked—in bed with him, but still pretty damn fabulous. She let out a happy sigh.

Ethan tugged her hair gently until her face was turned up to his. "Okay?" he murmured.

"Okay." She nodded.

"Good." He manoeuvred so they were no longer hugging, but he still had an arm behind her back for support. "I'll take you back upstairs so you can get cleaned up."

Alice looked at her watch. She had a little over half an hour to compose herself. It would be no mean feat, considering the fact her arse was on fire, and her lips felt so swollen it probably looked as if someone had punched her in the mouth.

"Come on."

Alice leant on Ethan more than she strictly needed to, finding comfort in having him so close. She wondered if he was still hard, and what he'd do about it if so. Would he leave when he'd taken her to her room and go and masturbate? Or would he put up with the frustration until this evening? If it was the latter, she had no idea how he'd have the willpower. Her pussy and clit still ached for attention, and the moment she was alone she intended to rub herself to a hasty climax before cleaning herself up ready for work.

Ethan's intentions soon became clear. He followed her into her bedroom and shut the door—which seemed pointless given the only other person currently in the house was Jeremy. Then he twisted her around so she was facing him and leant down to kiss her. His technique was just as delicious as she remembered—passionate, thorough, and perfectly capable of making her knees weak all over again.

Within seconds, Ethan pulled away, leaving her gasping. He then herded her towards the bed and bent her over it. There came the unmistakable sound of a zip, then the tear of a foil wrapper, the snap of latex, and he was inside her. Her walls stretched easily around him, and unintelligible sounds burbled from her lips as he began to move.

He reached around to trap her swollen clit between his fingers and thumb. He then rolled and pinched it relentlessly as he fucked her from behind. It was all over very quickly—they'd both been teased to the maximum in the schoolroom and Jeremy had been the only one to climax. So it was no wonder they both came so quickly and collapsed in a heap on Alice's bed.

There was no cuddling this time—Ethan heaved a huge sigh and stood up. He removed the condom and dropped it into the bin beside the dresser, then put his clothing back how it should be.

"I'm really sorry, sweetheart," he said, giving her an apologetic glance, "but I fucking needed that, and you look like you did too. We really must discuss contraception later, because I'm desperate to feel you properly around me. But anyway, I gotta go. We have to open up soon, and I think I need to change my underwear and squirt on some more deodorant. You little minx."

He tipped her a wink and left the room. Alice stared incredulously after him. *What the hell just happened?* But a glance at the clock on her bedside table reminded her that she didn't have time for wondering. The only thing she had time for was getting herself cleaned up and going downstairs to begin her working day.

How she was going to concentrate on work with an abused arse, mouth, and pussy, she didn't know. Her only consolation was the fact that Jeremy and Ethan would have the same trouble. She hoped.

Chapter Nine

Several days passed, and Alice became increasingly on edge. Since the schoolroom encounter, followed by Ethan fucking her over the bed, there had been no sexual advances from either man, or any more challenges.

They'd spent time together, of course, both in a professional and a domestic sense. They were living together, after all. Conversations they'd had made Alice feel much more at home. She would have the privacy she required; in other words, neither Jeremy nor Ethan would enter her room without permission. They had the mealtime rota sorted out too. Alice wasn't surprised to discover the cleaners Jeremy hired for the manor also took care of the private quarters. If she was totally honest with herself, it was just another perk to living there. All she had to do was keep up her end of the cooking rota, and take care of her own laundry, which she was more than happy about. The thought of the two men handling her underwear—in a non-sexual sense—gave her the shivers. And as for her washing their smalls… no. Just no.

They had also visited a private clinic—at Jeremy's expense—to be tested for STIs. Alice knew she didn't have anything, but she could hardly expect Jeremy and Ethan to get tested and not her. Unromantic and unsexy as it was, it was only fair that they were all checked out. Then they could continue their games without fear of health recriminations. She'd used the contraceptive injection for years as it was; loving the convenience of it, not to mention the lack of periods or the related mood swings. Now, it seemed it was going to be more useful than ever, as she could be having sex with Jeremy or Ethan, or both, at a moment's notice. She'd never have to turn them down because it was her time of the month.

Their test results had arrived that morning. All three of them, as she'd expected, were infection and disease-free. And something told Alice that this information would jump-start their sexy games once more. Only now, they could be even more spontaneous. Well, as spontaneous as a planned-out list of kinky sexual challenges could be, anyway.

It had been a busy day, so Alice had eaten dinner—a delicious pie and mash combination, courtesy of Ethan—then gone up to her room for a nice, relaxing bath before pulling on her comfortable pyjamas and curling up on her bed to read. She was so deeply engrossed in what she was reading that the knock on the door made her shriek and drop her book. Pressing her hand to her thumping heart, she took a couple of breaths to calm herself, then called, "Come in!"

The door opened and Ethan stepped in. Clearly, he'd showered recently, as his hair was wet. But it wasn't that which really drew Alice's eye. It was the fact that the only thing he was wearing, aside from trainers, was a pair of jeans that did wonders for him. They encased his muscular thighs, emphasising their power, and she suspected that his rear view looked pretty damn delicious too. She was suddenly hyper-aware of her totally unsexy pyjamas.

He flashed her a smile, and she had to resist the temptation to squirm on her bed. Ethan's smile could do that to a person—his straight white teeth, luscious lips and those *dimples*. Damn. On top of that, when he smiled, his whole face lit up; his mischievous-looking eyes crinkled at the corners, and he looked adorable and sexy at all at once. Alice wasn't sure how that was possible, but somehow he achieved it.

Running a hand through his hair, he took a step towards her bed, the grin leaving his face. He looked down at what she wearing.

Heat crept up Alice's chest and neck, and soon after her cheeks began to flame, too.

"Cute," Ethan said. She searched his face for signs of sarcasm, but found none. "Anything underneath?"

She shook her head. Hell, no. She never wore anything underneath her pyjamas. That was the whole point of pyjamas, surely? They meant you didn't have to sleep naked, but weren't encumbered by knickers or bras. She heaved a happy sigh every day when she took off her bra. The size of her breasts meant that going without a bra was absolutely not an option, but they were such a pain in the arse. Or tits, to be more precise. Some were too big, some were too small, some had straps that slipped down, others were too tight around her body. Shopping for them was a nightmare. She'd been measured by several different shops and specialists, and none agreed on her size. Therefore, she always tried new ones on in changing rooms, jiggling around to make sure her boobs stayed where they were supposed to be. Only if they passed that test would she actually fork out for them. And that was another thing that pissed her off—the price. Large sizes never came cheap, and getting them when a sale was on required a hefty dose of luck.

"…dining room."

She'd been so intent on her internal rant about bras that she hadn't listened to a word he'd been saying. The last two words alone meant nothing, and his quizzical expression indicated that he was waiting for her to say something.

"S-sorry," she said, slipping a bookmark into her book—she'd have to find the page she'd lost later—and putting it down on the bed, "I wasn't listening."

Ethan tutted. "Too right you weren't. You were miles away. What were you thinking about?"

"Um, bras." *No point in lying*. Hopefully the peculiarity of her answer would make him forget that she hadn't been listening to him. She didn't know if it was on the cards that evening, but she didn't want to earn herself a spanking.

A tiny line appeared between his brows. "O-kay. Anyway, as I was saying, I've come to collect you and take you to the dining room. And your outfit is just fine. You got some slippers?"

Their conversation felt like something out of the Twilight Zone to Alice, but she nodded and slid off the bed, then reached underneath it to grab her slippers. Thankfully they weren't too embarrassing—just black slip-on things with white spots on them. She wouldn't mention the big fluffy ones she had stashed in her wardrobe ready for winter. After pulling the spotty slippers on, she took the hand Ethan held out and followed him through the house. They went out of the private quarters and into the public area. She had to jog a little to keep up with his long strides.

When they arrived in the dining room, she wasn't surprised to see Jeremy already waiting there. He gave her a warm smile and looked her up and down. "I see you were all ready for bed. Sorry about that. We won't keep you long. Please, sit." He indicated a chair that had been pulled out of the immaculate display around the table and moved to an empty area of the room. She sat down, her buttocks spreading across the seat. The edges dug into her flesh.

"Good," he continued. "Now, I must inconvenience you and ask you to stand again. Remove your clothes, then sit."

Alice couldn't help the tremble in her hands as she moved to undo the top button of her pyjama top. She'd never been completely naked in front of the men before, and she wasn't looking forward to it. What if they went off her when they saw her lumps and bumps all displayed at once? What if they were horrified when they realised just how overweight she was?

Figuring there was nothing she could do about it either way, she stripped, dropping her clothes into a pile to one side of the chair, then settled back down into the seat.

It was even more uncomfortable now, without the layer of protection her clothes had afforded. The back of the chair was all carved wood with lots of pointy bits, so she purposely didn't lean on it. Discomfort on her bottom and the back of her legs was quite enough, thank you very much.

However, it seemed Jeremy and Ethan had other plans. They walked up to her, side by side. Jeremy reached into his pocket and pulled something long and dark out of it, then handed it to Ethan. It looked like a scarf. Next, Jeremy pulled another long, dark item from his pocket. Then, as if they were synchronised, the men knelt down, grabbed one of Alice's arms each, and tied her wrists to the back of the chair. They then stood and took a step back to examine their handiwork. She was now pulled tight against the chair, and she could clasp her hands together. So she did—it might help her deal with what was going to happen next.

Because this was challenge number two. It had been a while since she'd looked at the list, so she couldn't remember all the details, but she did know that this task wouldn't be quite as painful as the previous one. Though given the way the sharp angles of the chair dug into her, she was beginning to think it would be pretty close. It was certainly going to be no walk in the park.

Ethan stepped behind her and tugged at her bonds to make sure they were secure. "You remember the idea of this task, don't you? You're tied to this chair, and Jeremy and I will be playing with you however we wish. You are forbidden to come, and if you start to move around too much or don't do as you're told, we'll tie up your legs too."

She nodded. That was the part she'd remembered. About not being able to come, and not moving. She wasn't sure exactly what they were going to do to her. It wasn't specified on the list. Perhaps they were just going to make it up as they went along. A shiver rolled across her skin, and her nipples stood to attention. Whether it was the chill or arousal causing it she couldn't be sure, but Jeremy, who was standing in front of her, noticed.

"Ha. She's got stiff nipples already. Horny bitch. Gorgeous tits, though. I think I'll just…"

With that, Jeremy dropped to his knees once more and shuffled in front of her. He wrapped a hand around her left breast and pulled as much of it as he could into his mouth. The warmth of his lips and tongue were divine, and when he began to suckle at the tip of her tit, Alice knew it would take a colossal amount of willpower for her not to come during this task. She was already pretty damn horny, and at the moment she had just one man playing with her chest. When the manpower—and therefore the number of hands, fingers, and mouths—doubled, she knew they'd be teasing her relentlessly, pushing her to the very edge of climax, then denying her.

Ethan moved from behind her chair and stood beside it. He reached down and began to caress her right breast, idly at first, then with more vigour. He grasped her hard nipple between his thumb and index finger and pulled it away from her body, then let go. The bouncing flesh slapped back against her torso, and Alice looked down to see her right nipple standing out from her body like some kind of antenna. If it had been erect before, there were no words to describe what it was now.

She flicked her gaze left, to the dark-haired man still making a meal of her other breast. Jeremy was clearly very fond of playing with boobs because he licked, nibbled and suckled at her flesh with an enthusiasm it was impossible to fake. That enthusiasm, not to mention skill, translated to immense amounts of pleasure for her. She closed her eyes, enjoying the delicious sensations that rushed through her body, confident in the fact she never had, and probably never would, come through breast play.

A warm mouth closed around her right nipple. Her eyes flicked open. She couldn't *not* watch, now. There were two totally gorgeous men sucking her tits, and the thought crossed her mind that perhaps she'd fallen asleep the night of her interview at Davenport Manor and had just been having an incredibly vivid—and kinky—dream ever since. She hoped not.

A stinging pain from her right nipple brought her back to the present, and assured her that she most definitely was *not* dreaming. Ethan really had just bitten her. She sucked in a breath. A trickle of juice seeped from her pussy, down her perineum and to the surface of the chair below. Oh my God—she was leaking onto the furniture! The ancient, authentic, irreplaceable furniture. Jeremy was not going to be pleased. But then this had all been his idea, so it was his fault. He should have thought of that before he decided to tie a naked woman to an old dining room chair and pleasure her to within an inch of her life.

As delicious as it was to have the two men playing with her chest, the insistent throb from her clit and the ache of her pussy made her long for something more. Something *inside* her. It would be much harder for her to stop herself coming if she was penetrated somehow, but she was growing so horny she didn't really care. Despite being told she'd have her legs bound if she moved too much, she shunted her hips forward a little, bringing her pussy closer to the front edge of the chair. Hopefully one of the men would take the hint.

It made sense that it was Ethan. Both men were right-handed, and it was much easier for him given the position they were in, kneeling side by side in front of her. He pulled away from her breast, making her areola crinkle in the chill which was emphasised from the saliva he'd left cooling on her skin. Then he slipped his hand between her knees, skimming her right thigh as he crept his fingers closer and closer to where she wanted them most.

In the meantime, Jeremy had stopped suckling her and was pinching and slapping her pendulous breasts, clearly a ploy to allow him to sit back and watch what Ethan was doing to her. Or, more specifically, how she was *reacting* to what Ethan was doing to her. His gaze remained firmly on her face, an almost evil grin stretching across his lips. She tried hard to return his stare, but as Ethan's fingertips slipped between her swollen labia and began to stroke up and down her saturated slit, she rolled her head back and closed her eyes in bliss.

"Remember: don't come," Jeremy said.

"Mmm-hmm!" was all she managed as she pressed her lips together tightly, holding in the gasps, moans, and groans she would let rip in an ordinary sexual situation. But there was nothing ordinary about this. Not for her, anyway.

Deliberately avoiding her clit, Ethan continued to rub the sensitive skin of her vulva, lulling her into a false sense of security. There was no way she'd come if he didn't touch her clit.

Suddenly, two thick fingers slipped inside her. She gasped, then bit her lip immediately, not wanting to make too much noise. Noise hadn't been on the "forbidden" list, but the more she kept herself in check, the less likely she'd be to move around too much. She didn't want her legs to be tied up too. Her arms were bad enough. And now she was thinking about it, she felt much more acutely the beautiful yet sharp carvings of the chair back digging into her skin. Her thighs and bottom had gone a little numb, so the edges of the seat no longer felt quite so unforgiving.

As if he sensed her drifting away into her own thoughts, Ethan pushed his fingers deeper inside her pussy and bent his thumb up to press the sensitive bundle of nerve endings at the apex of her vulva. If he continued stimulating her clit, painfully swollen as it was, she'd come in no time. And then she'd really be in trouble. She didn't know if it would be classed as a failure of the challenge—invalidating their agreement and screwing her career prospects—or whether they'd just keep repeating any challenges she failed until she completed them successfully. Either way, she didn't really want to find out. She was a perfect-first-time kind of a girl, and she planned to continue that trend.

The soft pad of Ethan's thumb rolled over her clit, mercifully not pressing too hard, or moving too fast. If he carried on like that, she might be all right. She'd come eventually, of course, but with any luck Jeremy would deem the challenge complete before then, and she would be able to rush to her room, lock the door, and finish herself off.

Jeremy continued to touch her elsewhere. His nimble fingers stroked her neck, her décolletage, her breasts, her tummy, her hips. He slipped a hand behind her and grabbed as much of her right buttock as he could. Digging his fingertips into the ample flesh, he sent jolts of mild pain rushing through her body, where they centred on her groin. Great. Between them they really were pushing her to the very brink, however subtly.

"She's doing well, isn't she, Ethan?"

Alice rolled her head forward and opened her eyes so she could watch their exchange. Looking at them, a fresh burst of lust coursed through her veins. They had more clothes on than she did—Jeremy was fully clothed, in fact—which made her total nudity feel all the more erotic, but both still looked eminently sexual. Ethan's dimples appeared, and the look in Jeremy's eyes would turn any straight woman—and probably some lesbians too—into a gibbering wreck. She was lucky she was already sitting down, and her hands were tied, or else she'd have reached out to them. She tangled her fingers together and squeezed, trying hard to distract herself from the sights and sensations that were slowly pushing her up the slope towards climax.

After a beat, Ethan replied, "She's doing very well, mate. Do you think it's time to up the ante?"

Alice stared at them, horrified. They wouldn't, surely?

Both men looked at her, grinning. She was unable to respond. She didn't know how to. If she protested, they'd probably just tease her all the more. But she certainly wasn't going to welcome it. So she kept her face straight and took deep breaths to try to keep herself calm. Well, as calm as a person could be with one man playing with their pussy and the other touching every other exposed inch of skin.

Jeremy nodded. "Yes. Let's go for it. Look at her. She wants it, wants to come. If she bites her lip any harder she's going to draw blood."

Alice heard his words, but couldn't understand his meaning. Yes, of course she *wanted* to come, but she was biting her lip to *stop* herself from doing so. They'd told her she wasn't allowed to, for fuck's sake! What the hell?

As one, they pleasured her quivering body once more. Ethan's long fingers curved up to her G-spot, stimulating it as well as her clit. Alice squeezed her eyes closed and started thinking about unpleasant things—it was the only way she was going to get through this without gushing all over his hand. She chivvied herself on, convincing herself that the most powerful sexual organ in her body was her brain, and if it didn't want her to come, then she wouldn't.

Jeremy pinched and pulled at her nipples, then he stood and bent so his mouth was level with her bare shoulders. He peppered gentle kisses over her skin, surprising her with the occasional nip. Moving his lips up her neck, then behind her ear, he was so close she could smell him; a mixture of fresh sweat and expensive aftershave.

He murmured in her ear, "Do you want to come?"

It was an idiotic question, and Alice wasn't sure how to answer it. Then she realised that *because* it was an idiotic question, there was no point in lying. She'd just make things worse for herself.

"Yes, *please*." She put particular emphasis on the last word, almost begging.

"Ethan," he said, without turning his head, "Alice wants to come."

His friend's reply was instant. "I know damn well she does. She's absolutely soaking wet and so damn hot. I just want to fuck her."

"Well, you can't fuck her just yet. But you can make her come."

Alice met Ethan's eyes. She tried to send a silent message

with her gaze, but realised even if that were possible, she'd be giving mixed messages. She wanted to come, but she didn't, at the same time. It didn't matter, anyway. Ethan was playing the game; on Jeremy's side.

He pulled his thumb away from her clit, and Alice almost heaved a sigh of relief. That was until he bent his head and closed his lips around the distended flesh and sucked. She couldn't help herself—she yowled, wringing a dry laugh from Jeremy's lips.

Ethan licked and sucked at her swollen clit, his hair brushing the skin of her thighs and pubis, adding an extra layer of sensation. This was it. She was absolutely done for. Never in a million years could she hold out against this kind of sexual onslaught, and Alice wondered why she'd ever thought she could. Any minute now—even with her brain screaming out in protest—she'd come. And it would all be over.

Any… minute… now. So… fucking… close.

The words in her ear were so unexpected that she jumped.

"It's okay, Alice," Jeremy said quietly, but still loud enough for Ethan to hear, "you can come. You've earned it."

The words had barely left his mouth when her climax hit. It was like walking into a wall of water; it crashed into her with such intensity. Once again, she was glad she was tied to the chair, or she'd probably have wriggled herself right off it. Only her bindings and Ethan's steady hands on her thighs kept her—relatively—still.

Jeremy's permission had opened a door, and all her feelings had come flying out. She'd gone from a still, quiet woman teetering on the edge of orgasm but desperate to avoid it, to a wailing, spasming, highly passionate minx.

And, as she slowly came back to herself, her heart rate and breathing slowing, the contractions in her pussy waning, she opened her eyes and looked at the two men. They remained, frozen, in the positions they'd held when she started to come, and stared at her. As she flicked her gaze from one pair of eyes to the other, she realised just how much Jeremy and Ethan had liked what they'd seen. Their gazes were dark, dangerous, and hungry.

Somehow Alice knew that climax wouldn't be the only one she'd have that night.

Chapter Ten

Life went on as normal in Davenport Manor for a while. Or at least as normal as things could be when the owner and the head of security liked to play kinky sex games with the property manager. The three of them continued with their rotas, watched TV and films some evenings, exchanged books, talked, and acted like good friends living together. Except for the intense sexual undercurrent that simmered there all the time; when they were eating, lounging in the sitting room, working, everything.

It confused Alice. It was clear to her—though she still couldn't quite believe it—that the men were attracted to her. And the feeling was mutual. She'd hardly ever masturbated before getting this job and moving into the manor, but now it seemed that the saying was true: the more sex you have, the more sex you want. That, coupled with the fact Jeremy and Ethan's rooms were just down the corridor, had Alice shoving her hand between her legs on many occasions as she fantasised about them showering, dressing, stroking their cocks…

Other than the time with Ethan in her old place, she'd never had sex with either guy "just because". It was always linked with a challenge somehow, and she found that bizarre. Didn't free agents who fancied each other usually have sex? There was nothing stopping them. But then it occurred to her that maybe something *was* stopping them. Her. Gorgeous as Jeremy and Ethan were, all men—or at least the ones who weren't so arrogant that you wouldn't want them anyway—had their insecurities. So perhaps they were under the impression the whole thing was purely a business transaction of sorts for her. That she was simply doing her job during the day and spending occasional evenings doing whatever they wanted her to do, because it was their arrangement.

Maybe it hadn't occurred to them that she'd quite happily fuck, suck, lick, massage, and any other erotic thing a person could think of, with or to both of them. Repeatedly. Challenges or no challenges.

The more she thought about it, the more she believed she was right. They believed she was just in it for the glowing reference and Jeremy's contacts. She was, of course. But it was so much more than that too.

It seemed that if she wanted more than just task-related sex, she was going to have to ask for it. Which was all well and good for women with lots of self-confidence, but Alice had never come on to a man in her life, except in her younger days when she used to go out on the town. But back then alcohol gave her false confidence, and more often than not, she'd been blown out, anyway. Men just didn't want big girls. Or at least, they never used to.

It seemed society was changing; skinny women were starting to be vilified just as much as big ones once were. It was great that plus-sized girls were gaining acceptance, but Alice hated the fact that it was at the expense of thin girls. Not all of them went on silly diets and made themselves ill just to look how they thought the press wanted them to. Some of them were naturally slim and perfectly healthy.

Alice thought the press should just butt out, or launch a campaign on how *all* women were beautiful, no matter their size.

She knew for sure that just as women liked different types of men, it worked in reverse too. Guys had varied tastes; some absolutely adored Rubenesque women.

That thought gave Alice pause. If some guys liked big girls, then why couldn't Jeremy and Ethan? Just because they were both super-sexy and could have any woman they wanted? She had no idea what sort of girls they'd hooked up with in the past, but there was no denying that when they played with her, both of them had erections. And unless they were popping Viagra, then they were genuine.

She smiled to herself. They *did* want her. The physical evidence was overwhelming. But it didn't change the fact she was not the sort of woman to proposition a guy, much less two of them.

Maybe she'd write them a note, or something. She'd figure it out.

***

It turned out she didn't have to. Not that evening, anyway. She'd been thinking about the situation as she walked through the house, closing it up for the evening. On her way back to her office to tidy up, Jeremy found her.

"Alice," he said, smiling. "Are you all finished?"

"Sort of. I still have to tidy my office—"

"Ugh, never mind that. It'll keep until tomorrow morning, won't it?"

She nodded. It wasn't that untidy. Just a few things that needed to be put away. But it could wait.

"Excellent. Now, could you come with me to the library, please?"

He turned and headed in the direction of the library, and she followed without a word. It had been a rhetorical question, really. He knew damn well that she wouldn't say no.

When they arrived, Ethan was already there waiting for them. He grinned at her by way of greeting, and she smiled back, shyly.

Jeremy turned to her, and she blushed a little under their gazes. Particularly since those gazes held such promise. Hopefully of delights to come.

It was then she thought about how much things had changed. At the beginning, when all the challenge stuff started, she'd seen it as a chore. Something to be endured, with her eyes firmly on the prize. But the more time she'd spent with both men, the more she'd enjoyed herself; both sexually and socially.

Her heart sank as she realised what it meant. This had become about much more than just sex for her. She wouldn't go so far as to say she loved Jeremy and Ethan, but she *was* incredibly fond of them. And not in the brotherly sense.

Although the men were fond of her too, she knew that when her challenges were complete and her employment contract was finished, she'd walk away and be nothing more than a pleasant memory to them. She would have to do something about it, shove her emotions into a dark cupboard in her brain and lock it. Multiple times. Then pile a load of boxes in front of it for good measure.

The last thing she needed was to walk away from Davenport Manor with a broken heart. No, she was determined that she would have the same attitude as the men—she'd simply see their time together as fun, and would have lovely memories to keep her warm on cold nights. As well as some serious wank fodder.

Her decision made, she looked enquiringly from one man to the other, wondering what was going to happen next. They still looked at her with amused expressions.

"What?" Alice said, instinctively bringing her hand to her cheek. "Do I have something on my face?" She swiped at her skin.

Jeremy grabbed her wrist and pulled it away gently. "No, Alice. You're as perfect as ever. Stop fretting. It's just that you're so bloody cute when you start daydreaming like that. You do it quite a lot. You get a little line between your eyebrows which makes you look like you're trying to work something out, and a dreamy expression other times. I'm guessing that's when you're thinking of something nice."

Alice disentangled herself from his grip, eager to distract him before he asked what she'd been thinking about. If his assumption was correct, she'd probably had some kind of weird frowny, dreamy expression. "So," she said, with forced brightness, "what do you two buggers have planned for me in here?"

"Well," Jeremy replied, seemingly not noticing her diversion tactics, "I think you know, don't you? It's on the list."

Oh yes. The list. She hadn't looked at it for ages—it was pointless. Whatever was on it was going to happen, whether she memorised it or not. And even if she *could* remember the specifics of each and every task, she never knew when they were going to take place. The list hadn't included a timeline. So she just went with the flow.

However, she didn't want to admit to Jeremy that she hadn't read his precious list recently. It obviously meant a great deal to him, and she didn't want to upset or annoy him, so she just smiled and lowered her gaze to the floor. It sort of looked like a yes, but it meant she wasn't lying. Perhaps just by omission.

"Right," Jeremy continued, grabbing Alice's arm again and guiding her further into the room, "take your clothes off and put them on that chair."

He indicated the chair in question. Alice nodded and began to undress. Her gaze wandered around the room—her favourite room in Davenport Manor—taking in its size and grandeur. She'd never seen a library so big—except public libraries, of course. But they were purely functional spaces, and often not very attractive. This library was sumptuous and beautiful; it was a long room, the entire depth of the house. It was almost as wide as it was long, and the ceilings were very high. The windows at each end had built-in seats, and she often thought about taking a book from one of the many, many shelves and curling up to read it in one of them. She decided she would do just that before her contract expired. Although she was sure the other houses she'd work in throughout her career would have libraries, they'd have to be pretty damn impressive to be a patch on this. She should make the most of it.

Now she stood naked before the two men, and resisted the temptation to cover herself up. It wouldn't work, anyway. She'd need two hands to cover her large breasts, and that would leave her neatly-trimmed pussy on display. So she stood with her hands by her sides, waiting for the next command.

Ethan spoke first. “Fuck. I’m rock hard already. She’s just stunning, isn’t she? I must confess I’ve been looking forward to this task for some time.” He rubbed his hands together gleefully.

Alice remained still and silent.

“She’s being very obedient, isn’t she?” Jeremy moved over to where she stood and walked around her naked form. “Do you think we’ve turned her into a proper little submissive?”

Alice’s cheeks flamed at his words. How dare he say such things about her? And yet, other than the heat burning across her chest, neck, and cheeks, she made no response. So perhaps he was right—under the care, for want of a more suitable word, of these two handsome, dominant men, she’d turned into some kind of submissive. Sexually, anyway. She’d read enough kinky novels to know a liking for submission didn’t make a woman weak. It just meant they liked to be bossed around in the bedroom—and some of them even outside of it.

If that was what got her going—so what? They were all adults here, and free to do whatever they liked with one another, no strings attached.

Ethan replied to Jeremy. “If we have, the tendency must have been buried there beforehand. It doesn’t just happen overnight. Of course, it could just be that she wants to get this over and done with as soon as possible.”

“Or,” Jeremy said, narrowing his eyes as he looked at Alice, “it could be that she doesn’t want us to delay. She wants to get started with the task as soon as possible. Because she enjoys it.

Wants it."

He lowered his hand to her crotch, dipping a finger between her labia. "Huh. Seems I was right. All she's done is take her clothes off, and already she's getting wet."

Ethan strode over to one side of the room and retrieved the rolling ladder which reached up to the very top shelves of the library. He manoeuvred it so it was facing the wall, then locked the wheels. He turned and nodded at Jeremy, who took Alice's arm and led her over to Ethan and the newly-secured ladder. After positioning her in front of the ladder, facing its steps, Jeremy pulled the binds they'd used in the dining room—or at least ones that looked the same—from his pocket and handed one to Ethan.

Between them, they encouraged Alice up the first step of the ladder—mercifully, it was more like a flight of mobile stairs, with flat wooden slats instead of rungs, otherwise it would have hurt her bare feet—then secured her wrists to the handrails. Bending her neck so she could look under her arm, she saw she was just a little way off the floor, with her arse pointing into the room in all its fleshy glory.

She wondered if she was positioned this way so her bottom was in a good spanking position, but she'd wracked her brain to remember this particular task and couldn't recall any kind of corporal punishment. She pressed her lips together hard to suppress a smirk—if she couldn't remember, then there was a good chance that this was a nice, straightforward task with nothing untoward involved at all. Except being naked and bound to some rolling steps in a library, of course. And hopefully being given a good seeing-to.

Nobody spoke for a few minutes, but Alice was aware of

activity behind her—she suspected it was the two men mouthing plans to one another and using their hands to emphasise their meaning. Though she wasn't sure why they were bothering to keep it from her if they thought she already knew what was going to happen. Perhaps they'd changed the plan.

Seconds later, her ordeal began. Only it wasn't an ordeal. That made it sound bad, and Alice's experience was the complete opposite. Jeremy and Ethan were touching her lightly. The tips of their fingers swept over the back of her, from head—well, neck—to toe. Gentle caresses that made her want to writhe madly and had all the tiny hairs on her skin standing on end.

They continued this for some time, until she quivered with anticipation. Although her entire body had become an erogenous zone, she couldn't help wondering when they were going to touch her between her legs, or on her breasts. But she kept quiet—they were running the show, and if past experience was anything to go by, whatever they had planned would be well worth the wait.

Soon, the men upped the ante. They replaced their hands with their mouths, then kissed, licked, and nibbled their way over the skin they'd already sensitised with their fingers. Alice wished she was sitting down. All the stimulation was giving her shaky legs. And, despite the fact they hadn't even been *close* to it yet—except for Jeremy's earlier brief touch—her pussy was so wet that juices leaked down the insides of her thighs. She pressed her thighs together to stop the trickle going any further, and to try to get some stimulation on her severely-neglected clit.

"Hey!" Jeremy said, slapping her arse. "We'll have none of

that. Trying to get yourself off. Just for that, you can wait a little longer until we touch you where you really need it."

Alice hung her head. *Shit.* She wasn't sure how much longer she could wait. It wasn't the first time they'd both teased her before letting her climax, but before, the teasing had been more direct—her tits, her pussy, her thighs. This was just torture. The closest they'd currently got to her pussy was her arse cheeks. Part of her wanted them to start spanking her bum and thighs—at least the pain would transform into the kind of intense pleasure that might eventually make her climax. If she was lucky.

She arched her back, hoping the sight of her plump backside being thrust out would tempt one of them. Ethan laughed. "Mate, look at this. She's desperate. Gagging for it. Begging us without using any words. Clever girl. Shall we put her out of her misery?"

After aiming another slap at her arse cheek, Jeremy moved around to the side of the ladder and looked at Alice's face. "Is that what you want, Alice? To be fucked?"

Past the point of caring whether she came across as desperate or not, she nodded eagerly.

Jeremy chuckled. "I thought so. But here's another question for you. Which one of us would you like? Me? Ethan? Or maybe both?"

Alice's eyes widened at the final statement, and Jeremy's smile grew wider. He looked at his friend and said, "I think we have our answer. You should have seen her face when I suggested both of us. You ready?"

Alice peered over her shoulder at Ethan, who was nodding.

"All right if I go first?" Jeremy asked. "You've had her before, after all. I haven't."

"Be my guest. Just make sure she can still stand up when you're done, okay?"

"I can't promise anything, but I'll do my best."

She breathed out heavily, hoping the men wouldn't recognise it as a sigh of relief. She'd thought they were both going to fuck her at the same time. And, as hot as that notion was, she wasn't sure she was ready for it. Not just yet.

Jeremy untied her left wrist, while Ethan took care of the right. Then Jeremy moved behind her again. He put his hand on her back and pushed her into a bent-over position. She grabbed one of the steps for leverage. Somehow, she thought she was going to need it.

Jeremy's hand slipped between her legs and parted her labia. He dipped a finger into her wetness and sucked in a breath through his teeth. "Fucking hell—she's soaked! And red hot. God, I can't wait to get inside."

There came the unmistakable sound of clothes being removed and dropped onto the floor. Then the blunt head of Jeremy's cock pressed against her pussy lips. She resisted the urge to shove herself back onto his shaft, suspecting he'd just tease her further if she did. Anticipation made her breathless as she waited for the lord of the manor to shove his thick cock inside her aching pussy.

Jeremy grabbed his cock and rubbed the tip up and down Alice's wet slit, bumping against her clit with each stroke. She knew he was doing it on purpose, trying to break her. But he wouldn't succeed, not this time.

"Oh fuck it!" With that exclamation, Jeremy slid inside Alice in one slick movement. Once he was balls deep, she clenched her internal walls, determined to try to tease him like he'd teased her. He responded by shunting inside her even more, leaving her gasping.

Leaning over her back and reaching around to press a fingertip to her clit, Jeremy murmured into her ear, "No more holding out, Alice. If you need to come, then come. The more times the better, in my opinion." He gave a husky laugh, then straightened and grabbed her hip with his free hand.

As he started to find his rhythm, thrusting in and out of her, he pressed her clit against her body. Alice was extremely glad he'd given her permission to come how and when she liked, because his touch was already pushing her rapidly towards climax. She joined him in his thrusts, rocking back as he came forward, making his balls slap heavily against her and wrenching moans and groans from their lips.

Alice had been so engrossed in fucking Jeremy for the first time that she'd almost forgotten about Ethan. Suddenly her peripheral vision picked him up as he moved to one side of the ladder, watching her face as she was screwed by his best friend. Then he leant through the gap between the handrail and the steps and kissed her, hard. He possessed her mouth thoroughly, forcing his tongue between her lips and seeking hers. She didn't think she could possibly be any more turned on, but Ethan taking her mouth that way while Jeremy fucked her pussy and stroked her clit made her feel supremely desirable. And powerful. The result was a fresh jolt of arousal that buzzed through her body, before centring on her clit. Jeremy groaned as her muscles clamped around him once more.

Had her mouth not been occupied, Alice would have blurted out an apology. But the tiny part of her brain which was still able to function reached the decision that it was a ridiculous thing to do in the situation. After all, what straight man wouldn't want a tight, clenching pussy wrapped around his cock? Certainly not the two she was currently playing with.

Then, as though they'd communicated somehow, Ethan deepened their kiss and Jeremy increased the speed at which he stimulated her clit and pounded into her, both at the same time. Alice took it in her stride—kissing Ethan back just as passionately, and rutting back onto Jeremy's eager prick. All she could think about was the pleasure she was feeling. She could hardly discern where—or who—it was coming from, but all she knew for sure was that with a few more strokes of Jeremy's fingers, she would be undone. She tensed her inner muscles repeatedly, trying her hardest to take him with her.

As soon as the blissful tingling started in her abdomen, she pulled away from Ethan. He looked confused for a moment, but when she sucked in a hasty breath, it seemed he understood. The sensations that crashed through her grew steadily more powerful, keeping her teetering on the edge for what seemed like forever, until finally, Jeremy gave her clit a swift pinch and sent her tumbling over it.

Alice was vaguely aware of the noises she was making, but she didn't really care. The rest of her was much more occupied by the delicious feeling of the climax ripping ferociously through her body, leaving her bucking and twitching in its wake. She slowly, *slowly,* started to come back to reality as the orgasm waned. Just in time for Jeremy to remove his hand from her clit and grip her hips hard, thrusting faster and deeper until he let out a roar and spilled his own release. She gasped as his cock twitched and spurted powerfully inside her and he relaxed his hold on her hips. She'd have marks there later.

Finally, Jeremy slumped over her just long enough to press a warm, lingering kiss to the back of her neck, then pulled away, leaving her empty and leaking. She was about to say something about making a mess of the vintage carpet, when Ethan pulled his cock from his trousers and underwear and moved behind her.

Within seconds he had hold of her shoulders and was rocking her back and forth on his prick like she was a rag doll. He wrapped a hand in her hair and pulled her head back, tugging just enough that tiny shockwaves of pain danced across her scalp, but not so much that it truly hurt.

Watching Alice and Jeremy had clearly affected Ethan, as it wasn't long before he was muttering expletives and emptying his balls into her pussy. He pulled out quite rapidly, and Alice was surprised—and a little miffed—that he hadn't at least attempted to make her come before he did. When he turned her around and dropped to his knees, she suddenly understood why. He pressed his hands to the insides of her thighs, encouraging her to open them. Before the cum that filled her had chance to trickle out, he pushed his face between her legs and lapped at her pussy and clit until she tangled her fingers in his hair and held on tight in order to stop herself from wobbling.

Part of her wondered how he felt about licking Jeremy's spunk out of her as well as his own, but she figured that if they were so fond of sharing women, then sharing their own bodily fluids wasn't really an issue. Either way, it was pretty damn hot.

That thought—and any others—flew rapidly out of her head when Ethan pushed two thick fingers inside her and sought her G-spot, while he fastened his lips around her clit. When he began to stimulate them simultaneously, she had to reach back and grab the handrails of the steps instead of his head, otherwise she'd have been in danger of squeezing him until he popped.

The fact she'd not long climaxed and the skill with which Ethan pleasured her most erogenous zones meant that her second orgasm approached fast. She barely had time to tell him she was coming before it arrived. It wasn't as powerful as the first, but it still rocked her world—literally; her legs would have gone from under her if it hadn't been for her grip on the steps and Ethan's quick reaction. He'd slipped a hand behind her back for support before continuing to lick and suck at her clit until her cunt stopped spasming. She joined him on the floor and slumped over him, wriggling eagerly into the arms he held out before drifting into a blissful, orgasm-induced doze.

Alice was vaguely aware of being lifted up and carried in strong arms, but her sleepiness was such that she didn't recall anything else until she woke up the following morning, dressed in her pyjamas and snuggled up beneath her duvet.

Chapter Eleven

Alice knocked softly on the door to Jeremy's private drawing room.

"Come in."

She entered, then closed the door carefully behind her. Confusion hit as she glanced around the room to find Ethan wasn't there. It was also odd that Jeremy had asked her to come here in the first place—if his request was work-related, it would usually take place in his office. Or, less often, in hers or Ethan's. And if his summoning was task-related, then where was Ethan?

He scribbled something onto the piece of paper he'd been reading—probably his illegible signature—then looked up from his desk. "I guess you're wondering why I asked you here?"

No shit, Sherlock. "Yes, I am."

"Well, I suspect you've worked out it's not for a challenge. But it is related. Please, sit." He indicated the chaise longue that stood at an angle a few feet from the side of his desk. The sunlight from the large window bathed the purple-velvet-covered piece of furniture, and Alice sunk happily onto it. She almost purred like a contented cat as the beams warmed her body.

"I just wanted to talk to you in a neutral setting."

It sounded odd, but she knew what he meant. By now, many of the rooms in the house held certain memories; of work-related things, domestic stuff, or their more debauched activities.

"Okay," she replied, giving him what she hoped was an encouraging smile. "What did you want to talk to me about?"

"Our… situation." He smiled coolly, and Alice's heart gave a sudden, painful leap. What did he mean? Had he changed his mind? About the challenges? About her references and his useful contacts?

"There's no need to look so alarmed, Alice. This is nothing bad. Or at least, I don't believe it is." He pushed his chair back and stood, then crossed the room in a few long strides and sat beside her on the chaise longue. Took her hand.

Alice gulped, his fingers stroking over her palm sending sparks of arousal through her body. She dropped her gaze to where their skin made contact. Why the hell did he make her feel that way from a simple touch? How?

Jeremy put the fingers of his other hand beneath her chin and tilted her head. Their gazes met, and she resisted the temptation to look down again. When it came to intensity, Ethan was the one who took the cake, but Jeremy came a close second. "Listen. I just wanted to speak with you about what we've been doing since you arrived and took on the challenges. Ethan and I are incredibly pleased with your progress. You've taken what we've given you so far, and taken it well. Also, unless I'm very much mistaken, you're actually enjoying our games now, as opposed to simply seeing them as a means to an end."

He still held her chin high, so she couldn't hide her expression—and therefore her emotions—from him. The answer was probably written all over her rapidly-heating face, but it was clear he expected a verbal reply. "No," she said, "you're not mistaken. I do enjoy our… games. I enjoy them, my job, and spending time with the two of you."

She hadn't meant to blurt out so much information,

particularly the last part. But it was too late now, and she knew that Jeremy would never let it go until he was satisfied he had a grasp of her meaning. Alice prepared herself for the inevitable questioning.

Jeremy raised an eyebrow, then straightened his face. "Good, I'm very pleased. We feel exactly the same. And we also feel that you've settled into the role of being a woman who we can share perfectly. It couldn't possibly have worked out any better."

Alice nodded emphatically, but in fact she had no idea what he was getting at. It was obvious she'd been in the role of someone they could share—because the challenges involved them sharing her! If she said no to sharing, she said no to the whole thing, and her career went up in smoke.

"I'm very glad you're happy with the situation, Alice. Because we're more than happy with you."

He shifted his hand from her chin to cup her jaw, then leant towards her and planted a kiss on her lips. It was chaste at first, but then the pressure increased. Jeremy shuffled closer, his thigh against hers, their upper bodies twisted from the hip and pressing together. He removed his other hand from hers and slipped it around the back of her head, then tangled it in her hair. Using the leverage he now had, he deepened the kiss further, slipping his tongue between her lips.

She felt as though she was going to melt. Jeremy's tongue moved sensuously around her mouth, teasing her own tongue, her teeth, the most sensitive parts of her lips. A rapid movement later, and he had her bottom lip between his teeth. He licked, nibbled, and sucked at it until she writhed on the chaise longue like some kind of wanton hussy. Only it wasn't faked. Every touch of his tongue, teeth, and lips increased her excitement to the extent that she felt how wet her pussy was without even moving.

Jeremy pulled away from their kiss, but kept his face mere millimetres away from hers. "Alice," he murmured, fixing her with that intense gaze once more, "can I make love to you?"

She gaped, surprised he'd even asked. Not that she thought he'd ever do anything against her will, of course, but her astonishment was twofold. One, he just wanted to have sex with her. No challenges involved. Two, he didn't just take what he wanted. It had to be startlingly obvious she wanted him too. Granted, she didn't have an erection pressing against the front of her skirt, but her nipples strained against her blouse, her lips were swollen and parted, and unless she was imagining it, she'd got so horny that she could actually smell her own pussy juices.

She was so lost in her bewilderment she forgot she was supposed to answer Jeremy's question.

"Alice?"

Blinking, she replied, "Wha—? Oh my God. Yes, of course. Please… do." She couldn't bring herself to use the phrase he'd used, because it didn't feel quite right. To her, it meant what the words implied—that there was love, or at the very least affection, involved. Something reserved for relationships and romance. Not being screwed by your boss in a more traditional fashion as a break from the highly kinky sexual games you'd been playing.

Though, if she was completely truthful, there *was* affection involved. On her part, anyway. Jeremy was undoubtedly fond of her, but he certainly wasn't thinking of her on a relationship level.

Seconds later, as he made short work of the buttons on her blouse, she froze. Or *was* he thinking of her on that kind of level? He'd made such a big deal of saying how she fitted into the role of being a woman he and Ethan could share. Was he hinting at something more than just ticking items off his list? Surely he was the sort of man who didn't *need* to drop hints. He was rich, gorgeous, confident, and powerful. He could have anything—or anyone—he wanted, right?

She was yanked out of her train of thought when Jeremy shoved aside her underwear and slipped two fingers inside her pussy. "You're so fucking wet. I think if I put my cock in there, I'll come straight away."

A whimper tumbled from her lips before she could stop it.

He smirked. "What was that for, Alice? You really want me to put my cock in your pussy?"

This was the kind of language she was used to from him. More comfortable now, she whispered, "Yes. Please put your cock in my pussy."

Jeremy groaned, long and loud. He swiftly removed his clothes, then hers, before laying her gently back on the chaise longue. She writhed against it, the luxurious material heavenly against her skin. He kissed her again, hard. Juices seeped out of her pussy, down her perineum, across the tight bud of her anus and onto the purple velvet. For once, she didn't worry about whether that would piss Jeremy off. It was his fault, after all. Right now, all she really cared about was him making love—no, *fucking* her.

She twisted her face away from his. "Please," she begged, "please fuck me, now."

He pushed his weight up onto his hands, and looked down, studying her face. "You know, I usually like to make a woman come before I penetrate her."

Alice stifled a giggle at his use of the word "penetrate". So formal, so clinical. And yet she knew damn well that the man was far from either of those things when it came to sex. "Don't worry," she said, slipping a hand between her legs, then coating her fingers in her juices and pushing them into his mouth, "I'm plenty wet enough already. I'm sure it won't take me long to come. And if I don't, you can always make it up to me later."

Eagerly, Jeremy sucked and licked at her fingers until they were clean. Then he pushed them out of his mouth with his tongue. A smile tugged at his lips. "Mmm, you *are* wet. And you taste sublime. Well, if you insist. Saucy wench."

With that, he leant down and captured her mouth in another scorching hot kiss. At the same time, he used his legs to push hers apart, then dipped his hips so his cock slipped up and down her slick seam. Their groans mingled in the silence of the room. Jeremy stopped teasing both of them and angled his cock so the thick, blunt head pressed against her entrance. Remembering they weren't taking part in any kind of challenge, therefore there were no rules and she could do what she wanted, Alice tilted her hips up, popping Jeremy's cock into her.

He growled. "I say again, you saucy wench." He pushed himself all the way inside her, balls deep, crushing Alice's swollen clit between them and sending a burst of pleasure coursing through her. "God, you feel good. So wet, tight, and hot. You won't hold it against me if I come too quickly, will you?"

Alice couldn't think why he'd come more quickly from the relatively vanilla sex they were about to have, when his stamina was just fine during their kinky encounters. But at that moment, she didn't really care. She just wanted him to fuck her. She shook her head.

"Good. And I will make it up to you, I promise." He rearranged himself so his weight was on his elbows and knees, and cupped her face, looking into her eyes as he began to thrust in and out of her.

It was at that point Alice felt as though Jeremy had meant exactly what he'd said. He *was* making love to her—that was, fucking her but with lots of meaningful eye contact and strokes and caresses. And compliments.

"Fuck, Alice. You are just so gorgeous. I love the fact there's plenty of you to go around. A man could get lost in your curves forever. And I know I can treat you roughly and not break you. Ethan and I are very lucky to have you."

She had no idea how to respond to that, so she simply made some encouraging noises and rocked her hips to meet his, hoping to distract him before he realised she hadn't replied. It worked, and his gentle thrusts became faster and harder until the blissful sensations sweeping through her body forced her to close her eyes. Her cunt felt like it was on fire, but in a good way. With each upward stroke, Jeremy was managing to tease exquisite sensations from both her G-spot and her clitoris. If he thought he was going to come before she did, he had another think coming. Each movement pushed her closer and closer to the edge, and she curled her hands against his muscular back, her nails digging into his skin.

"Uh, fuck, Alice!" Jeremy's tone and the extra forceful jerk of his hips told her he didn't just like to give pain, he liked to receive it too. *Interesting.* She didn't think it was possible, but his cock grew harder inside her, indicating just how close he was to his own climax.

"Hey," she whispered, opening her eyes and urging him to do the same. "I'm almost there. Keep hitting that angle and we might just get there together."

He said nothing; nodded once. He kissed her, then pushed himself up on his hands again. Alice could no longer wrap her arms around him, so she got hold of his biceps instead. They weren't quite as large as Ethan's, but still felt damn good beneath her fingers. She couldn't help herself—she squeezed the muscles, digging her nails into their firmness and smirking as the pain caused Jeremy to grunt and pick up his pace even further.

Alice bowed as the sensations rushing through her body reached fever pitch and her climax became a dam on the edge of breaking. She dug her nails harder into Jeremy's arms, curled her toes, and let out a stream of unintelligible sounds as she inched closer and closer to her peak. A handful more thrusts—and the consequent strokes against her clit—later and she yelled as her climax hit. It was long, hard, and intense, and she was vaguely aware of Jeremy calling out his own release as her internal walls gripped his cock like a vice.

Writhing beneath him, she sucked in hasty breaths as her orgasm raced through her body. Eventually it began to wane, and she relaxed into the soft, cushiony material beneath her.

Jeremy slumped onto her and dropped gentle kisses to her face and lips, before snuggling his face into the crook of her neck. He sighed happily, and murmured something that Alice didn't catch.

"What did you say? I didn't hear."

He raised his head enough that he could whisper into her ear, "I said that was absolutely amazing."

Alice smiled and reached up to stroke his hair. He gave another contented sigh, then moved off her and sat up with a wry expression on his face.

She looked at him questioningly.

"I'm okay," he said. "I just thought I'd better get up before I fell asleep and crushed you. Maybe another time we'll do it in a bed so we can fall asleep together."

It wasn't a question, so Alice didn't answer it, but the thud of her heart and flip of her stomach told her all she needed to know about her own feelings on the matter. She followed his lead when he started pulling his clothes back on, glad to cover herself up again, but disappointed she could no longer drink in the sight of his gorgeous nakedness.

They returned to the living quarters and reached Alice's bedroom first. Jeremy grabbed her before she opened the door and gave her another kiss that left her breathless and more than a little horny, before tipping her a wink and continuing on down the corridor to his own room.

She dashed inside and closed the door, then launched herself onto the bed and buried her face in the pillows. Her head was a mess. She was happy and satisfied from the lovely fuck she'd just had with Jeremy, but she couldn't stop herself from wondering what it all meant. She wasn't being oversensitive and reading too much into things. It was *him* who had implied it was becoming about more than just sex for him—and possibly Ethan too.

If he meant what she thought he meant, then the three of them were in trouble. Big fucking trouble. Erin's maternity leave would end in a few months and she'd return to the manor, forcing Alice to move elsewhere for work. And she doubted she'd be lucky enough for it to be close by.

No, she'd already used up her luck quota when she landed the job and the two smokin' hot men who went with it. She couldn't possibly have any more.

Things like that just didn't happen to girls like her.

Chapter Twelve

It was with some trepidation that Alice made her way to the servants' quarters of Davenport Manor. She'd received orders from Jeremy that she should go and take a shower and not apply any lotions or sprays of any kind when she was done. Then she was to put on her dressing gown and head to the back kitchen. The request had confused her enough that she'd found her copy of the list so she could see what the men had planned for her. And now she knew, she was nervous. Details of her conversation with Jeremy about him and Ethan sharing her floated back into her brain. He'd said how well she'd fitted into the role.

And now it appeared she was going to be shared in the literal sense.

When she entered the room, both men were already there, waiting for her. They were also both topless, and Alice's pussy twitched involuntarily as she drank in the delicious sight of their gleaming skin and flexing muscles.

"Alice," Jeremy said, smiling warmly. "We're so glad you're here. Now the fun can begin. You know what to do next, yes?"

For the first time in a while—due to her recent consultation of the list—she knew exactly what he was talking about. So, as expected, she moved next to the chair in the corner of the room and removed her clothes, folding each item before laying it on the seat.

Then she walked over to the enormous trestle table in the centre of the room—noting that all the usual props had been removed—and sat on its edge, before twisting her body and swinging her legs up onto its surface. Now she shuffled as gracefully as possible—which wasn't very—to the middle of the table and lay down.

Without moving her head, she looked as best she could to where the men still stood at the edge of the room. She hadn't been reprimanded or ordered to move, so she figured she'd got it right. Her suspicions were confirmed when Ethan moved closer with a length of rope in his hand. He walked towards the top end of the table and was lost from sight. Soon, she felt tiny movements in the table as Ethan secured the rope to one of its legs, before wrapping the other end around her wrist and tying it securely. He checked to make sure she was comfortable before repeating the process three more times on her remaining limbs.

Now she lay spread-eagled on the enormous table and could hardly feel more exposed. Her pussy was splayed open, her tits bobbed on her chest with every breath she took, and she couldn't do a damn thing to cover herself up. Not that she really wanted to.

No, all she wanted was for the men to touch her. And she knew that was going to happen soon enough.

The clink of metal drew her attention, and in her peripheral vision she saw Ethan and Jeremy approaching, carrying enormous silver trays. Ethan disappeared from view; she guessed he was walking around the table to reach her other side. She hadn't been told not to, so she turned her head and saw her guess was correct. Now there was a man on either side of her. Their trays were held aloft, so she couldn't see what they carried. It was food of some description—she knew that much—but wasn't sure exactly what. She hoped it wasn't something disgusting, like caviar or snails.

Milliseconds later, the rich scent of chocolate hit her nostrils. *Oh, thank God for that.* Chocolate she could handle. The only downside to this task was the fact she'd rather the roles were reversed—she would much rather be licking and sucking chocolate from Jeremy and Ethan's bodies, and she'd bet her last pound any other straight female who met them would feel the same. Unless they didn't like chocolate, in which case they were crazy anyway.

"Close your eyes, Alice," Ethan murmured.

She did as he asked. She had no reason not to, after all. She trusted him. Trusted both of them.

Now she relied on her other senses to tell her what was happening. Her ears picked up the pinging of cutlery. She could still smell the chocolate, and *ohhh,* now she felt it being drizzled over her breasts. They'd melted it, and were pouring it over her. The sensation was ticklish—as well as incredibly sensual—and she did her absolute best not to move. She didn't want to spill any of the confectionery from her curves—she wanted every last drop to be licked or sucked off by a warm, wet mouth.

There were some clanging and scraping noises, then Alice got her wish. As if they'd signalled to one another, both men closed their mouths over one of her nipples at the same time.

She gasped. Her sense of touch—or, rather, feel—leapt into overdrive. Lips on her tits, hands stroking her thighs, cooling liquid chocolate trickling down the sides of her breasts… It was heaven. Soon, chocolate wasn't the only thing trickling towards the table—her pussy was wet and ready, eager for a tongue, fingers, or even better, a cock. Juices seeped from her core and gravity did its job, leading them down her arse crack and onto the wooden surface beneath her.

But it seemed Jeremy and Ethan had more teasing in mind before she'd get the touch she wanted; no, needed. Once they'd laved her skin clean of the sweet goo, they grabbed their bowls and spoons and repeated the process, trickling more chocolate over her boobs, stomach and thighs. They'd obviously decided to use it all up on her skin before it solidified in the bowls.

Alice writhed on the table—no mean feat considering how tightly she was restrained—as the sensations swarmed through her body. She'd given up trying to stay still—it was just impossible. Then Jeremy and Ethan began licking and sucking once more. Jeremy clambered up onto the table and knelt between her legs, then bent to clean the sauce from her thighs and lower abdomen. They'd deliberately not allowed any to get onto her pussy—either because they were concerned about the health implications, or because they knew it would drive her crazy to explore all around the area without actually touching it. It was probably a combination of both.

She craned her neck to watch Jeremy's progress as he inched closer and closer to her pussy, then let her head fall back onto the table and closed her eyes. There was no sense in tormenting herself further by avidly watching the men. They'd do exactly what they wanted for as long as they liked. Only when they were ready would she be allowed to come.

Since she wasn't looking, she was surprised when Ethan moved his tongue suddenly from her chest down to her belly button. Then lower, and lower, until he was hovering at the very edge of her short pubic hair. Alice held her breath. Surely he wasn't going to lick her pussy? Given their positions, it would be much easier for Jeremy to work his way up and bury his head between her spread thighs than for Ethan to lean over and eat her out.

They were just teasing her. Pushing her and pushing her to see how much she could take before she begged and pleaded. Or screamed for it. Well, she wasn't going to give them the satisfaction. They might be the masters of the tease, but they'd done it to her so many times now, she was becoming the mistress of patience. She might not be able to stop herself wriggling, but she sure as hell wasn't going to beg.

Ethan continued to lick, suck, and kiss her tummy, while Jeremy did the same to her thighs. Alice basked in the delicious pleasure they were bestowing on her—and the best part was the knowledge that there was much more to come.

Suddenly, the lips teasing her upper body were gone. She opened her eyes to see what Ethan was up to, and was greeted by the sight of him removing the rest of his clothes. She barely had time to admire his sexy naked form before he was climbing onto the table and straddling her head, facing her feet. The heady scent of his musk hit her nostrils and she opened her mouth instantly, eager to suck his cock.

Ethan leant forward, bracing his hands against the table and moving into a position where she could reach him. He dipped his pelvis, and Alice closed her lips around the head of his prick. She received a slick of salty pre-cum on her tongue, and hummed contentedly around his shaft as it grew harder and thicker in her mouth.

She was so fixated on sucking Ethan off that she was only vaguely aware of Jeremy as he stopped touching her thighs. She felt the table shift slightly, then nothing. Shrugging to herself, she continued to tease the sensitive head of Ethan's dick, growing steadily more turned on as he moaned and cursed above her, and as more evidence of his arousal seeped from the tiny slit at its tip.

When she moved her head to fit as much of Ethan into her mouth as she could, she was rewarded by some incredibly feral sounds. His passion only served to push hers higher, and her clit and labia filled with more blood—eager to be stroked, rubbed, licked, and sucked.

The table jolted, and then she felt warm, slightly abrasive skin on her legs. She surmised that Jeremy had joined them once more and that his hairy, naked thighs were moving against hers. Moving where, though? Ethan's positioning meant that if she opened her eyes, all she'd see was his crotch and muscular upper thighs. Not a bad view, to be fair, but not one that would help her work out what Jeremy's next move might be.

She didn't have to wonder for much longer. A warm tongue swept up her juicy slit just once, then, after a brief pause, Jeremy lifted her bottom and pressed the blunt head of his cock against her labia. She moaned loudly around Ethan's shaft, and both men chuckled in response.

Then Jeremy gave a firm push. His prick slipped easily through her wet folds and hovered briefly at her entrance before slowly sliding in, deeper and deeper, until his balls pressed against her. A noise that sounded something like "fuck" worked its way from her mouth around Ethan's shaft, and Jeremy mirrored it, though his speech was much more intelligible.

For the second time, it seemed as though the men were using an unspoken signal. Earlier, they'd started to tease her nipples at the same time. Now, they began to fuck her in unison—one man in her mouth, one in her pussy. They were sharing her—literally.

Four hands worked in unison. They explored her breasts, nipples, and tummy, and toyed with her clit. The vast majority of her erogenous zones were being taken care of at once, and the sensory excess sent her into a kind of trance. She let herself be carried away on the waves of decadent bliss as she offered and received erotic pleasure. She felt like some kind of fucking machine—sucking, being fucked, stroked, caressed, pinched. The room filled with moans and groans which grew steadily more animalistic as the three of them worked their way toward climax. The scent of fresh masculine sweat tickled Alice's nostrils and added another layer of arousal to her already overloaded body. After one more stroke of her clit—from whom, she had no idea—she was done.

Twisting her head to pull away from Ethan's cock, she screamed her ecstasy, holding nothing back. She couldn't move because of her bonds and the two men on top of her, so she yelled again as the pleasure that had centred in her pussy exploded out, sending ripples of orgasmic bliss through her body. The spasms of her cunt gripped Jeremy's cock tightly, and she heard him muttering expletives as she triggered his orgasm. Anticipating the feel of his twitching shaft inside her as he came, Alice was surprised when, instead, he pulled out and emptied his balls over her stomach. Ethan knelt up, grabbed his cock and stroked himself to completion, his spunk mixing with his friend's on her pale skin.

Soon the swearing, the talking to God, and soft moaning tailed off, and Ethan and Jeremy's breathing slowed down and returned to normal. Alice wanted nothing more than to curl up with them, the meaty filling in a very sexy sandwich, but until they released her she couldn't do a damn thing. So she allowed herself to drift into a doze until they recovered and saw fit to untie her.

The next thing she was aware of was being lifted gently from the table. She opened her eyes to find she was cradled in Ethan's arms. He followed Jeremy—both of them still naked—from the room and back to their living quarters where he sat on her bed, still holding her, while his friend ran a bath. She heard the gushing water, and soon the scent of her favourite bubbles reached her. With a smile, she snuggled into Ethan's chest.

He stroked her hair and kissed her forehead. "You all right?" he whispered.

Alice nodded lazily. She was more than all right—she was in heaven. She'd just had the most intense climax of her life, and now one incredibly sexy man was looking after her while another ran her a bath. What was not to like?

A few minutes later, Ethan disturbed her from her doze again. He carried her to the bathroom, then leant down and gently put her in the tub.

"Hey," Jeremy said, from his position on the floor beside the bath, "are you going to wake up, or should one of us stay with you?

We don’t want you falling asleep and drowning in there!”

A shrug was the only response she was capable of mustering. She sank into the bubbles, then rested her head on the bath pillow stuck to the surface behind her and drifted off yet again as hands dipped into the water to wash the sweat, saliva, and spunk from her skin.

Chapter Thirteen

Alice walked along the corridor to Jeremy's office. The house had been closed to the public for hours, and she'd showered and changed, then headed to the kitchen to see what the plan was for dinner. It was Ethan's night to cook. But neither of the men had been there. She'd waited a while, then left and knocked on both their bedroom doors in turn. There'd been no answer, so she figured they were still working. She'd decided to offer to cook tonight, since they were so busy. And she was hungry.

When she got close to Jeremy's office door, she got a strange feeling of déjà vu from when she'd inadvertently caught him having sex in there. She never had found out who he'd been having sex *with*, and she stuffed that question into her memory bank to return to at a later date. When he was in a talkative mood, perhaps after a couple of glasses of wine, she'd ask him. Purely out of curiosity, of course—not because it was any of her business who he slept with. Though as far as she knew, the only person he was having sex with at the moment was her. She doubted he had time for anything else between running the manor, crossing things off his kinky list, and the three of them spending time together. He did go out to meetings a fair bit, though. Perhaps he was…

A snatch of conversation from inside the room caught her attention. It was Jeremy and Ethan. She leant closer to the door and listened carefully, praying that the ancient floorboards beneath her feet wouldn't creak and give her away.

"We have to tell her," Ethan was saying. "Because otherwise it's going to be too late."

There was a loud sigh, presumably from Jeremy. "I hear what you're saying, buddy. Really I do. But I don't think we should. The poor girl would probably run a mile. And we don't want that now, do we?"

"Of course not. That's the last thing I want, which is why I want us to tell her. She's a smart woman, remember; she's probably figured it out already. But the sooner we spell it out to her, the sooner she'll be able to start getting her head around it. I'm not denying that it might come as a surprise to her, but I reckon she can handle it."

Jeremy sighed again. "Just give me a while to think about it, okay? Figure out how best to do it, and when."

Alice didn't hear Ethan reply, so she assumed he'd nodded or something similar. She heard the dragging of chairs across the wooden floor and realised she'd better announce her presence quickly, or it would be the second time she'd been caught loitering outside Jeremy's office. The difference was the first time had been a mistake, a misunderstanding; this time she'd been deliberately eavesdropping. In her defence, they were talking about her. How many people would be able to resist listening in on a conversation about themselves? She definitely couldn't.

She knocked and entered the room, finding them on their feet and about to leave. "Ah, there you are. I just came to see what was happening about dinner. I figured you were both busy so I was going to offer to cook."

Ethan slipped an arm around her shoulders and pressed a soft kiss to her hair. "That would be lovely, thank you. But you're not doing an extra shift. We'll swap, and I'll cook tomorrow instead. And to make it up to you, you can choose anything you want, and I'll make it. Even a dessert, if you like."

"It's not a problem," she mumbled, glad neither of the men could see her face, buried in Ethan's chest as it was, and reddening rapidly as a result of his amorous attentions, "honestly. I don't mind."

"No," Jeremy said, as they left the room and he closed and locked the door behind them, "Ethan's right. We lost track of time, and we should have let you know where we were. It's not fair for you to cook two nights in a row. We had an agreement, and we'll stick to it."

"Okay." She shrugged. "You two go get showered or whatever, and I'll put something together."

Jeremy reached out and gave her hand a squeeze. "Thank you, Alice. You really do look after us, don't you?"

Alice blushed harder but said nothing, and the three of them made their way back to their living quarters in silence. They separated; the boys heading to their bedrooms, and Alice to the kitchen. She hummed contentedly as she prepared dinner. To an outsider, she probably looked like a very happy woman who was enjoying herself as she cooked a meal. But in truth, her mind was a maelstrom of unwelcome thoughts.

Recalling the conversation she'd overheard from outside Jeremy's office, she wondered what they'd been talking about. It was clear *she* was the person they had been discussing, but she had no idea what they actually meant. According to Jeremy, it was something that would worry or scare her. And for the life of her, she couldn't think of what that might be. Perhaps they'd changed their minds about their agreement, endangering her job prospects, not to mention her heart. But she couldn't see that happening, not at this late stage. The tasks they'd set for her were proving incredibly fun and pleasurable for all concerned. They wouldn't call time on that. Plus they were acting the same as they always did towards her. Surely they'd seem different if they were cooling off towards her?

Unless… Alice's heart gave a little leap. Perhaps they'd come up with another challenge to add to the list. Something so extreme, so terrible, that they thought she would run a mile when she heard about it. Well, she'd show them. There was nothing they could do or say to stop her checking off every single item on that damn list. *Nothing.*

The evening passed pleasantly; Jeremy and Ethan came back from their respective rooms showered and ready to eat. Their damp hair and fresh scent wasn't wasted on Alice; she drank in the sight and smell of them, smiling when her body responded favourably. Her pussy throbbed, and her nipples tingled and pressed against the soft fabric of her bra. Damn, the boys were fully clothed and not doing anything remotely sexy—except existing, of course—and she was super horny. There was only one thing for it; she'd have to disappear to her room as soon as possible and get herself off.

She ate her dinner quickly, though not so fast she'd get indigestion. That wouldn't do her libido any good, would it? Then she took her used plate, glass, and cutlery, and loaded them into the dishwasher.

"Hey," Jeremy said, after swallowing a

"Leave that. I'll sort it out. You go and chill."

"Okay," she said, smiling. "I'm actually gc

So I'll see you in the morning."

Ethan glanced at his watch and gave a little fr ...hen he recovered himself and grinned at her. "Goodnight, Alice. See you tomorrow. Thanks again for sorting out the dinner."

Jeremy echoed Ethan's words.

With a wave, she retreated to her room. Once there, she locked the door behind her and stripped her clothes off, leaving a trail of garments between the door and the bed.

She slipped beneath the duvet, enjoying the feel of the cool sheets against her skin. She didn't usually sleep naked, but for some reason, tonight she wanted to. After she'd given herself an orgasm, that was. A Jeremy-and-Ethan-induced orgasm. The only question was, should she use her hands or her vibrator?

After a few seconds' deliberation, Alice decided on the latter. That way, if she was really lucky she could have more than one climax, to help get those naughty thoughts out of her head and purge the arousal from her body. Damn it, what were those men doing to her? They'd turned her into some kind of nymphomaniac.

Alice cursed herself. Here she was, lying in bed about to pleasure herself, yet there were two seriously sexy and very willing men just down the corridor. Why on earth hadn't she asked one of them to come to bed with her? Actually, she knew the answer to that question. It was because she couldn't possibly choose between them. And, if she was honest, she enjoyed having the two of them to play

e. But she simply couldn't summon up the courage to ask of them to come to bed with her. It wasn't just the fear of rejection—it was the intimacy of the situation. The three of them had done some very physically intimate things over the past few months, but they'd never actually slept together in the traditional sense. She felt that would take the situation to a whole other level. An emotional one.

As much as *she* liked that idea, she didn't think Jeremy and Ethan would. They were fond of her, she knew that much. But, like it or not, she'd developed feelings for the two men that went beyond fondness, beyond lust. And when the time came when she'd have to move on from Davenport Manor, she knew she'd be devastated. And not just because she loved the place.

Heaving a deep sigh, Alice rolled over to grab a book from her bedside table, instead of her vibrator. Her depressing thoughts had killed her horniness. But when she caught sight of the sexy shirtless guy on the front of the romance novel, she changed her mind. Fuck it; she'd spent enough time admiring Jeremy and Ethan's naked forms, not to mention enjoying what they did to her. She'd conjure up some wank fodder and shove those unwanted thoughts to the very back of her mind.

She retrieved her rabbit vibe and slipped her arms under the covers. Touching her pussy with her free hand quickly revealed that lube wouldn't be necessary. Despite the fact her mind had taken a dark path for a little while, her body clearly hadn't caught up. Thank God for that. She inched the vibrator inside herself, positioned the ears where she wanted them, and switched the toy on. Immediately, low waves of pleasure coursed through her. She closed her eyes and let her imagination go to work.

In her mind's eye, Jeremy and Ethan were lying in a large bed with a space between them big enough to accommodate a third person. Her. They beckoned her to join them, and naturally, she did. She crawled up the length of the bed and moved into the gap they'd left for her, then paused. The only problem with having two men to choose from was being spoilt for choice. She couldn't kiss them both at once; she only had one mouth. That gave her an idea.

Having encouraged them to scoot closer together, she reached out and grabbed a thick cock in each hand, then kissed each man in turn. It was tough to concentrate on stroking as well as kissing, but she managed it. And the guttural sounds coming from their throats made it all worth it. Not to mention the ache of her clit, and the juices coating the insides of her thighs. Pleasure wasn't a strong enough word to describe the way she felt. Bliss, perhaps. Or heaven. Yes, heaven.

Back in the real world, her clit was past aching and rocketing her towards climax. Notching up the sex factor in her imagination, she pushed a button on her rabbit to make the vibrations faster. She gasped, then tangled her free hand into the sheets as the unparalleled ecstasy of orgasm began to take over her body. Her abdomen tightened and she held her breath as the delicious pressure built. Then, with a rather graphic image of herself, Jeremy, and Ethan in her mind, and a flick of her wrist, she came. The sensation of a dam bursting flooded through her and her pussy spasmed wildly around the shaft of the toy.

A moan escaped her throat, then she sucked in a hasty breath as another wave of contractions overtook her. Her clit suddenly became too sensitive and she switched off the vibrator and pulled it out, before dropping it to the mattress beside her. As she rode out her orgasm, her stiff limbs relaxed, and she felt as though she was sinking into the bed; melting, boneless. Her eyelids grew heavy, and in spite of the relatively early hour, she knew she'd be asleep in seconds.

A knock at the door startled her from her almost-sleep, and caused her heart to lurch painfully. She clasped her hand to her naked chest and responded, "Yes?"

"Alice? It's Ethan. I just came to check you're all right. You went to bed really early. You're not feeling poorly, are you? Do you need anything?"

She grinned. What a sweetie. "I'm fine thank you, Ethan. I'm just knackered for some reason. But I don't feel ill. Lovely of you to check, though."

"Ok-ay," he said, sounding a little disbelieving. "But you know where we are if you need us. Goodnight. Sweet dreams."

Sweet dreams were practically a given after that little fantasy and the resulting orgasm. "You too, Ethan. Goodnight."

She heard his heavy footsteps retreating down the corridor, then the faint sound of a door being closed. Sighing happily, she rolled over and shoved her vibe back into the cupboard—making a mental note to clean it first thing in the morning—then sunk into the pillows. She was delighted and flattered that Ethan had cared enough to come and see if she was okay, but couldn't help thinking it was bad news too. Without meaning to, she was getting in deeper every day, and her heart was in serious danger of being broken.

When she fell into a fitful sleep she had no dreams at all, much less erotic ones.

Chapter Fourteen

Jeremy sat on one of the steps leading to what had once been the servants' quarters. "Bend over," he said with a smile, "and put your hands on my knees."

Alice did as she was told, instinctively looking down, which of course meant her gaze was on his crotch. Already it was clear he was excited at the prospect of what was going to happen. She was too, actually. The games she'd played with Jeremy and Ethan over the past months had opened her mind to many different sexual pleasures, and she'd discovered that receiving pain was one of them. She didn't crave it, like some more devout submissive masochists, but she enjoyed the sweet pain that was inflicted on her. It helped, of course, that the men knew this and would only go so far with their sadistic torture.

As soon as she was in the correct position, Ethan flipped up her skirt. He gave a murmur of appreciation as he took in the sight of her naked arse and pussy. His fingertips caressed her hold-up stocking tops for a few seconds, then moved to the bare skin above them. He stroked and squeezed at the pale flesh of her thighs before journeying higher still.

There came a chuckle, then, "Wet already, Alice? You are a horny bitch, aren't you?" He coupled his words with a light slap on her bum, which made her yelp.

Jeremy grasped her forearms and steadied her. She smiled gratefully, although he couldn't see her face, then retorted, "Well, it's only because you two have made me this way. I never used to be bothered about sex."

She imagined the two of them exchanging looks over her head. Jeremy's body shifted slightly, as though he'd nodded at his friend, then Ethan spoke again. "We'll take that as a huge compliment. I suppose if you've only ever had mediocre sex up until now, then there was no real reason for you to miss it when you weren't getting it. And unless you're the queen of faking it, you've enjoyed every single sexual encounter—task or otherwise—with Jeremy and me. So, yes, you're absolutely right. We have made you this way. We've made a monster… a sex monster!"

Ethan and Jeremy's laughter rang out. Although she desperately wanted to giggle too, she daren't. The fact she'd spoken out in the first place had probably earned her a few extra smacks, so she wasn't about to make things worse by joining in with their mirth. She bit her lip hard. With her face concealed, she pulled herself together and waited patiently for what would happen next.

After a few seconds, the men managed to get a hold of themselves and the atmosphere reverted to its previous seriousness. She heard the soft whisper of material, indicating that Ethan was moving around. Then the whoop of something being swung through the air. Purely on instinct, Alice stiffened, readying herself for the inevitable impact.

It never came. Not right away, anyway. Ethan was clearly getting a feel for his new instrument, as there were several repetitions of the strange, intimidating sound before he stepped up behind her and trailed his hand across her bare buttocks. He continued to do this for a minute or so, sensitising her skin. If she hadn't known better, he would have lulled her into a false sense of security. But Alice wasn't fooled, not for a minute. She forced herself to relax, knowing that the blows would come, and the more tense her bum was, the more it would hurt.

When she sensed Ethan step away from her again, she knew it was time. The handle of the tool he was employing on this occasion was so long that if he stood right behind her and administered it, he'd smack her head, and probably Jeremy's too.

She heard a couple more swoops through the air, a pause, then the next swing landed on her naked skin. The surface of the implement was so large it reached both her buttocks at the same time, and the rattan material of which it was made left one hell of a sting in its wake, though it took a second or two to register.

She let out an anguished yell and flung her head back, narrowly missing head-butting Jeremy as she moved.

He cupped her face in his hands and gave her a reassuring smile. "Come on, Alice, you can do this, you know you can. I've long thought there was a much better use for a carpet beater than its intended one, and you're helping to prove my theory correct." He looked at Ethan and gave a nod.

With that, Ethan laid another smack on her arse. She gazed into Jeremy's eyes, attempting to lose herself in them, to shut everything out and stop her natural reactions to what was happening. Her eyelids fluttered slightly at the next blow, and she clenched her teeth so hard that she feared her jaw would pop, but didn't make another sound.

Jeremy stroked her hair. "Good girl. I told you you could do it." He reached down and rearranged himself in the crotch area.

"Sorry," he said, grimacing, "things are getting rather tight down there."

She couldn't prevent the corner of her mouth curving up at his words, but mercifully all he did was smile back. Her miniscule grin clearly wasn't cause for further punishment, thank God. The blows she was receiving were more than enough, in her opinion. Somehow, they hurt more than anything she'd been previously subjected to. She didn't know if it was the stuff the carpet beater was made from, or whether it was because the pattern of its surface made the points of contact so much more unpredictable. The only thing she *did* know was that it fucking *hurt*, and Jeremy was confident she could take it without flinching. She'd do her best to please him, of course, but it would be tough.

In the end, it turned out that trying not to react was the perfect antidote to the pain. She was concentrating so hard on not rocking her body away from the blows, not gripping Jeremy's thighs until *he* squealed, not making a noise, not pulling a face... Each distraction kept her brain so busy that it was almost as if a barrier had been formed between the beater and her bottom. A barrier of thoughts and pure determination.

Ethan continued to whack her bottom, and despite the fact the pain almost felt like it was happening to someone else, Alice couldn't ignore the blood rushing to the surface of her arse cheeks and the intense heat it caused. It burned so hot she reckoned it would be possible to fry an egg on her butt. It was awful and incredible all at once, the discomfort morphing into pleasure, making her so wet her pussy juices seeped down towards her knees. She felt sure a glance at her clit would confirm it had grown to an enormous size. But she didn't move; she continued to lock gazes with Jeremy, stoically taking everything Ethan had to give, aware that each and every blow brought her closer to the end of the task and the no doubt delicious fuck that would follow it. And she didn't care who fucked her—Jeremy, Ethan, both at once. Whatever they offered, she would take and take it greedily until she climaxed.

Jeremy reached down to rearrange himself again; the task was clearly getting to him, exciting him further with each spank. Then he cupped her head once more and pulled her towards him, slanted his lips over hers, and kissed her. It was no peck either. It was about as far from chaste as a kiss could possibly get and still be on someone's mouth. He tangled a hand in her hair and used it to hold her tightly to him, his lips crushing bruisingly against hers. His tongue possessed her mouth without an ounce of tenderness; he was forceful, stopping just this side of cruelty. Alice loved it. The passion with which he kissed her was a non-verbal way of telling her just how much he wanted her, needed her. And it thrilled her to her very core.

After pulling back ever so slightly, Jeremy sucked her plump bottom lip into his mouth and toyed with it for several minutes. Every second that passed pushed Alice closer and closer to an erotic meltdown. She'd never felt so hot just from a kiss. But then, there was also a man tormenting her arse. Eventually, with a final cheeky nip, Jeremy released her lip. The devilish smile and the look in his eyes told her that he had been just as affected by their kiss as she had. She was sorry it had ended, and hoped there would be many more like it in her future. Her near future, hopefully.

As her brain regained some of its function, she realised that she'd long ago lost count of the number of blows that had been rained down on her ample bottom. However, somewhere inside herself she knew it would be over soon. The two men never gave more than she could take, and she was getting close to the point where the feeling stopped being an incredible mixture of pleasure and pain and started becoming unpleasant and unwanted.

Sure enough, a couple of whacks later, Ethan put down the carpet beater. He gave a huge sigh, as though he was relieved to have stopped. Spanking her was probably as physically draining for him as it was for her, if not more so. Jeremy had definitely got the best part of this particular deal. He smiled, then slid gently out from beneath her, leaving her still bent over the step, her hands now on the rough wooden surface. She wondered why she hadn't yet been given permission to get up. Oh God, Jeremy wasn't going to have a turn, was he? She couldn't take any more, not today.

She needn't have worried. It soon became apparent all he wanted to do was inspect Ethan's handiwork.

"Fuck," he said, with a feather-light touch to her flaming skin, "that really does pack a punch, doesn't it? I don't think I've ever seen her arse that red. It's almost purple! But those patterns are amazing, aren't they?"

Ethan murmured his agreement, then cleared his throat. "Right," he moved to Alice's side and took her hand, "shall we get you upstairs? I'm absolutely dying to fuck you and there's nowhere suitable here."

It crossed her mind that the easiest—and certainly quickest—solution would be for him leave her where she was, take his cock out and fuck her from behind. He was a smart guy, surely he'd realised that? But, she surmised, he was also a very nice guy, and had probably decided her backside had had enough torture for one day, without him slamming against it as he screwed her.

She struggled up, her trembling legs barely able to support her weight. Immediately, Ethan slipped his arm around her back, then the three of them made their way upstairs.

With every step Alice took, the material of her dress swept against her bum. It was barely a stroke, but the pain in her arse was such that even someone breathing on the tender flesh would probably make her cringe. Fortunately, the throb of her clit, which reminded her that none of them had had any release so far, spurred her on enough to get back to her room.

Once there, Ethan started to undress her as Jeremy closed the door behind them. When she was naked, Ethan commanded her to climb onto the bed and wait for him on all fours while he took his own clothes off. She twisted her head to watch him strip—a sight she never grew tired of. She enjoyed seeing each exposed part of his body; from his broad, muscular shoulders and the mop of brown hair that almost brushed them, to the long, lean expanse of his legs. Regardless of how delectable he looked naked, though, her absolute favourite part of him was his smile. He treated her to one, his dimples appearing and his kissable lips and straight white teeth combining to create an image that Alice could happily drink in again and again for the rest of her life.

Her favourite part of Jeremy was his eyes. For two relatively small parts of the human anatomy, his were very expressive. It was easy, now she knew him better, to tell when he was happy, sad, angry, curious… and aroused. A further movement of her head confirmed he was indeed, still horny. The gaze he fixed on her was laden with intent, with promise and longing. But, unfortunately for him, he wasn't going to get her. Not right now, anyway.

Ethan joined her on the bed, clambered towards the pillows and settled on his back. He beckoned to her, and she went quickly, eagerly. She straddled his hips, then shuffled up so she could kiss him. Out of the corner of her eye, she saw Jeremy move, then became aware he was standing at the foot of the bed where, when they began fucking, he would have the most graphic view. She heard the flap of his belt being opened, and the zip of his fly. Clearly he was intending to get his own release, just as they would get theirs.

She leaned down and pressed her lips to Ethan's. Immediately he moved his hands up to her head, cradling it as he reciprocated. He was much gentler than Jeremy had been earlier, but equally thorough. His tongue tickled the sensitive inside edges of her lips, her teeth, and then got into a delicious rhythmic dance with her own tongue. A fresh burst of energy rushed through her veins, and she kissed Ethan with renewed vigour, gripping his firm biceps and pulling in a deep breath through her nostrils. She closed her eyes as bliss overtook her. Another trickle of juice ran down her thigh and onto Ethan's stomach.

Alice imagined Jeremy had a totally pornographic view of her wet and splayed pussy as she straddled his friend. Not to mention her severely reddened arse cheeks. When she listened carefully, tell-tale sounds indicated he had already begun to stroke his cock. At this rate, he'd come before she and Ethan had even started fucking. But as long as she got her orgasm, she wasn't really bothered who else came and when. She was just that horny.

Soon, her and Ethan's kiss got to the manic stage where usually they'd start rolling around on the bed until they finally fucked. But on this occasion, it was clear that wasn't going to happen; for that, Alice was supremely grateful. She definitely didn't want her bum to touch the bed, or anything for that matter. She'd be sleeping naked, on her front, and with no sheets tonight, she knew. She'd have to skip a shower too. Even cold water on her tormented skin would be excruciating, like when a person was sunburned. Ouch. But it wasn't all bad—every smart and sting would remind her of the kinky fun she and the men had enjoyed.

Ethan distracted her from her thoughts by snaking a hand down past their torsos and slipping it between her legs. He let out a grunt as he touched her soaked pussy, then pulled away from her mouth so he could speak. "Good God, Alice. You are *so* wet, absolutely sodden. I'm surprised Jeremy has been able to resist fucking you, given the amazing view he's got."

Jeremy's response was deadpan. "Trust me, the only reason I've been able to resist is the fact that if anyone fucks her from behind now, or for the next few days, they will be making her scream with the unpleasant kind of pain, not pleasure. And I only like hurting her in the good way."

"You and me both, mate," Ethan shot back. Then, to Alice,

"Sit on my cock."

She needed no more encouragement. The smarting of her butt had lessened to a dull throb, so she was able to shift back down Ethan's body and position the blunt, purple head of his prick at her entrance without too much discomfort. Then she relaxed her thigh muscles and let gravity do its job until he was buried inside her to the hilt. Their groans filled the room, and Ethan reached up to squeeze and stroke her tits as she began to rock back and forth on his shaft. They grinned at one another, revelling in their combined pleasure. Then he pinched her nipples, eliciting a squeal and a clench of her pussy walls around his dick, which in turn made *him* shout out a curse.

"Serves you right," she said with a grin. "Don't you think I've had enough pain to deal with for one day?"

He had the good sense to look apologetic. "Sorry, but those nipples of yours are just so… pinchable."

She leant down so her tits dangled above him, but his height—and her lack thereof—meant they didn't quite reach his mouth. "Suck 'em instead, then."

Ethan sat up and did as she said.

Still riding his cock, Alice flung her head back and purred like a contented cat as her pussy and tits were stimulated at the same time. If she moved in the right way, she could add her clit to that list too. She began to circle her hips, pleasuring herself against Ethan's pubic bone as she screwed him slowly.

A deep moan issued from his throat and the faint tremors vibrated through the breast he was suckling. Another spike of arousal overtook Alice's body and suddenly she sat up straight, popping her nipple from Ethan's mouth.

"I'm sorry," she said, blinking and pushing her hair away from her face, "I'm just… I just… I need to come. Don't you?"

Ethan nodded emphatically, then grasped her waist and held her steady as she began to bounce up and down on his cock, one hand between her thighs. Heavy breathing came from behind her—apparently Jeremy was getting close to his orgasm. Figuring she'd already helped him along the way, but couldn't physically do anything else to make him come, she concentrated on herself and Ethan and where their bodies were joined. She used her index finger and thumb to pinch and roll at her heavily-distended clit as they fucked. Before long, she felt the delicious sensations in her abdomen that meant her climax was drawing close.

She notched things up a level, riding Ethan harder and faster. His fingers tightened on her waist and she suspected he too, was experiencing the first signs of impending release.

"Help me," she gasped, out of breath as she was, "help me fuck you harder. I need to come, and I know you do too."

He said nothing, only nodded. His hands still on her hips, he pushed her up, then slammed her down on his thick cock, time and time again until she stiffened and froze, with the exception of the hand that still stimulated her clit. Then she came. The tightening of her abdomen increased, then popped like a balloon full of water, orgasmic pleasure rushing through her at an incredible speed and making her laugh, then scream, with joy. Her pussy contracted, gripping Ethan's cock in a tight sheath and triggering his own orgasm.

Jeremy's release made three, and a spurt of something warm and wet landed on the back of Alice's legs as the room filled with grunts, moans, and pleas to any deity who would listen. She collapsed onto Ethan, moving up and down slightly with the rise and fall of his chest, and smiled as she felt just how fast his heart was beating. Hers was the same, of course, but he was much fitter than her, so it was gratifying to discover she'd got him going so much.

She heard Jeremy's retreating footsteps, and was about to roll over to see what he was doing, and to take the weight off Ethan, when she remembered. The last thing she wanted to do was roll onto her arse. So, in a totally ungraceful move, she extricated herself from Ethan and flopped onto the bed on her front. As the other sensations throughout her body died down, the intense heat from her buttocks became more apparent. Which just made the sudden cold all the more shocking.

She squealed. The men laughed, then Jeremy said, "Relax, babe. I grabbed some moisturiser from the bathroom and I'm going to cover your luscious arse with it. Hopefully you'll be able to sit down again at some point this week."

Mumbling obscenities into the pillow, she allowed Jeremy to moisturise her bottom. And, to be fair to him, he was being as soft and gentle as possible. He smoothed a layer of the cool cream onto her skin, then advised her to leave it to soak in overnight. It would help with the pain.

Personally, Alice thought he was full of shit, but the tiny stroking motions, combined with the chilly ointment, had been soothing. Soothing enough to let the exertions of the evening take their toll and pull her into a light doze, which grew rapidly deeper. Just before she nodded off altogether, she heard someone close her bedroom window. Then Jeremy spoke. “I’ll turn the heating up in a minute. I don’t want her getting cold.”

She had a smile on her face when she fell asleep; the last thought in her mind as she drifted off was that she wished her contract at Davenport Manor would never come to an end.

Chapter Fifteen

"Right," Alice said, then drained her glass of apple juice and put it in the dishwasher, "I'd better go and get the ballroom set up for the meeting. I'll see you two later."

Jeremy had a mouthful of cereal and so didn't say anything, merely looked at her questioningly. Ethan, who'd just returned from his en suite, having brushed his teeth, said, "Hey, wait. What do you mean, get the ballroom set up for the meeting?"

"In the past, meetings have always been held in Jeremy's office, haven't they? But the number of people attending this time makes that impractical, so I'm setting up some temporary tables and chairs in the ballroom. We can't have a meeting in the library or parlour, using the incredibly valuable furniture now, can we?"

"No," Ethan said, grinning, "I suppose not. But can you hang on a few minutes? Let me just go and check everything's okay in my office, the CCTV cameras and stuff, then I'll come and help you. You're not moving all those tables and chairs around by yourself."

Jeremy's spoon clanged down into his bowl, startling the other two. He looked at Alice and pressed a palm to his forehead. "Shit. I'm so sorry. I never thought about having to use a different room, or setting anything up. And I've already arranged to pick up our attendees from the train station, or I'd help too."

Alice smiled softly. "I know you would. But it's not a problem. I won't say no to Ethan's help, but I could manage on my own, if I had to. I'm not made of glass—I won't break. Now, you two do what you have to do, and I'll make a start."

She turned and left before either of the men got a chance to protest, then grinned widely once she was out of sight in the corridor. She couldn't help it—the two of them were just so sweet to her and looked after her incredibly well, sometimes to the point of being over the top. Like today—she could manage perfectly well by herself, but she was happy to let Ethan help and save her some of the graft. Plus, it would be a nice opportunity to watch those delicious muscles of his get a workout. He was lucky she wasn't a total bitch, because if she was, she'd just stand there and order him around while admiring his body, rather than getting stuck in herself.

It seemed Ethan really was eager to help out, as he got to the ballroom only a couple of minutes after she did. "So, where do you want me?"

Several possible responses flitted through her mind. Every single one of them was sexual, involving him being in a state of undress. Instead, she gave him a wicked grin and said nothing.

His lips twisted into a filthy smile as the penny dropped, and he wagged a finger at her. "You naughty girl." He crossed the room towards her. "But I suppose had the roles been reversed, I'd have had a similar response."

"Can you blame me?" Alice replied. "Especially since it's been a while since we last… you know."

Ethan grunted. "Don't I know it. Things have been crazy, haven't they?" He glanced at his watch. "You know, we could probably make up for it a little bit now, before the place opens."

She raised her eyebrows even as her heart rate picked up. "Are you serious? Here? Now?"

He reached out and pulled her into his arms. Their proximity meant she could feel his cock beginning to stir in his trousers. "I can't think of anything better, can you?"

Without giving her a chance to reply, he leant down and slanted his mouth over hers. She responded, wrapping her arms around him and opening her mouth to allow his tongue entrance. As always, she thoroughly enjoyed kissing him. He was damn good at it, with his wicked lips, versatile tongue, and thorough knowledge of what to do with them. The large, strong hands currently inching up her dress went a long way in ramping up her arousal too.

She shifted her own hands down to grab his arse, pulling him more tightly to her. The insistent press of his now fully-erect cock against her stomach made her hungry for it. For him. Breaking away from their kiss, she sucked in a hasty breath. "H-how long have we got?"

He grabbed her wrist and pushed her hand onto the bulge of his crotch. "Long enough." A deep groan escaped his throat as she squeezed and stroked his cock through his clothes. Without an iota of warning, he took her hand and led her to a stack of chairs at the edge of the room, manoeuvred her so she was facing them, and flipped her dress up. As she'd been commanded all those weeks ago, she wasn't wearing any underwear. So, in the absence of anything to tuck her dress into, Ethan had to let it drop again while he undid his belt and fly and took out his cock.

He slipped a hand back under her dress and sought her pussy. "Can you take me now?" he murmured, his breath hot against her ear. She knew what he meant; he was asking if she was wet enough because he didn't want to hurt her. His very words turned her on even more and the unmistakable sensation of her cream trickling out of her pussy had her nodding frantically.

With a hand on her upper back, he encouraged her to bend and grip onto the stack of chairs. Once she was in position, he held the hem of her dress in one hand and angled his shaft with the other until it butted up against her pussy. There was a brief pause, then he shunted his hips forward until he was buried inside her to the hilt. She was very wet, but there was still a resistance, a tightness, that made them both gasp. Remembering the only other person in the building was the chef, who'd be busy working to loud music in his kitchen right at the other end of the house, Alice groaned loudly, a sound that was echoed by Ethan.

A couple of seconds passed, then he asked, "Okay?"

Again, Alice knew what he was getting at, and she nodded yes. Yes, she was ready; yes, she wanted him to fuck her. Hard.

Having received his answer, Ethan gripped her hips and began to pound into her, ferociously and fast. Their positioning caused his cock to stimulate her G-spot with every thrust. Alice stuck her hand between her legs and rubbed her clit. At the rate they were going, she suspected it would soon all be over. But she didn't mind; there'd be plenty more fucks where this one came from. Ethan and Jeremy were more than generous when it came to giving her orgasms in between tasks. It was just the past couple of weeks that had been dismally sex-free.

In fact, they'd probably had non-task-related sex with her more than they had during challenges. And now their dry spell was clearly over, in spectacular fashion.

Her approaching orgasm coiled a spring in her belly, a spring which tightened with every passing moment.

And it seemed Ethan wasn't too far away, either. "Unh—Alice, I'm going to… Unnnh!"

She sped up the ministrations on her clit until her hand hurt. But it was worth it. She zoomed up and across the pleasure plateau and hurtled down the other side with the most perfect timing. Her inner walls twitched and spasmed along with Ethan's spurting cock, and their yells and curses filled the ballroom until Alice worried that even the faraway chef would be able to hear them.

"Fuck!" Ethan slumped over her, bracing his hands on the chairs so he didn't squash her against them. He pressed a kiss to the back of her neck. "That was… amazing. Not to mention unexpected. Surprise sex is awesome!"

Alice giggled. "I couldn't agree more. I confess I was getting a bit antsy. Masturbating just isn't the same."

"No," he said, suddenly serious. "It isn't. Let's not leave it so long next time, eh?"

"Okay." She smiled as she said the word, but it soon dropped from her face when she thought about the future, and the fact she wouldn't be at Davenport Manor with two hot guys on call for frequent, top notch, and sometimes kinky sex, forever. Ethan couldn't see her face, of course, so he had no idea her thoughts had taken a turn for the maudlin.

By the time they'd disentangled and rearranged their clothes, she was beaming. Putting a brave face on it. She stood on tiptoes and kissed him. "That was fantastic, but we should do some work now.

I'm going to pop to the loo and clean up. If you could start arranging the tables and chairs, that would be great. I won't be long."

She wasn't either. When she re-entered the ballroom, Ethan had his back to her, so she did what she'd fantasised about earlier—watched him work his sexy body as he hefted the tables and chairs around. After a couple of minutes, he turned and caught her staring.

"Hey," he said, with a good-natured grin. "Are you helping, or just observing?"

"Much as I would love to do the latter, we're getting short of time, so guess I'll have to help out."

A little while later, the furniture was set up and ready for the meeting.

Ethan went to open up the house to the rest of the staff, and then Alice briefed them in the ballroom so she could continue distributing notes around the table as she talked. The room was closed to the public for the duration of the meeting so they wouldn't be disturbed.

Soon, Jeremy arrived with their guests. After making sure everyone had drinks and refreshments, Alice began the meeting. As she threw the first point on her list out for discussion, she happened to catch Jeremy's eye. He and Ethan sat next to each other, and it was clear they'd been discussing something that wasn't work-related. The smirks on their faces gave her the impression *she* was the topic. More specifically, she suspected, what she and Ethan had been up to earlier. Perhaps Ethan had scribbled a note or something. God, it was just like being at school—attempting to misbehave without being caught.

Well, she could play their silly games too. Luckily, her first talking point had opened up many channels of discussion among the group, and someone else was taking minutes so she didn't have to give proceedings one hundred per cent of her attention. She picked up her pen and adopted a thoughtful expression before slipping the tip between her lips. An innocent onlooker would think she was merely thinking and chewing on her pen as she did so. Jeremy and Ethan, however, were pretty damn far from innocent and picked up on her teasing right away.

Mimicking a very, very slow and subtle blowjob, Alice looked around the table to make sure no one else was paying attention to her. They weren't. She flicked her gaze back to the two men, who shifted uncomfortably in their chairs as they watched her intently. Jeremy slipped his hand beneath the table, presumably to rearrange himself. Alice pulled the pen from her mouth and grinned widely at him.

Ethan didn't look much better off. She repeated her sexy ploy a few more times throughout the duration of the meeting, still managing to get involved in several discussions. Alice multi-tasked to the extreme—teasing the men while running a successful meeting about the manor, events, and fundraising.

Afterwards, Jeremy took their visitors back to the train station, and the other staff members who had been present at the meeting helped her and Ethan put the ballroom back to rights. Then everyone continued with their regular tasks. As a result, she wasn't alone with either of them until much, much later in the day. But as soon as she walked into the living quarters, they pounced on her—

verbally.

"You," Jeremy said, totally deadpan, "are a very, very bad girl."

Alice shrugged. "Just getting my own back, that's all. You two were clearly trying to wind me up with your grinning and the *looks* you were giving me, so I thought I'd turn the tables. You're just pissed off because you couldn't stand up for a while."

Ethan smirked. "Well, I won't disagree with that. I'm just glad we had the tables to hide behind. Or underneath, should I say."

"Me too," Jeremy put in. "We'd have looked terribly unprofessional if any of the guests or other staff had seen us sitting there with erections." He fixed Alice with a steely glare. "You, my darling, are going to be punished for this misdemeanour. And you might not like it."

He and Ethan exchanged grave looks, then turned back to Alice. She stifled a gulp. What on earth did they have in mind for her now?

Chapter Sixteen

It wasn't long before she found out what they had in store. The very next day, in fact.

Jeremy and Ethan had acted strictly professionally around her throughout the morning and afternoon. If it hadn't been for the knowing glances she caught them giving each other, she'd have thought they'd forgotten all about their threat.

She could hardly wait for the house to close, so she could find out what was going on. Good or bad, she just wanted to know.

But it turned out they had no intention of telling her. They were going to *show* her.

"Follow me, Alice," Jeremy said curtly, he and Ethan having appeared in her office once all of the visitors and staff were out of the building.

She did as she was told, hyper-aware that Ethan was close behind her. As they moved through the big old house in silence, Alice wracked her brain, trying to work out where they were going. Jeremy hadn't said whether this was a task or not. Maybe not, as whatever was going to happen was a result of her "misbehaviour" the previous day. But equally they could have adapted one of the remaining items on the list to make it into more of a punishment.

Her wonderings didn't get her anywhere, not until they arrived in front of the door that led to the chapel. Then her brain went into overdrive. Surely not? She wasn't at all religious, but using a holy space for their nefarious activities seemed wrong, somehow. Not a task, then. She'd have remembered the chapel being on the list.

Jeremy opened the door and indicated she should go in ahead of him. She'd walked a few paces into the quiet room before she realised there were no footsteps echoing hers. Spinning around, she saw that Jeremy and Ethan were still standing in the open doorway, watching her interestedly. Alice gave them a querying look, and was answered by a few seconds of complete silence. Nobody moved, or spoke.

"Go and stand in front of the altar, Alice." Jeremy's expression was unreadable—not helped by the gloom in the chapel. The old-fashioned wall mounted lights weren't very bright.

Heart racing, Alice walked up the aisle and stepped onto the raised stone platform the altar stood upon. She looked back towards the door to await her next command.

"Take off your clothes." Ethan spoke this time, and despite the lack of light, Alice could see the gleam in his eye.

She wanted to balk, to shake her head, to refuse. But it was pointless. They wouldn't force her, but if she didn't do as they asked, the resultant punishment would be even worse than the one they planned to mete out now.

Glad the room was reasonably warm—thankfully, Jeremy wasn't stingy when it came to heating the house—Alice started to remove her clothes. She made no attempt to be sexy or alluring as they hadn't specified that, so in a few seconds she was completely naked, with her rounded bottom and the backs of her shapely thighs on display to both men.

She was gratified to hear sharp intakes of breath from behind her. It helped her claw back a little bit of the power they'd taken from her when they'd made her strip in front of an altar.

It didn't last long. The control seeped away from her once more when Jeremy's next words reached her ears. "Now kneel down and ask for your sins to be forgiven."

She bit the insides of her cheeks to keep any words of protest emerging, and got to her knees as carefully as possible. Dropping down was for rooms with nice, thick carpeting—not cold, unforgiving stone. And it was seriously fucking cold. Suddenly, Alice's previous thought that the room was bearably warm was obliterated from her brain as the chilly stone beneath her sucked all the heat from her body, leaving her with uncomfortably erect nipples and skin covered in gooseflesh so tight it almost hurt.

She couldn't suppress the shiver that raced through her. A spark of anger ignited. What the hell were Jeremy and Ethan thinking? Other than the fact she was naked, there was nothing at all erotic about this situation, this game they were playing. She'd be more likely to catch a cold than make anybody come. A series of admonishments crowded her brain, and she was desperate to let them out, to tell the men exactly what she thought of this idiocy. But something made her hang on just a little longer, to see what would happen next.

Her patience was rewarded. She heard the shuffle of clothing, then footsteps moving towards her. Two sets, if she wasn't mistaken. Jeremy and Ethan came to stand either side of her. Even better—they were topless. A flicker of warmth fought the freeze permeating to Alice's bones. It grew considerably when they took an arm each, lifted her, placed their shirts beneath her knees, then lowered her back down. She could still feel the chill from the floor, but it was no longer biting.

Tilting her head to look at each of them in turn, she gave a grateful smile.

"Have you repented for your sins, Alice?" Jeremy said, looking at her sternly.

She nodded rapidly, thinking fast as she knew what his next question would be.

"And what do you have to say?"

"That I'm very sorry, sir. Sorry for teasing you and Ethan… Mr Hayes, yesterday in the ballroom. I shouldn't have done it, and I apologise."

"Very good," Jeremy replied. "Now we'll give you your punishment, then we'll forgive and forget, yes? And you mustn't touch yourself at all as we do it."

Punishment? Fuck, wasn't being made to kneel in front of an altar in the buff enough of a reprimand?

"Alice?" Jeremy prompted.

Clearly not. She nodded, less enthusiastically this time, and prepared herself for whatever they had planned.

Jeremy and Ethan glanced at each other. Jeremy gave a single nod, then the two of them undid their trousers and pulled out their cocks. They were both hard, clearly much more turned on by the situation than she was. However, Alice's libido soon picked up at the mouth-watering sight. She had to resist the temptation to reach out and take their pricks into her hands and, in turn, her mouth. It was likely what she'd be expected to do, anyway, but she knew the rules—she had to wait until she was told.

Their next move took her completely by surprise. Instead of doing what she'd suspected they would, they grasped their own shafts. Large hands circled engorged flesh and began to pump. Ethan even used his free hand to palm his balls. Alice glanced from left to right and back again, taking in the graphic imagery before her. And then it hit her; their intent became clear.

Jeremy noticed her shocked expression. "Come on, Alice. It's not that terrible a punishment. And you do deserve it." He chuckled.

Nodding meekly, she tamped down the resistance that threatened to burst out of her. Especially since it was a knee-jerk reaction. She didn't mind, really. It was quite kinky, in fact, and as she continued to observe the two men wanking over her, her pussy grew swollen, juices coated the insides of her thighs and her clit throbbed. The urge to touch herself, to masturbate along with the men, was enormous. But she'd been forbidden to do so. Alice gritted her teeth in frustration. Why did they have to be so damn sexy, so arousing?

They picked up the pace, their respective fists becoming a blur. She raked her gaze up each of their delicious bodies in turn, finally alighting on their faces. It was clear from their expressions and the tension in their muscles that they were getting incredibly close to climax. Seconds later, Jeremy began to make noises deep in his throat and Alice arched her back, thrusting out her chest, ready to catch his spunk. The groans grew louder, then were echoed by Ethan's. Alice closed her eyes.

Almost as if they'd choreographed it, Jeremy and Ethan fell silent, except for the soft swishing of skin against skin, and the slight clicking sound of the quickened strokes on their uncircumcised cocks. She heard hastily sucked-in breaths, then, finally, stripes of warm ejaculate landed on her skin. Alice let out an involuntarily gasp, then pressed her lips together to stop herself making any more noise and getting into further trouble. It seemed both men had had testicles full to bursting, as the amount of warm, sticky liquid coating her tits and décolletage seemed never-ending.

Eventually, though, their orgasms waned and Alice tentatively opened her eyes to be greeted by a vision of two red-faced, gasping, sweaty men. She stifled a grin. There was no question that they'd been in charge of the situation, but knowing she was the one to make their cocks hard, to make them come, filled her with a sense of power so extreme she felt like her head was going to pop. Unfortunately, her clit also felt fit to burst. Obeying, as she always did, the order not to touch herself meant she was still unfulfilled, and desperately horny.

"Wow," she said, her need to escape, to relieve herself, spurring her on to break the silence. "Are you feeling better, boys?"

Clearly not quite back on earth, they said nothing, instead moving to help her up. Ethan then grabbed their discarded shirts and used them to wipe Alice's chest and breasts. She smiled her thanks, then gave Jeremy a questioning look.

He nodded. "You can go, Alice. Thank you. That was…" Shrugging, he gave a wry smile. The sense of control still coursing through her body making her bold, she gave a saucy wink, bent to collect her clothes, and walked towards the door.

Just before she left the room, she looked over her shoulder and said, “Any time, gentlemen.”

Then, before her newfound bravery gave out, she scurried naked—breasts and bottom bouncing—back to her room and locked the door behind her. She shoved her clothes into her wash basket, then went straight into the bathroom and switched on the shower. She pulled the tie out of her hair as she waited for the water to reach the desired temperature. After a few seconds, she stuck her hand beneath the spray and nodded in satisfaction before stepping into the bathtub and closing the shower curtain.

Letting out a loud sigh of contentment, Alice tilted her head back, allowing the pressure of the water to pound her into a state of blissful relaxation. She turned so the spray was directed at the area that needed it most. Although Ethan had given her a thorough wipe-down, he clearly hadn’t got all the cum off, as smears of it were drying on her skin and making her itch. She grabbed her sponge and scrubbed until she was satisfied every trace of the sticky stuff was gone. Then she set about washing and conditioning her hair, followed by soaping up and rinsing her body.

It was only when she reached between her legs to make sure she was soap-free down there that she realised how swollen her clit still was. Damn, she’d have to do something about that. Jeremy may not have given her permission to masturbate in the shower, but he hadn’t said she couldn’t, either. And how would he know, anyway? As long as any sound she made was drowned out by the running water, it didn’t matter.

Throwing caution to the wind, she pressed her finger to her clit, jumping as a fresh jolt of arousal zinged through her body. She thought for a moment how much she'd prefer it if Jeremy or Ethan were doing this to her, then cast the sentiment aside. *Needs must.* And right now, what she needed was to come.

Despite the fact she'd washed, her pussy was slick once more. She spread the juices over her bud and manipulated it the way she loved best. Stroking and pinching the sensitive flesh caused her orgasm to approach swiftly, and before long she was stuffing the fingers of her free hand into her mouth to stifle the sounds she made as she was engulfed by immense pleasure.

Alice's shudders slowed as her release waned and she laid her hands against the wall behind the shower head, enjoying the hot water sluicing down her back as she waited for her breathing and heart rate to return to normal.

Finally, she felt able to move. She stepped out of the shower and turned it off. Then, after grabbing a towel, she headed into her room, dried off, plaited her hair so she didn't have to bother drying it, and pulled on her pyjamas and dressing gown. She really wanted to snuggle into bed with a book, but it was still early and a grumble from her stomach reminded her she hadn't eaten yet. Happily, she remembered it was Jeremy's turn to cook, which was a bonus, because she certainly couldn't be bothered.

On arriving in the kitchen, she found Jeremy couldn't be bothered, either. He smiled at her and brandished a set of takeaway menus. "My treat. As it should be, since it's me who's crying off the cooking. What do you fancy?"

Casting her gaze over the two men, whose wet hair and change of clothes told her they'd showered too, she sat down at the breakfast bar. Resisting the temptation to give a smutty reply to Jeremy's question, she took the menus from him and quickly sifted through, then handed one for takeaway pizzas back to him. "Any toppings you like, I don't mind. But make sure you order sides."

Jeremy flipped the menu over and looked for the section for side orders. "Which ones?"

"All of them. I'm starving! And I'm sure between the three of us, we'll eat them all."

Giving a nod, Jeremy turned to Ethan. "That all right with you, old chap?"

"Yep. You know me, I'll eat anything. Tell 'em to make it snappy."

Half an hour later, the three of them were sitting around the coffee table in the living room, digging into their food with gusto. It wasn't sophisticated, and it definitely wasn't romantic, but Alice still couldn't help her mind wandering down that path as she surreptitiously glanced at the men sitting either side of her. She loved their company, felt comfortable with them, and hated the fact their companionship—and the kinky benefits that went with it—wouldn't last forever.

A lump appeared in her throat, and she tried not to draw attention to herself as she blinked rapidly to try to prevent the prickling sensation behind her eyelids turning into full-blown tears. Fuck, what was the matter with her? She was behaving like some soppy love-struck teenager.

The moment the word entered her consciousness, she zoned in on it. *Love*. She wasn't in love—or falling in love—was she? If so, who with? Again, she sneaked glances at Jeremy and Ethan and experienced similar feelings of extreme fondness, not to mention sexual attraction, for each of them. She frowned. If she felt the same about both of them, then she couldn't be in love with one of them, could she?

Relief washed over her. That was all right, then. Love would be a complicated thing to contend with when the time came for her to leave the manor. She'd stick with extreme fondness and sexual attraction, thanks very much. It would still hurt when she left, but she'd get over it.

Eventually.

Chapter Seventeen

Alice jumped when the knock came at her bedroom door. She'd been about to go for a shower after a busy day, and before she was due to go and make dinner for the three of them.

After pulling her dressing gown on and tying it tightly around her waist—which, she realised, was pointless, given that it could only be Jeremy or Ethan who had come to her room, and they'd both seen her naked more times than she could count—she moved to open the door.

It was Jeremy. He'd been out at a meeting and was still wearing his suit. He'd taken off his tie, though, and his hair was a little messy, as though he'd been running his fingers through it. He looked incredibly sexy—there was just something about a man in a suit. And Jeremy wasn't just any man. Yum.

After a moment, she realised she hadn't actually spoken to him yet. She cleared her throat. "Hi, Jeremy. Good day?"

He raised an eyebrow and smirked, then returned the favour by looking her up and down. She tried not to fidget beneath his scrutiny. Finally, he moved his gaze back to her face. "My day was fine, thank you. Am I interrupting something?"

"N-no. I was just going for a shower. Can I help you with something?" She didn't mean work, and they both knew it.

Jeremy smirked again. "Well, you can forego your shower. For now, anyway. Ethan and I have another task for you, and you'll need a shower more afterwards than you do now."

Her heart pounded, but she willed her voice not to give away her emotions as she replied, "Okay. I'll just get dressed." She turned into the room, but he grabbed her arm and twisted her back to face him.

"Don't bother. We both know it's pointless. Just put something on your feet."

He released her, and she did as he said, shuffling into the nearest footwear, which was a pair of flip-flops. Jeremy gave a nod, then indicated she should follow him. The flip-flops slapped loudly on the wooden floor of the corridor as she walked. Alice cringed—the sound was hugely annoying. Jeremy would probably be very irritated by the time they got to their destination. Wherever that was.

She was a little surprised when they arrived at the kitchen in their living quarters, until she saw Ethan sitting at the breakfast bar. They were clearly just collecting him on the way. Alice waited for him to get up and come with them, but he didn't. He merely nodded at the two of them, then spoke to his friend. "Everything is ready."

Alice frowned, then spotted the items perched at the end of the breakfast bar. Rope, and… she gasped. They might have totally thrown her with the location, but now she'd seen the items, she knew exactly what was in store. And she wasn't particularly looking forward to it. It being their private kitchen, as opposed to the main one in the house, didn't change the fact. The only possible bonus was that she wouldn't have as far to go to get back to her room afterwards. She wished she hadn't answered her door in the first place. She should have pretended she was in the shower and hadn't heard Jeremy knocking.

Sighing, she resigned herself to her fate. Ignoring him would have made no difference. She'd have to complete the task at some point, so she might as well get it over and done with. An unexpected shiver raced across her skin, and she looked up to find both men staring at her.

Ethan got up, moved around the table towards her, and slipped his arm around her shoulders. "It'll be okay, Alice. We'll look after you, you know that."

She gave a small smile and nodded, because she knew he was right. They *would* look after her—they always did. But it didn't change her feelings towards the task—she still wasn't looking forward to it one bit. She sucked in a breath and forced a wider smile onto her face. "Okay," she said, the brightness in her voice belying her true feelings. "Ready when you are, gentlemen."

"That's my girl." Jeremy reached over and gave her a pat on the arse. "Now take off your dressing gown and flip-flops, and we'll help you onto the breakfast bar."

Just like during her last task in the chapel, Alice was thankful for the warmth of the room. But now she was prepared for the chill of the surface she was about to be put onto. She dropped her dressing gown to the floor and kicked her flip-flops on top of it. Then she moved to the end of the table nearest to her and stood with her back to it. Its edge pressed against her lower back and she was glad the men were going to help her up—her lack of height gave her a distinct disadvantage.

Jeremy and Ethan came to stand either side of her. "Ready?" Ethan asked.

She nodded in response, and they hoisted her onto the hard, unforgiving surface. It wasn't quite as cold as the floor of the chapel had been, thank God, but it made her grit her teeth nonetheless. Eager to move things along, she lay back on the table and spread herself out, then stared resolutely at the ceiling. She could almost see them exchanging a look at her hurry to get started. But then, if they'd been in her position, she was sure they'd feel the same way she did.

"Okay, Alice," Jeremy said, walking alongside the breakfast bar, trailing his fingertips up her naked body as he did so, "we're going to tie you up now."

She said nothing, since it was a statement, rather than a question. He was probably giving her a chance to back out, but the thought had never entered her head. She'd come this far; there was no way she was going to quit now. Plus, there'd probably be *some* element of pleasure in the task for her, since Jeremy and Ethan were involved. It was hardly going to be Chinese water torture.

The men secured her to the two poles supporting the breakfast bar—she suddenly wondered if they were strong enough to hold her weight. They made sure the rope was tight but comfortable, and not cutting off her circulation. Then they began to touch her. Their actions were strangely reminiscent of the task they'd completed in the servants' quarters but, sadly, without the melted chocolate. This time, though, as much as she loved fucking both men, she hoped neither of them would decide to join her on the bar—it wasn't designed to hold one person, never mind two.

She needn't have worried—that wasn't their plan. Alice quickly grew aroused as a result of their caresses, though she was a long way from orgasm.

"Alice, you're not permitted to come while we're touching you, okay? When we use the… implement, you may. But not just yet," Jeremy said.

She nodded, while secretly thinking they were mad if they thought she'd come while they used the implement, as Jeremy had called it, as opposed to when they touched her. In other words, she wasn't going to come at all. Looked like she was destined for another bout of masturbation when she got back to her room, then. *Damn.*

Her frustration grew the more they caressed her, particularly since they were exploring everywhere except in between her legs. Given the amount of time the three of them had spent playing together, the men were as familiar with her body and what she liked as she was. Her rapidly increasing wetness, swelling clit, and rock-hard nipples attested to that. Jeremy and Ethan sure knew how to push her buttons.

Jeremy stopped playing with her breasts for a second and spoke to his friend. "Ethan, see how wet she is. You're nearer."

Ethan moved a hand to her groin. He slipped his fingers between her folds and let out a groan when he discovered she was, in fact, *very* wet.

Jeremy laughed. "I'll take that as a good sign?"

Ethan stroked up and down her slick vulva, periodically knocking against her clit as he did so. Alice bit back a moan. "Yep," Ethan said. "On a scale of one to ten, I'd say she's at nine."

Alice raised her eyebrows. *Really?* She was horny—and getting more so by the second—but she hadn't realised just wet she'd grown, and how quickly.

"Excellent," Jeremy replied, removing his hands from Alice's breasts, then stepping out of her eyeline. She heard him pick something up. "So do you think she'll be able to take *this*, then?"

Alice had already seen the item in question, so she didn't bother trying to twist her head to glimpse what he was holding. But the knowledge alone caused dread to trail a chilly finger up her spine, then dip down to clasp her stomach in its icy hand.

Ethan was silent for a second, assessing the thing that Jeremy held aloft, then nodded. "Yeah, definitely. It's no bigger than either of our cocks, is it? And she manages them pretty well!"

They laughed. The sound sent a wave of anger through Alice's body. Ethan's words hadn't helped, either. What he'd said was true, but the difference was she *wanted* their cocks inside her. Their warm and hard—yet slightly pliable—cocks, which were attached to two of the sexiest men she'd ever met.

The pestle, on the other hand, was *not* something she wanted inside her. It was cold, completely and utterly rigid. It was designed for grinding things, for God's sake! And yet Jeremy had got it into his head that it would be erotic to put it in her pussy. She gritted her teeth again. She would endure it, *she would.* It was just one little task, and she'd been through much worse—she'd been forbidden to wear underwear and spanked with a wooden ruler and a carpet beater. A mere pestle would not defeat her.

She smiled tightly, then fought to make the grin more genuine. "Okay then, boys," she said, wriggling in what she hoped was a seductive fashion and pulling against her restraints a little. "So what are you waiting for? I'm ready."

"Oh, Alice," Jeremy said, moving back to where she could see him and stroking her hair. "You're not fooling anyone, sweetheart. We know you're not keen on this task, but we also know you'll do it anyway. How about this? We're nice, really, so let's sweeten the pot. You do this, and we'll fuck you afterwards. How does that sound?"

It sounded a great deal more bearable. Certainly preferable to scurrying off to her room to come by herself. She nodded, mildly annoyed that he presumed having sex with the two of them was such a wonderful thing. But of course, the arrogant bastard was right. She'd never hidden the fact she enjoyed screwing them, and even if she had, her body would have betrayed her, traitor that it was.

"Good girl." He stroked her hair again, then leant down to kiss her forehead. "You can lie back and think of England if you like, darling, but I don't think it's going to be as bad as you believe it will be."

She shrugged—not easy, bound as she was—and bade him get on with it.

"As you wish, my darling. As you wish. Ethan." He handed the pestle to Ethan, who took it with a grin.

Fuck, this was it. She knew she was being stupid—it really wouldn't be that bad—but she couldn't help the flutters of anxiety that ran through her. There was something about the prospect of having that damn thing thrust up her that turned her right off.

Which, presumably, was why Jeremy and Ethan had indulged in a fair amount of foreplay with her beforehand. And now they were going to make the most of it.

Ethan settled the end of the pestle against her pussy lips. She closed her eyes. Felt the cold marble tracing up and down the edge of her outer labia, then slowly, slowly, being pushed between her folds. The delicate skin there was even more sensitive to the chill. She gasped, jerking away from the pending intrusion, though her bound wrists and ankles meant she didn't get far. To his credit, Ethan didn't laugh—though as her eyes were closed she wasn't sure if he smiled—he just continued his task. As she'd moved, he had to start again. This time she was determined to grin and bear it.

He repeated his previous movements, and pushed until the bulbous end of the cool marble phallus was against her entrance. She pulled in a breath through her nose and puffed it out through her mouth, harnessing all the calm she could manufacture to stop herself resisting the penetration. It worked. She still wasn't entirely happy, but her eyes flew open with surprise when the pestle slowly made its way inside her. It felt… good. Strange, and nothing at all like a hot, stiff cock, but good.

"Fuuuuck." The word tumbled from her lips, causing Ethan to glance at her face, his own creasing into a frown. Once he realised she was exclaiming in pleasure, rather than dislike or discomfort, his frown turned into a grin.

"All right?" he asked.

She nodded vigorously, growing more aroused as the makeshift dick filled her pussy. Barely realising what she was saying, she told him, "Don't stop."

Ethan's eyebrows shot up almost into his hairline. "Well," he said, smirking at Jeremy, then back at her, "you've certainly changed your tune. And here I was, thinking you were hating it. And me."

I could never hate you, she thought, but didn't say it. "I didn't think I'd like it. But it actually feels really good. Nothing like a real cock, but in a pinch it would certainly get the job done."

Both men burst into sudden laughter, then Jeremy said, "So are we going to have to hide the pestle from you after tonight? We don't want you wanking with it. Not when there are two perfectly willing men to assist you if you're feeling the need."

She stifled a giggle. Did they honestly think she didn't masturbate? Granted, she was getting more sex now than she'd had in all her previous sexually active years put together, but it had only served to make her libido more rampant. If she went to one—or both—of them every time she felt frisky, they'd never get any work done. Or sleep.

She said nothing, though, instead rolling her hips to pull the pestle deeper inside her. "All right, Little Miss Impatient," Ethan said, twisting his wrist so the marble pressed deliciously against her G-spot, "you'll get your orgasm, don't worry. And at least a couple more besides." He winked at Jeremy, and the two of them laughed again.

"Good," she all but choked out, then lay back and took what was coming to her. And boy, was Ethan skilled with a pestle! She had no idea if he was any good at grinding herbs and spices, but he was brilliant at manipulating her where she most wanted and needed it. Before long, she'd had an almost violent G-spot climax which made her squirt out all over the pestle, Ethan's hand, and the breakfast bar.

"Bloody hell!" Ethan said, slowly pulling the marble shaft out of her. "That was incredible." He looked to his friend for confirmation.

Jeremy gave a small nod, looking astounded. "Yes, that's one word for it. I've seen her squirt before, but not quite like that. Maybe we should use the pestle more often." He looked over at Alice, who smiled beatifically.

"Well, I think you'll find I've completed my task, gentlemen. So how about you keep your promise? Who's first?"

Neither of them replied, instead moving to untie her as quickly as possible. She sat up, then rubbed her wrists and rotated her ankles until they felt normal again. When she was done, she let Jeremy and Ethan help her down from the breakfast bar. "Thank you. So, where to?"

"Not far," Jeremy said, taking her hand and leading her into the living room. He turned her around and pushed her back onto the sofa. She landed on the soft cushions with a giggle, her smile widening as the two men began taking off their clothes. They were clearly in a hurry, and she laughed as they struggled to get naked without falling over or getting stuck. It was only then she realised they were in some kind of race—they hadn't actually said anything, but she suspected whoever undressed the fastest would be the one to fuck her first. She wasn't bothered either way—she was going to have both of them, and it really didn't matter which order they went in. Or whether she sucked one and fucked the other. It would be fantastic, whatever happened.

She didn't have long to wait. Ethan won their impromptu race and quickly knelt down on the floor in front of the sofa, pushed her legs apart, and buried his head between them. She let out a hiss of pleasure as his warm, agile tongue began to explore the area that had not so long ago been touched by the cold marble of the pestle. A fresh gush of juice came from her pussy and coated Ethan's tongue and lips, and he groaned in response. His enthusiasm and enjoyment were what made him so damn good at eating her out. She'd quite happily sit back all day and let him bring her to climax after climax.

Actually, that wasn't strictly true. As much as she loved getting head, she knew that after a while, she'd be gagging to have his cock inside her. Or Jeremy's. Or even that damn pestle. Whatever.

Thoughts of Jeremy made her turn her head to see what he was up to. He stood a pace away from his friend, watching her writhe at Ethan's ministrations. His hand was wrapped around his cock, pumping it slowly. A bead of pre-cum sat at its tip. Suddenly, she wanted nothing more than to taste it. She beckoned to him, then indicated he should get up on the sofa so she could suck him. He did so eagerly, placing a hand on the back of the sofa to steady himself while he used the other to feed his prick into her waiting mouth.

She tasted the saltiness of his pre-cum, then licked it all off his skin and poked her tongue greedily into his slit to get more. Removing his hand from his shaft, Jeremy tangled it in her hair and groaned as she sunk her lips further down his cock. Had her mouth not been otherwise occupied, she'd have smiled at his reaction.

She soon forgot all about that as she struggled to concentrate on two things at once—teasing Jeremy's dick while Ethan used his talented tongue on her cunt. Ethan had picked up the pace, using one hand to pull back the hood of her clitoris while slipping two fingers from the other hand inside her. The touch of his tongue directly on her nub was almost too much. She groaned.

The sound sent vibrations onto Jeremy's shaft and he gasped at the unexpected sensation. His cock twitched, coating her tongue with another hot slick of liquid. Alice's pussy creamed in response, and a muffled groan from between her legs told her that Ethan was licking it up eagerly, and happily.

Alice wondered if Ethan's cock was as hard as his friend's. Suddenly, she wanted nothing more than to find out. She twisted her head to pop Jeremy's shaft from her mouth. "Ethan, are you ready to fuck me?"

"Fuck, yes. Shall I?"

She beamed at his response. "Absolutely. Oh, and while you're there, make me come."

"Don't I always?"

Not bothering to answer the rhetorical question, she took Jeremy's dick back into her mouth and continued to suck it. She deliberately didn't go too fast or too hard, because she didn't actually want to make him come. Not in her mouth, at any rate. Her plan was to have him fuck her straight after Ethan. Then, who knew, by the time Jeremy was finished, Ethan might be ready to go again. She was quite happy to screw both of them until they were all completely spent.

Ethan slipped his tongue around her vulva and flicked it

across her clit while he pushed his fingers back inside her, making sure she was ready for him. She shoved her hips forward, silently urging him to get on with it. She was more than ready. Thankfully, he took the hint. The sofa dipped and his body bumped against hers as he shifted himself into a suitable position for fucking her. Yet more juices trickled from her pussy in anticipation. Ethan used them to lubricate his cock as he rubbed it up and down her slit, then he moved so the tip notched against her entrance.

Remembering this was no longer part of the challenge, and she could do what she damn well wanted, Alice reached out and wrapped an arm as far around Ethan's broad back as she could—which wasn't far at all—and pulled him into her. He exclaimed and quickly moved his own arms to support his weight and avoid crushing her—and getting his face too close to his friend's backside.

From the corner of her eye she saw Ethan's delicious body as it worked to pleasure hers. His hair had flopped over his face, so she couldn't see his expression, but she sure enjoyed the rest of the view. The muscles of his torso flexed and rolled as he thrust slowly in and out of her. His biceps bulged. And she was pretty sure his arse looked gorgeous too. She made a mental note to try to fuck one of the men when there was a mirror behind him, so she could see his tight buttocks as he fucked her. Or maybe a mirror on the ceiling would be a good idea.

If her mouth hadn't been full, she'd have giggled. Here she was, thinking like the lady of the manor, fantasising about changes of decor as though she was going to be here longer than a few more weeks, or that it was anything to do with her.

The thought was driven from her head as Ethan began to thrust into her powerfully. He'd clearly had enough of going slowly, and now planned to fuck her fast until it drove them both to climax. Somehow, he managed to angle his body so his pubic bone pressed against her clit with every movement, and her pussy rippled in delicious sympathy. It would be easy to reach down and stroke herself, but she trusted him to make her come before—or at the same time—as he did. When he sped up further, a flicker of doubt passed through her mind, but she shoved it away. Even if he didn't make her come, it wasn't the end of the world. He could finish her off with fingers or tongue, or leave it to Jeremy.

She needn't have worried. He altered his technique so instead of pistoning in and out of her, he rotated his hips so their groins never parted. Her eyes rolled back in her head at the divine sensation. She passed it along to Jeremy, reaching up to cup and caress his balls, which she knew he enjoyed. But even though much of her mind was taken over by bliss, she remembered not to overstimulate him. It didn't seem to matter. Either because of the length of time she'd been sucking and licking his dick or the situation in general, he began to jerk, forcing himself deeper into her throat—a sure sign he was close to coming. She allowed it for a little longer, until he grew so frantic she worried it was too late.

She pulled him from her mouth and squeezed her fingers around the base of his shaft. "Not yet! It's your turn next."

Jeremy's breathing was heavy, his face red. He didn't speak, just nodded. He wrapped his hand around his shaft and stroked so slowly he hardly moved. Watching him for a second or two, Alice figured he was keeping himself hard so he could jump in as soon as Ethan was done. Satisfied he wasn't going to come just yet, she turned her attention back to Ethan, who was also red-faced and panting. She was impressed she'd been able to divide her concentration between the men so well—obviously she'd got better at it the more often they played together.

Vaguely aware that Jeremy had clambered off the sofa, she shifted her hands to grip Ethan's upper arms, giving her leverage to meet him thrust for thrust. The added bonus being how good he felt beneath her fingers—the man truly had biceps to die for. And she intended to hold on to them as he screwed her into oblivion. This time, her mouth unimpeded, she let out a peal of laughter. It distracted Ethan from his rhythm, but not for long.

She soon shut up when he started grinding against her, stimulating her clit where it was crushed between their bodies. Her grip on his arms was so hard she was surprised he didn't yelp. But then, he was no wimp. It probably felt like a tickle to him.

Soon, yelping and tickling were the furthest things from her mind. The tightening of her abdomen and slight fluttering of her pussy that always signalled the start of her orgasm had increased. "Ethan…" she murmured, looking at him earnestly.

Luckily, he knew exactly what she was getting at and picked up his pace until he was moving at an almost impossible speed. All those hours he spent working out, and she was the one reaping the benefits.

Their moans and groans filled the air; as did the slick noises given off as his cock plundered her soaked pussy. As she grew closer and closer to climax, she happened to glance over at Jeremy. He was watching her, utterly rapt. When he realised she was looking at him, he gave a devilish grin and winked salaciously. "You are sooo fucking hot, Alice."

His words helped tip her over the edge. She clung on to Ethan like a limpet as intense pleasure ripped through her. Her pussy milked his cock, causing him to yell as his own release overtook him. They gasped and spasmed together, and she held his head in her hands and looked into his eyes for a second before pouring every ounce of her feelings for him into a toe-curling, passionate kiss. Her heart actually skipped a beat when they eventually parted and she saw the look in his eyes that seemed to convey that his feelings mirrored hers. But she couldn't hope that was true—it would all end in tears. Hers.

Jeremy broke the silence. "Hey, you two. Isn't it my turn?"

Confusingly, Alice wasn't at all irritated by his words. She was happy to hear them, despite the interruption of the "moment" that had just taken place between her and Ethan. Jeremy wanted her. And as she looked at him, she realised how much she wanted him too. She pressed a brief kiss to Ethan's lips and motioned that he should swap places with his friend.

Jeremy clapped Ethan on the shoulder as the two men passed each other, then knelt on the floor in front of the sofa. "Hey you," he said, gently brushing her damp hair back from her face, "lie down. I'm not a martyr like him; I want to screw you without getting carpet burns on my knees."

She giggled and did as he said. He quickly joined her on the sofa and moved between her legs. Then he covered her with his body, propping his elbows either side of her chest and leaning down to capture her lips in a searing kiss.

Alice didn't think it was possible to get any wetter—particularly as Ethan's cum was now making its way out of her—but the intent behind Jeremy's kiss was powerful, so powerful it made her head spin. Her heart pounded as the startling realisation hit her that she really did feel the same way about both men. And, as much as she tried to deny it to herself, that feeling was love. Pure and simple.

She was so fucked.

When Jeremy pulled away, she managed to get out of that particular headspace. Just because she'd had the revelation didn't mean she had to tell them about it. In fact, it would be much better to keep quiet. If she said something, she had no doubt things would become massively complicated. It was unlikely that *one* of them felt the same way, never mind both. And would she be content with just one of them? Especially knowing how close they were and that they pretty much came as a package, along with Davenport Manor.

Fortunately, Jeremy was so busy burying his head between her ample breasts that he didn't notice she wasn't one hundred per cent into what they were doing. When he bit one of her nipples, she let out a screech born more of shock than pain, and gave him all of her attention. She heard Ethan chuckle behind her and tilted her head back to see him standing at the end of the sofa, playing with his balls and rapidly growing erection. Damn, these men had stamina. Perhaps she'd get her screwing-until-they-were-completely-spent wish, after all.

For now, though, she was still on round one with Jeremy and he was clearly very eager to get inside her. His foreplay, though skilful as always, wasn't quite as enthusiastic as normal. She decided to put him out of his misery. "Go for it, Jeremy. You know I'm wet—though granted, some of it is Ethan's spunk—and the sooner you get going, the more likely you'll be to make me come again. I refuse to let either of you leave until you've *both* given me at least two orgasms each."

Jeremy didn't react to her comment about Ethan's cum, but when she made her orgasm demand, he looked over her head at his friend and grinned. She could only assume Ethan was beaming back.

"Hey," she said, reaching up and lightly slapping Jeremy's cheek, "stop gawping at him, and get on with it."

"As you wish, my lady."

A snort escaped her at the thought of being a lady, but the sound quickly morphed into a groan of pleasure when Jeremy sunk his cock into her in one smooth movement. He leaned on his hands and started to fuck her in earnest. She grabbed his buttocks and held on for the ride. Moments later, she squeezed her eyes closed and let her head loll back as another climax approached. A series of unintelligible sounds filled the room, and it took a few seconds before Alice realised it was her making them.

Jeremy's grunts and gasps joined hers in a chorus which grew louder and more frequent, until they reached a peak as their climaxes hit, one after the other. For the second time that evening, Alice's pussy clenched around an eager cock and milked it dry. Her own orgasm was more powerful than the last, and by the time she came down she was aching and lethargic. Thoughts of showering, then sinking into bed began to invade her mind. Dinner be damned. If the boys were hungry, they could make themselves a sandwich.

A movement in the corner of her eye made her turn her head. Ethan stood there, still naked and gorgeous, with his stiff cock in his hand.

She smiled. It looked as though she wouldn't be having that shower or heading to bed any time soon.

Chapter Eighteen

Alice sat in her office, flipping through the pages of her diary for that week. After a minute, a startling realisation hit her. She checked the date again, and the colour drained from her face. Her contract was almost up—she only had four weeks left at Davenport Manor. Beautiful Davenport Manor and her dream job, and the dream men she'd been fooling around with for months. Her heart jolted uncomfortably, and she suddenly felt so sick she actually scrambled around under her desk for her bin.

She alternately gasped and dry heaved over the waste basket for a minute or so, until it became clear it was a false alarm. Heaving a sigh of relief, she grabbed the half empty bottle of water from her desk and drained it, before throwing it away. Sitting silently for a few minutes, she rubbed her temples and waited until she felt a little better before continuing what she'd been doing.

Then another realisation hit her. Since she only had a month left at Davenport Manor, surely that meant her tasks were almost complete? Jeremy had obviously planned it so they were spread out over the nine months, and as a result, were never that close together. So perhaps she only had one or two left.

She hurriedly retrieved the book she was currently reading from the top drawer of her desk and opened it to the last page. There, tucked inside the back cover, was her copy of the list. It looked a little worse for wear, having been transferred from bags to pockets to drawers and, finally, to this book. But the writing was still clearly legible, and Alice saw she was right—her tasks were almost complete. Only one left. A huge smile crossed her face as she took it in. She'd expected the final task to be horrendous—saving the worst until last, in this case. But she couldn't have been more wrong. It was going to be a great deal of fun.

A few days later, on the day the house was closed to the public, Jeremy came to her in her office. "Alice," he placed his hand over the paperwork she'd been reading, forcing her to look at him, "leave that. Ethan and I have planned your final task for today."

"B-but the cleaners, and the gardeners… Won't they see…?"

"No, they won't. I've made an excuse for them not to come in today—though I've still paid them, of course—so the three of us will be totally alone. I could have just made sure the gardeners were at the other end of the grounds, and the cleaners wouldn't have been able to see us from the windows of the house, anyway. But I suspected you'd feel uncomfortable if they were on the premises, which is why I took that particular decision. It's just us three, sweetheart."

"Um, okay." She had no more excuses. Secretly, she was pleased, since this task was no chore. In fact, it would be an absolute pleasure. A glance out of the window revealed that the weather gods had even conspired to help them. The sun was out, and there wasn't a cloud in the sky. Perfect. She took the hand Jeremy held out, and walked with him through to the back of the house, out through the patio doors in the parlour and onto the grass. Once they passed out of the shadow of the manor, the sun caressed the exposed skin of her arms, lower legs, neck and face. Alice grinned—she'd always loved the sun. Even though she never tanned, she still enjoyed basking in it, the sensation of it on her skin.

As they moved past the lawns and parterres, Alice spotted their destination. The view opened up when they rounded the outside corner of the walled garden.

Ethan sat on one of the benches surrounding the maze, waiting for them. He smiled as he spotted them, and even from a distance, Alice saw the way his face lit up, and just how damn gorgeous he was when he smiled. Well, all the time, actually, but particularly when his eyes twinkled and those dimples appeared in his cheeks.

The depressing thought that she'd have to commit such things to memory as she wouldn't be around much longer slipped into her brain. She shoved it away roughly and picked up her pace to get to the maze, and Ethan. Jeremy made a sound of surprise at her sudden burst of speed, but went along with it. He probably thought she was eager to get on with it—which was true, but not because, like the last task, she wanted to get it over and done with. It was because she wanted to have some *fun* with it. To drive the unwelcome thoughts from her mind for as long as possible, and lose herself in the eroticism the two men supplied in buckets.

She grinned at Ethan as she and Jeremy reached him. He winked back. "You ready for this, Alice? Your final task?"

Her smile widened. "Sure am. I think this will probably be my favourite task of all."

"You would say that." He ran a hand through his hair, which was creeping past his shirt collar—he was obviously overdue for a haircut. "You're guaranteed action and you won't have to work for it."

"That's true." She looked from Ethan to Jeremy and back again. "But I think I've earned it already, don't you? After what you two have put me through."

"Hey," Jeremy interjected, his tone serious, "you signed up for this, sweetheart. Nobody forced you—"

"I *know*." She shot him a glare. "I never said you'd forced me. I'm just saying I think I've earned the fun I'll have in this task, that's all. It's more of a task for you two, really."

Jeremy and Ethan exchanged a look which Alice couldn't decipher, so she didn't bother to try. "So," she said brightly, grinning at them, "shall I head to the middle?"

Jeremy opened his mouth to protest—perhaps because she'd taken charge somewhat—but Ethan put a hand on his arm.

"Yes," Ethan replied, returning her smile, "that would be great. Give us a shout when you're in the centre of the maze and Jeremy and I will take our positions."

"Okay." She turned away and headed for the nearest entrance.

"Alice," Jeremy called, stopping her in her tracks. She looked at him over her shoulder. "Just remember, although it'll be Ethan and I competing, you'll be expected to do whatever is required of you by whichever one of us reaches you first."

His expression was deadly serious, and Alice wondered what he had planned if he were to win the race to the centre of the maze. Surely there wasn't much he could do to or demand of her that hadn't already been done or demanded in the time she'd been at Davenport Manor. She gave a nod, then continued towards the maze.

Soon after, she passed through the nearest gap in the huge yew "walls" and entered a world of greenery.

As much as she was looking forward to what was about to happen—she loved the idea of the two men competing for her—she didn't rush to the centre of the maze. She'd only been inside it once before as she'd been so busy with work in her time at the manor, and she hadn't been alone. This time, she had the chance to take in and admire her surroundings. Jeremy was right—the maze was so tall that even the attic windows of Davenport Manor didn't provide a view inside it. But still, he'd sent everyone away today, so the three of them could partake in this final challenge without fear of interruption.

Desperate not to dwell on the *final* element, Alice pushed on, having no idea where she was going. It was eerie, actually, as though she was in a world of her own. There were no sounds—not even birdsong—and all she could see was endless green, unless she looked up at the cloudless sky. The sun hadn't yet reached its height, so it didn't penetrate the gloom surrounding her. A shiver rippled through her skin, leaving goose bumps in its wake, and she was suddenly eager to get to the centre—a clearing large enough that there should be some sunlight. Hopefully. Plus, she'd then be able to call out and start proceedings, ending her solitary state in a matter of minutes. Thank God—she'd enjoyed the alone time at first, but the longer she wandered between the yew hedges, the more on edge she became.

She concentrated harder on remembering where she'd already been, so she didn't keep getting stuck in dead ends, or have to retrace her steps. Soon, she entered an area she didn't remember. Her heart leapt. Yes—she was getting somewhere! She walked faster, taking turn after turn, turning back only a couple of times until finally, *finally*, she was at one end of a long, green corridor. At the other end stood the large stone bench that marked the centre of the maze. Behind the bench was the path that led back out of the maze on its other side.

So basically, if she sat sideways on the bench she'd be able to see who was going to reach her first. Though she wasn't sure "bench" was quite the right word for it—it had no legs, arms or back. It was a carved stone, rectangular structure that looked more like a plinth for an effigy of some kind. It wasn't, of course; it was just an ornamental piece that had been put in the manor garden who knew how many years ago. It had seen plenty of weather, that was for sure. Its edges were worn, and the inscription on the top was barely visible. But it was clean—Jeremy made sure of that by having it professionally taken care of once a year. She remembered him telling her that on her only previous visit to the maze.

She hurried down the path, glad to see the sunlight that bathed the bench. Hopefully its surface would be nice and warm on her bottom while she waited for her first suitor. She giggled at the choice of word. It was so old-fashioned, and yet it was exactly how she felt, having two men fight—sort of—over her. Like the jousting tournaments of the Middle Ages. Though the more she thought about it, the more she realised it didn't really matter who won—they were both going to have her, but whoever reached her first would be calling the shots.

Then, remembering that no one would come at all unless she let them know she was ready, she called out, “Okay, boys, I’m in the middle!”

They yelled in unison, “Okay!”

They continued speaking, but at a normal volume, so she couldn’t hear what they were saying. She assumed they were making arrangements for what happened next.

Silence followed, then, after a few seconds, Ethan called out, “I’m here!”

More quiet. Then, “Me too! You ready?”

“Ready. On three!”

The countdown began. After they both shouted out the final number, there was quiet once more. That was it—they were on their way.

Alice couldn’t help but wonder who would reach her first. Ethan, being taller and with longer legs could probably move faster. But perhaps his bulk would slow him down? Jeremy, on the other hand, had lived in the manor all his life—bar his university years, of course—and likely knew the maze better. Both men had positives and negatives, so it really was impossible to guess who would win. She would just have to wait and see.

If she listened carefully, she could hear the shuffle and scrape of shoes on the paths, and sighs and curses as the pair made their way to the middle. It was impossible to tell who was closest—just because one man sounded nearer didn’t mean he had the shortest distance to go before reaching the centre. It was misleading—which, of course, was the whole point of a maze.

She'd taken up the position which meant she could see both of the passageways that led to the centre of the maze, and she looked left to right, then back again. Over and over. It was like watching a game of tennis—only much more exciting. A prickle of anticipation ran up her spine, and made the tiny hairs on the back of her neck stand up.

Who would it be? Who was going to win?

The sound of footsteps grew louder; she couldn't be entirely sure whether it was one set, or two. There came heavy breathing and the swish of clothing. Finally, movement from her right. Goosebumps raced over her skin as Jeremy appeared at the end of the yew corridor and began to jog towards her. She smiled, and he returned it.

It was hardly surprising he was first. Speed and muscle were no match for the intricacies of a maze, unless you were going to crash through the walls. Both men were incredibly intelligent, but Jeremy had the advantage of years of practice. She wondered how far Ethan had to go.

Almost immediately, the man in question emerged from the gloom and caught sight of her. His gaze flicked to his friend, then back to her. After a beat, both men began sprinting towards her. Jeremy was closer, but Ethan was faster. Fuck. They were running at full pelt towards the stone bench. It could all end horribly if they didn't stop in time. Visions of a collision, or at the very least, badly-bruised shins, passed through her mind. She shuddered and closed her eyes, unable to watch.

Pulling her knees up to her chest and wrapping her arms

around her legs, Alice waited. She didn't care about the draught which now had full access to her lady parts. All she could think about was the crash that would happen in seconds. Milliseconds, even.

She heard scrabbling, harsh breathing, and then the slap of a hand on stone. Followed by an "Ouch!" She opened one eye and squinted at the scene, before opening both eyes properly. Jeremy was cradling his hand and, on the opposite side of her, Ethan had stopped a pace away.

She raised an enquiring eyebrow at Jeremy. He grinned sheepishly, shrugging. "I whacked the bench a little too hard." He shook his hand from the wrist. "I'll live."

"I bloody hope so," Alice said, returning his smile. "I'd feel terrible if you died of your injury. This wasn't supposed to be a fight to the death, you know."

Jeremy winked at Ethan, then looked back at her. "Yes, I do know. We both do. Which is why we like to share. It saves arguments all round, you see. And we've never had any complaints."

Alice looked from one man to the other. "No, I can't imagine you have. Being shared by you two is certainly nothing to moan about."

"Except in the good way," Ethan piped up, his dimples flashing.

"Huh?" After a beat, the penny dropped. She laughed and nodded. "Agreed. The pair of you definitely make me moan in the good way."

"Speaking of which," Jeremy interjected, holding his

uninjured hand out to help her up, "shall we?"

She frowned. "Where are we going?" She'd assumed they would get down and dirty right there in the maze.

"Not far," Jeremy replied. "Stand up on the bench." He continued to hold her hand for support as she climbed up onto the stone surface. Ethan moved to stand behind her—a reassuring move, should she lose her balance and fall. It wasn't a long way down, but landing on the hard ground would still hurt both her body and her pride.

As she straightened, Alice's mind whirled with the possibilities. Was he going to join her on the seat and fuck her standing up? Or move behind her and bend her over? No, that didn't make any sense, because Ethan was standing behind her, and she was pretty sure he didn't want a view of his best friend's arse as he fucked the woman they were sharing.

The pieces finally slotted into place when Jeremy lifted her skirt. Ever on the ball, Ethan reached out and gripped her hips, holding the material in place while steadying her at the same time. As Jeremy manoeuvred himself to the right level, Alice was supremely grateful for Ethan's presence. The last thing she wanted was to be admitted to hospital for head trauma brought on by orgasm and a resultant fall. That would be pretty embarrassing to explain. She reached down and gripped Ethan's wrists for extra support.

And not a moment too soon. Jeremy pushed the insides of her thighs, forcing her to shuffle her feet further apart. He hooked his thumbs into her outer labia and separated them, exposing her delicate and sensitive skin. Alice had been so absorbed in the men's race through the maze that she hadn't thought properly about what would happen when one of them won. As a result, she wasn't particularly horny. That changed when Jeremy's warm tongue touched her pussy. She gasped and dug her fingers into Ethan's wrists, causing him to pull in a sharp breath.

Jeremy's talented tongue danced over and between her folds, rapidly arousing her and making her pussy and clit swell. She grew more sensitive and her body quickly responded, sending lubrication where it was needed most. Gravity pulled it slowly down her channel and, seconds later, into Jeremy's receptive mouth. He swallowed it enthusiastically, rolling his tongue up and slipping it inside to taste more of her. The action coaxed out yet more liquid, and a delicious cycle began. When she was good and soaked, Jeremy moved his attentions to her clit, slicking her juices over the swollen nub and teasing it exactly how she liked it. And it was just *teasing*. He knew she wouldn't come this way. Not that what he was doing didn't feel good, but he was clearly treating her to a slow burn; making her hornier and hornier, while avoiding her self-destruct button. Then, when he was ready, he'd push that button and send her kicking and screaming—or should that be creaming?—into blissful oblivion.

She could hardly wait.

Jeremy moved his face away from her and slipped one finger inside her saturated channel. He quickly pulled it out, only to replace it with three. She was so wet that he entered effortlessly, and she soon adjusted to the invasion. Particularly when he manoeuvred so the tips of his fingers pressed against her G-spot. As he began to pleasure her, causing her legs to tremble, Alice was once again incredibly grateful for Ethan's steadying presence.

As Jeremy tormented her G-spot into submission, he put his lips and tongue where she wanted them most—her clit. She yelped as he pulled the sensitive bunch of nerve endings into his mouth and sucked, while flicking his tongue around it. The quivering in her legs increased, and she tensed up to avoid flopping either forwards or backwards and squashing one of the men. At first, the tension increased as her body scrabbled towards climax. Then, after a few more minutes of enthusiastic licking, sucking, and fingering on Jeremy's part, Alice came undone. At least that was what it felt like—as though she was unravelling, and pieces of her were floating away on the wind. She cried out, which brought her back to herself and the fact that both men were holding her up now. She made eye contact with Jeremy and gave him a goofy grin.

He smiled back. "Come on, let's get you in the house. I have further plans for you, young lady."

She giggled, a sound which abruptly turned into a squeal when Ethan spun her around, then positioned her over his shoulder in a fireman's lift. He landed a hearty smack on her arse. Alice squealed again, then retaliated. Ethan laughed, then groaned when she grabbed both his buttocks and gave them a squeeze.

"This could go on forever," Alice said. Her voice sounded strange, but then she *was* hanging upside down.

"You're right," Ethan replied. "Let's go back to the house and get on with something even more fun than arse slapping." With that, he headed down the narrow pathway he'd entered the maze from and made his way out. He slowed down as he approached each turning, working out which way to go. After only two wrong choices, they emerged into the sunlight, with Jeremy close behind.

Chapter Nineteen

"Are you going to let me down now?" Alice asked. "You must be about ready to collapse beneath all my weight."

He slapped her bottom again, harder this time. "Don't say such silly things, Alice. You're perfect as you are—and besides, I've been eating my spinach."

"Ethan's right," Jeremy put in, "you mustn't be so self-deprecating. So you're not a size ten. So what? It doesn't make you any less beautiful. Now be quiet, while us men drag you back to our cave."

Alice let her head drop back down, which provided her with an excellent view of Ethan's rear end—never a bad thing. Her face grew warm, and it wasn't just as a result of gravity making the blood rush to her head. It was because of what Ethan and Jeremy had said. They'd called her perfect, and beautiful. Warm, fuzzy feelings infused her body and had her floating on cloud nine until they reached their living quarters and the men had a my-room-or-yours? conversation.

She was brought back to earth with a bump when she was dropped onto Jeremy's bed. Ethan had tried to lower her as carefully as possible, but physics meant she still landed heavily, and the mattress springs gave her a shove or two back. Alice gasped as she took in her surroundings. She'd thought her room was nice, but this was *stunning*. It was ridiculous to think she'd been living in Davenport Manor for eight months and yet she hadn't set foot in either man's room. They were probably the only rooms in the whole building she hadn't explored.

Now, as she drank in every detail, she couldn't help but think she'd saved the best until last. The décor was very similar to that in her bedroom, but the differences in everything else were striking. The room was much bigger, with more windows. A glance towards the open door of the bathroom told her that Jeremy didn't have a bath—he had a hot tub. And then there was the furniture. There were beautiful chairs similar to the antiques that had pride of place in various other rooms throughout the manor, and a gorgeous dresser and bedside cabinets. As for the bed itself… well, words didn't describe. Without looking at it properly she didn't know if the oak four-poster was original or replica, but either way it was breath-taking. The drapes and duvet were far from authentic—they'd been replaced with something much more suited to a 38-year-old male living in the 21st century. But they didn't detract from the splendour of the bed, and the room in general.

It was then Alice finally came to the conclusion that she was way out of her league. She had no idea how much Jeremy was actually worth, but it was an amount someone like her could only dream of—and try desperately to achieve with the aid of frequent lottery ticket purchases.

She wondered for the umpteenth time what he and Ethan were doing with her. Ethan wasn't the lord of the manor, of course, but she suspected Jeremy paid his friend way over the going rate for a head of security role. That way he could keep him close so they could continue to cause the havoc they'd clearly been leaving behind since their university days.

"Hey," Jeremy barked. "Whatever thoughts are going

through your mind to make you frown like that, get rid of them right this minute. If you don't, I'll *make* you."

His tone sent shivers down Alice's spine. Her thoughts had indeed dissipated, which was kind of unfortunate, because she quite liked the idea of him *making* her.

"Are you with us now, Alice? Back in the room?"

He didn't sound angry, exactly. Perhaps bossy or domineering were better descriptors. Either way, the exchange had left Alice seriously horny and unable to speak. She nodded.

"Good. Now, if you could remove your clothes, Ethan and I will do the same."

"We will?" Ethan asked.

"Yes, of course. I may be the victor, but we're still sharing our dear Alice."

"Fantastic—I thought I might just have to watch you with her."

"Nope. Though I am going first."

"Fair enough."

Alice undressed. It didn't take long, given all she wore was a dress, a bra, and her shoes. The men were wearing more than she was, and they'd been far too busy talking to do anything else. So now she sat in the middle of the huge bed, watching them get naked and wondering exactly what was in store for her.

She didn't have to wait long to find out. Soon she was feasting her eyes on two bare male bodies as they advanced on her. Jeremy asked Ethan to go and sit on the other side of the bed, while he clambered up alongside Alice. He knelt in front of her, then cupped her face in his hands and kissed her. It was deep, possessive; probably the hottest kiss she'd ever had. So hot, in fact, that she grew wet almost immediately. Juices trickled down her crack and onto Jeremy's no doubt designer bedspread. *Oh well.* He had enough money to buy a thousand duvet covers. What was a little cum in the scheme of things?

His tongue swept in and out of her mouth with each movement of their lips, alternately fighting with and slipping against hers. It continued for some time, sometimes heavy, sometimes gentle, and by the time Jeremy pulled away, Alice was breathing heavily. Her nipples were erect, her clit swollen, and he'd only touched her face and mouth.

She bit her bottom lip to prevent herself blurting out how much she really just wanted to fuck. A glance down at Jeremy's crotch told her that he did too. And they would; all in good time. Or, more precisely, when he said so.

"Alice," Jeremy said, his voice low and laden with intent, "lie back and make yourself comfortable."

She obeyed, squeaking in surprise as she settled on the enormous pile of cushions and pillows and found there were so many that she wasn't lying down at all, just leaning back a little. Ethan laughed and grabbed her hands to pull her forward, then helped her remove some of the soft furnishings so she could actually lie flat—well, almost flat. She flashed him a grateful smile. At once, Jeremy lay down beside her and beckoned Ethan to join him on her other side. Alice caught Ethan's confused frown before he wiped it from his face and cuddled up against her.

"I require Ethan's help for a little while, Alice. I hope that's okay. You see, I'm going to do something to you that neither of us has done to you before, and I'd like you to be as prepared as possible." He pressed a kiss to her cheek. "After all, I'd never hurt you—in the bad way."

Alice suddenly knew exactly what Jeremy had in mind. What was more, she wasn't remotely concerned about it. She'd always known it would be on the agenda sooner or later, and was only surprised it hadn't happened before now. She'd been preparing herself for months—by lubing up her fingers and her slimmest sex toys and pushing them inside her bottom. In actual fact, once she'd got used to the alien sensation, she'd started to enjoy it, and now she found that if she penetrated her anus at the same time she was masturbating—either with her hand or a toy—she would come an awful lot quicker, and much more powerfully. She'd even progressed onto using thicker toys, so she was certain that with lots of tender loving care and lubrication, she'd be able to take Jeremy's cock. And Ethan's too. Though not at the same time, of course—she wasn't insane. Just horny.

She had no intention of enlightening Jeremy and Ethan with regards to her anal experimentation. She'd simply enjoy the skilful, plentiful foreplay before Jeremy went where no man had been before. Perhaps she'd tell them her secret afterwards. Maybe.

Jeremy didn't seem to notice she hadn't made any kind of response to his words. He flicked his tongue across her earlobe, then began to pepper kisses and nibbles down the side of her neck. Alice's nipples stiffened almost painfully—she was super-sensitive on her neck and ears.

Ethan joined in; mirroring his friend's moves on her other side. He rushed to catch up, but soon they were trailing their lips in unison down opposite sides of her body. Craning her neck to see what they were doing, she was surprised they didn't move from her shoulders to her chest, then her breasts. Instead, they continued on down her arms, with some eye contact and gesturing to communicate their plan to one another. When they reached her hands, they sucked her fingers, one by one—and sometimes two—into their mouths.

She'd never had anyone suck her fingers before, and the sensation was bizarre but strangely erotic. Her pussy responded, growing steadily wetter and more swollen as Jeremy and Ethan teased and pleasured her. After each of her digits had been well and truly sucked, they continued down the outsides of her thighs and to her ankles. She tensed—oh God, there was no way she wanted them to give her toes the same treatment they'd given her fingers. Her feet were ticklish beyond belief, and had been shoved into shoes for a good couple of hours. *Not* sexy. Thankfully they took the hint and after a hastily mumbled conversation, parted ways.

Jeremy shifted back up the bed and unleashed his wicked mouth and tongue on her tits, while Ethan did the same between her legs. Before long, Alice was melting into a gooey puddle of ecstasy. She was so overwhelmed with sensation that she couldn't concentrate on who was doing what, but she didn't really care. All she cared about right now was that she was going to come, very soon.

Just as that thought passed through her head, Jeremy lifted

his head. She opened her eyes and watched as he turned to face his friend, and said, "Don't make her come, Ethan. It's supposed to be easier to—you know, with a first-timer if they haven't come yet. She'll get her orgasms afterwards—or possibly during!" He laughed.

With a final, lingering lick of her pussy, Ethan pulled away, seeming reluctant. Alice gritted her teeth to stop the whimper that threatened to escape her throat. Bastards. She'd been so close. So fucking close.

Jeremy caught her expression and laughed again, before giving her a kiss. "Come on now, Alice, this is for your benefit. As much as I want to fuck your arse, and have been wanting to for a very long time, I want it to be pleasurable for you too. Okay? So how do you want it?"

"From behind, so you can't see the faces I pull. And so I can bite the pillow," she replied wryly.

"Assume the position then, my dear. I'll get the lube and condoms."

"How can I resist that? It's pure romance."

He gave her thigh a playful slap. She stuck her tongue out at him and rolled over, then got onto her hands and knees.

Jeremy reached around her to the bedside table, pulled open the top drawer, and retrieved an unopened bottle of lube and box of condoms.

"Aww," she said, her voice dripping with sarcasm, "just for me, huh?"

"Well, aren't you just the little firecracker today? I'd suggest curtailing your cheeky comments, otherwise you'll be punished."

She couldn't help herself; now she'd started speaking her mind, she found it difficult to stop. "Punished?" She snorted. "And what can you do to me that hasn't already been done? Spank me? Whip me? Use a carpet beater, or a ruler?"

"You're right, of course, Alice. But what I have in mind isn't something you've already done. It's much, much worse. You remember how Ethan and I have tied you up on more than one occasion? Well, we'll do just that. Except we won't beat you, spank you, or tease you. We'll just leave you to it. Horny as you are now, you'll go crazy because you won't be able to get any relief. What do you say to that?"

Alice gasped as her stomach gave an unpleasant lurch. "I say yes, sir, I'm going to be good now. No more cheek, I promise. Just don't do… *that*. Please."

"Shh." He stroked her arse cheeks lightly. "Relax. Don't wind yourself up, or I'll never get it in. Now we've finished messing about, shall we crack on?"

She nodded frantically. The sooner he fucked her, the better. Because, tough as he could be, he wasn't strong enough to stop fucking her once he'd started. So he wouldn't be able to make good on his threat, no matter what she said or did.

Not that she was going to do anything else he didn't approve of—she wasn't stupid. Instead, she wiggled her bottom from side to side, as if beckoning Jeremy in.

He gave the nearest buttock a slap. "Getting impatient are we? Give me chance!"

She heard the condom wrapper being opened and, a few

seconds later, the snap of rubber as he secured it at the base of his cock. At first, she'd been a little confused about why he was using a condom, but then she realised it was because he might want to fuck her in the usual way too. If he didn't use a condom, he'd have to go and wash before sticking his cock in her pussy, and that would probably ruin the mood. For him, at least. She, of course, would have Ethan to keep her company in his absence.

There was a click from close behind her, then the unmistakable sound of lubricant being squeezed from a bottle. She gripped the duvet—this bit wouldn't hurt, but it *would* be cold. Jeremy hadn't had the time, or the foresight, to warm the lube before using it.

The touch of his fingertip against her anus made her flinch. Then, having prepared herself for his next move, she stayed still, allowing him to slick the chilly substance around her rear entrance. Then he was gone. Another squelch. This time, he worked it inside her, making her slippery and ready for the foreign invasion. It also served to open her up, helping her to relax against the penetration.

"Good girl," he murmured, like some kind of kinky horse whisperer.

Alice gritted her teeth to stop herself giggling at the mental image. The last thing she needed was to start laughing when his finger was up her bottom.

He spent a little longer getting her prepared, then, seemingly satisfied, removed his finger from her. She heard more liquid sounds, which she assumed was him covering his condom-clad cock with the lubricant. There was a click and a tiny thud—he'd discarded the bottle on the bed. The mattress behind her dipped, then Jeremy gripped her hips.

A movement in the corner of her eye distracted her from her nerves. Ethan had moved up beside her and was resting on the pillows. He flashed a reassuring smile. She trailed her gaze down his body. His hand circled his shaft, stroking so slowly as to be almost imperceptible. She had no doubt that by the time she and Jeremy got going, he'd be pumping it a damn sight faster.

Jeremy's knuckles bumped against her buttock, then his shaft rested in the crack of her arse. He rocked his hips a couple of times, sliding his cock up and down the smooth skin, before positioning the tip against her slick anus.

She gripped the duvet, ready to take any discomfort out on it.

"Are you ready, Alice?" Jeremy asked softly. "I'll do my absolute best not to hurt you. But if you absolutely want me to stop, you must let me know."

"Yes… understood." She ground the words out, then gasped as Jeremy slowly began to penetrate her. There was a build-up of pressure—and pain, which was just the right side of unbearable—as he shoved against her resisting hole. Alice breathed hard and tried to relax, remembering that if she pushed back against him, it would make things easier and less painful. In theory. She was in enough discomfort that she was willing to give it a try—Jeremy's cock was neither as slim nor as smooth as the toys she'd used up her bottom before, and therefore it was definitely a challenge to accommodate him.

She looked down and saw she was holding the duvet so

tightly her knuckles had turned white. Something touched her head and she flinched before realising it was Ethan, stroking her hair to help soothe her. He grinned again. “You can do it. You’ve taken everything else we’ve thrown at you. This is your last task. You’re not going to fail now, are you?”

She frowned. He was absolutely right. It *was* her last task. And no, she *wasn’t* going to fail now. She pulled in a breath through her nostrils, gritted her teeth, and bore down on Jeremy’s dick. He popped past the tight ring of muscles and pushed slowly inside her, until his balls were pressed against her buttocks. She reached around and put a hand on his arse to stop him from moving.

He leant down and murmured into her ear, “You okay, sweetheart?”

She said nothing, just nodded. Then she managed, “Please stay still until I say. I’m just getting used to you. You can move when I tell you to.”

Jeremy didn’t comment on the fact she was the one giving commands, but the circumstances were different this time. She had to be calling the shots in this situation if he didn’t want to hurt her—and he kept saying he didn’t. So he’d do as he was damn well told. For now, anyway.

“No problem,” he said, then dropped a couple of gentle kisses between her shoulder blades. “Just let me know.”

Straightening, he stroked his fingers up and down her sides, across her back and onto her buttocks. The tiny hairs on Alice’s body stood on end, and a shiver rippled across her skin. Involuntarily, she tensed, wringing a strangled yelp from Jeremy.

"Hey! Do that again and you won't have to worry about me moving, because I'll come."

The giggle escaped before she knew anything about it. "I'm sorry. I didn't mean to. Okay, in a second, you can move. But go really slowly at first. I'll let you know when you can go faster."

"Understood," Jeremy replied. "I don't want to hurt you."

"I know. All right… go for it."

Jeremy gripped her hips again and began to rock slowly in and out of her. The copious amount of lube meant there was almost no friction. The stinging sensation soon melted away, and Alice began to enjoy herself. She let Jeremy carry on at a snail's pace for a little longer, just to be sure. Then, when she was confident she could take more, she told him so.

"Okay… But the agreement stands: you want me to stop, you know what to say."

"Yes, I do. I wouldn't have said it if I didn't mean it. So just pick up your speed and I'll shout if there's a problem."

He said nothing more. Instead, he increased the speed of his thrusting, and Alice closed her eyes as the sensation became more and more pleasurable. More what she was used to when she used toys up there. Which gave her an idea. She opened her eyes and looked at Ethan, who was watching her face intently. In a way, she was surprised he hadn't situated himself at the business end, watching her almost-virgin arse take a pounding. He probably wanted to be there, but he also wanted to make sure she was all right.

"Hey," she said, beckoning him closer with a jerk of her head. He moved over to her, and she whispered into his ear, "Get underneath me and play with my clit. That way, you can both make me come."

Ethan didn't reply, but the speed at which he lay back on the bed and shuffled underneath her spoke volumes. Soon, his deft fingers parted her slick folds and sought her clit. He rubbed and pinched it for a few seconds, before leaning up and closing his lips around it. She felt the brush of his hair against her stomach and thighs, and wished she could tangle her fingers in it while he teased her aching nub. But it was necessary to keep both hands on the bed; otherwise the force of Jeremy's thrusts would make her fall flat on her face. Or, to be more precise, fall flat on top of Ethan.

It wasn't long before Ethan slipped two fingers inside her soaking pussy. She let out a throaty groan. Her first experience of double penetration—sort of. She'd have to get used to the sensation, because now she'd been fucked up the arse by Jeremy, she knew actual double penetration would be on his and Ethan's agenda. Not that she minded. Now she was confident anal sex could not only be bearable, but extremely pleasurable if done right, she was more than happy to have the two men inside her at the same time.

In fact, she could hardly think of anything more erotic.

Inevitably, the ministrations of both men were driving her closer and closer to orgasm. She gripped the duvet so tightly her fingers hurt, then squeezed it some more. Finally, her release crashed into her like a tsunami. Waves of intense pleasure rolled through her, and she screamed until her throat burned.

Behind and beneath her, Jeremy and Ethan were having some erotic experiences of their own. The spasming of her core was milking Jeremy's cock, causing him to spurt into her while cursing like a sailor. Ethan had clearly been using his free hand to stroke himself, and she watched as his movements almost turned into a blur as he sought his own climax.

Alice shifted forward to gently disengage Jeremy's softening cock, waited until he was all the way out, then hurriedly moved and lowered her head to Ethan's crotch, ready to catch his cum. A couple of seconds later, he fed the tip of his prick into her mouth and yelled loudly as he came. She swallowed eagerly until he was done, then licked and sucked at him until he was clean.

Alice settled back onto the pillows for a well-earned break. She had no doubt it would be short-lived, however. Jeremy and Ethan were sexy *and* insatiable. Much to her surprise, though, they crawled up the bed and flopped down on either side of her. She was quickly snuggled between two hot, male bodies, their arms thrown possessively—yet sweetly—across her stomach and chest. Flicking her gaze between them, she still half expected one or both of them to liven up and instigate round two. Instead, their breathing deepened and, within seconds of one another, they fell asleep.

Well, that was a first! But at least she'd come. Ethan had made absolutely sure of that, and if he hadn't, she knew Jeremy would have. For all their kinky games, they always made sure she was satisfied. She grinned as she looked at the two men cuddled up to her. Whether it was post-sex hormones, she didn't know, but warm, fuzzy feelings bubbled up inside her, forcing her brain to address them. After several minutes of her thoughts going around and around, driving her crazy, she came to a definite—and totally astounding—conclusion.

Whether it was right or wrong, she was in love with them both. There was no point denying it any longer. But deciding whether she'd tell them or not was another matter altogether. She still had no idea if the men just saw her as a pleasant distraction and would wave her off happily in a few short weeks, or if there was more to it. Did they want to share her on a more permanent basis, or not?

The pressing question was whether she would be brave enough to find out.

Chapter Twenty

Alice groaned as her alarm clock went off, wanting desperately to shut it up, pull the covers over her head, and go back to sleep. She hadn't slept well for the past couple of nights. The realisation she was in love with not one, but two, men—men she'd have to leave in a couple of weeks and go God knows where for another job—was playing on her mind. She hadn't said anything. It was a waste of time. There was no way they felt the same, and even if they did, how could it work if she was employed somewhere else? Granted, it could be a property close by, but equally it could be hundreds of miles away. No, it was better just to keep quiet and hope she'd get over them. Eventually.

As her brain kicked into gear, another thought reinforced her wish to go back to sleep. Preferably for the rest of the day. It was her birthday. The round old number of thirty had now ticked over to thirty-one. Not that getting older bothered her at all; it was just the actual birthday thing—she'd never liked them, not since her parents had had that blazing row on her tenth birthday and her dad had walked out and never returned. Unsurprisingly, the memory had stayed with her and hovered over each of her subsequent birthdays like a big, black cloud.

At least she'd be able to work today and find plenty to distract her. With that thought, she gave her alarm clock a whack and swung her legs out of bed. No sooner had her feet touched the carpet than a knock came at the door. She sighed. Yes, she loved them, but couldn't they just let her wake up before they started in with their demands for conversation?

After hastily raking her hair back, then rubbing her hands over her face and sweeping the sleep from her eyes, she moved to the door. She opened it a crack and peered out. The two men stood there in their boxer shorts, looking somewhat sleepy themselves. What was this? They wanted a morning shag, did they? She certainly wasn't opposed to the idea—what better way to forget her depressing past?

They smiled, and Ethan spoke softly, "Morning, Alice. We just wanted to swing by and wish you a happy birthday. And tell you not to wear your work clothes today. In fact, a T-shirt and some tracksuit bottoms would be more suitable."

Alice frowned, struggling to process what he was saying. After a few long seconds, the hopeful smiles on Jeremy and Ethan's faces waned, and turned into expressions of concern. It was then she spotted the cards in their hands. Suddenly her brain switched on.

"H-how did you know it was my birthday?" she asked, her heart racing and mouth gone dry. God, the last thing she wanted was for them to start making a fuss of her, and wondering why she wasn't pleased about it. Her past family dramas were not something she wanted to talk about. Then, the other part of what Ethan had said finally computed. "And why shouldn't I put my work clothes on?"

Looking hurt, Ethan replied, "Your date of birth is on your employment paperwork. And casual clothes would be better for where you're going."

She raised an eyebrow, then shook her head. "I'm not going anywhere. I've got work to do. I'm not like you two—I can't just skive off any time I like." With that, she slammed the door closed and turned the key in the lock. Not wanting to hear their knocks or pleas, she dashed to the bathroom and switched on the shower, stripping and jumping under the spray as quickly as she could. Now all she could hear was the pounding of the water against her skin, the walls and the tub. And that was just how she wanted it.

The water pummelling at her helped the wave of anger to dissipate, only for it to be replaced with guilt. She shouldn't have snapped—they hadn't done a thing wrong and she was taking her dislike of birthdays out on them. Just because they'd made the effort. God, what a bitch.

As she washed her hair and body, she decided that *she* would make the effort, too. She'd apologise for being such a cow, make up some excuse for her behaviour, and be more thankful. If all else failed, she'd demand a birthday shag. That ought to distract them, right?

Her mind made up, she switched off the water and hopped out of the tub. She wrapped her hair in a towel and slipped on her dressing gown before heading back into her bedroom in search of the type of clothes Ethan had suggested. Whatever they had planned, she'd go along with it. Though it couldn't possibly be a task. They'd been completed—her references assured, her future bright. Except for the absence of Jeremy and Ethan, of course.

Alice dressed, then towel-dried her hair before pulling it into a high ponytail. She had no idea why she'd decided to put it up like that—she rarely wore it that way—other than it seemed to go with her sporty attire. Well, as sporty as a girl like her ever got.

Looking in the mirror, she forced a smile. She could do this.

She'd damn well try, anyway. Jeremy and Ethan had been so nice to her—smoking hot sex aside—since she'd arrived at Davenport Manor. The least she could do was be appreciative of their efforts. Her grin widened as she thought about all the lovely things they'd done for—and to—her, and she left the room, head held high, ready to face the day. Mostly.

As she moved into the kitchen, she saw the men sitting at the breakfast bar, gazing gloomily into their cups of coffee. A stab of guilt lanced her heart. She cleared her throat, and their heads snapped up immediately. Expectantly.

"Guys," she began, not quite sure what she could say to make things better, "I-I'm really sorry for what I said and did earlier. You didn't deserve that behaviour. It's utterly my fault. I've got some… issues with my birthday, and I took them out on you. It was wrong, and I apologise wholeheartedly." She smiled tightly and tried to look as contrite as she possibly could, hoping they would forgive her.

Neither of them spoke for a few seconds, then Jeremy got up and poured her a glass of apple juice. He put it on the breakfast bar in front of one of the empty stools. "Come and sit down. Tell us what your issues are, Alice, and we'll do our best not to exacerbate them."

Alice was frozen to the spot. He wanted her to talk about her issues? She was torn between sitting down and spilling her guts in the hope Jeremy and Ethan would make her feel better, or locking herself back in her bedroom. She decided to be an adult, and walked over to the breakfast bar before climbing onto the stool which had her drink in front of it. Buying herself a few more seconds—so much for being an adult—she took a sip of her drink and swallowed it.

When she looked up, both men were watching her expectantly. She stifled a sigh. There was no point in making something up, plus she was hardly awake enough to do that. The truth it was, then. Gripping her glass, she sucked in a deep breath and recounted her woeful birthday story as quickly as possible, eager to get it over with.

When she was finished, she met each of the men's eyes in turn, wondering what they would say. And what they were thinking. A few seconds passed, then Jeremy broke the silence. "Alice," he said, his eyes full of sincerity, "I'm really sorry you have that crappy birthday memory, through no fault of your own. But here's a suggestion: how about you make some new birthday memories? Better ones?"

She tilted her head to one side as she considered his words. His idea was great, in principle. But how? Granted, just being here with the two of them was already a shit-ton better than all of her previous years' birthdays put together, but she wouldn't be in the manor for her next birthday. Hell, she wouldn't even be here next month. Suddenly, the blood drained from her face and tears pricked at her eyes.

"Whoa!" Ethan said. He jumped up and came around to her side of the breakfast bar, then slipped an arm around her shoulders. "What's the matter? Jeremy's not perfect at all this emotion stuff, but I thought he did pretty damn well there."

Alice fought back the tears that threatened to spill and gave Ethan a watery smile. "He did. He did really well. It's just… hard. I want to make new, improved memories. I can try to do that today, but what will I do next year? I'll remember this year's events, for sure, but I won't be able to forget the bad ones that went before."

The men exchanged a look. Then Jeremy reached for a pile of envelopes which sat at the end of the table and slid them towards her. "I don't know about next year, Alice," he said softly. "But Ethan and I will do all we can to make you happy this year. And perhaps the happy memories will make the bad ones fade, at least a little bit."

Now the tears fell. But, to her surprise, they were tears of happiness. She really should stop being such a sad sack and make the most of the next two weeks. Afterwards, she'd have nine fabulous months to reflect on, both from a professional and personal perspective. There were people much worse off than her, after all. So she sucked it up, and gave a genuine smile. "Thank you. Both of you. I don't deserve you. You're so nice to me."

Another look was thrown across the table. Ethan ruffled her hair affectionately. "You ain't seen nothin' yet, babe. Open the top envelope."

She glanced suspiciously at each of them. They were grinning from ear to ear. What exactly did they have in mind? Surely not another task? No, they couldn't do that—she'd done everything on their list. Any sexual encounters they'd had since had been purely for pleasure. Pushing thoughts of pleasure from her brain for fear of getting utterly distracted from their current conversation, she reached for the envelope. It was quite big, bordering on A4 size, and was heavier than it looked, as though it contained either several sheets of paper, or some thick card. Maybe it was just a large birthday card.

She ran her fingers over the surface, searching for something that felt like a badge. Okay, maybe not.

She stuck her finger under the flap and lifted it open. She was still none the wiser. All she could see was some shiny paper, and it was blank. Damn. Quickly, she pulled out the contents and turned them so they were facing up, and the right way around. It was a folder, made of thin card. As she took in the words on the front cover, she gasped, and opened it up to see what was inside. She skim-read the characters on the smaller piece of card within, then her mouth dropped open.

Wide-eyed, she stared at the pair, who looked supremely smug—and with good reason. They were sending her to a spa for the day. And not just any spa—one of the most exclusive ones in the country, which was just up the road. They'd paid for her to have the works: use of all the facilities, any classes she wanted to take, and as many treatments as she liked.

"They've got my credit card details too, Alice, so if there's something you want that's not covered by that voucher, just charge it to the card. Anything you want."

Alice was speechless. Just when she'd thought the two men couldn't possibly be any nicer to her, they'd gone and outdone themselves. "Th-thank you. So much. I don't know what else to say." Tears threatened yet again, and Ethan pulled her into a hug and dropped a kiss to her damp hair.

"There's nothing else *to* say, sweetheart. Just go and get whatever stuff you need to take with you, then come back here to say goodbye before you leave."

Jeremy nodded encouragingly, so she slid from the stool and went off to do as they said. It was only when she'd shoved swimwear, toiletries, clean clothes, underwear, and a book into a bag that she realised she hadn't opened any of her other envelopes. Bollocks. She'd have to do it when she got back.

She finished packing her bag, then headed for the kitchen once more, to find the men sitting down again, and a bacon sandwich waiting for her. Oh yes, she hadn't eaten either.

"Lunch is included, but I thought you should have something before you go. We don't want you passing out in the sauna or anything, do we?" Jeremy nodded towards the sandwich. "Now hurry up, before I eat it for you. And your lift is waiting too."

"My lift?" She'd assumed she'd be driving herself. Which was no problem at all. Making a half hour journey in the car to an exclusive resort was no hardship. Especially when it was an all-expenses-paid day out.

"Eat your sandwich, before it goes cold," Jeremy said.

She shrugged and took her seat. Soon afterwards, her plate was empty and her taste buds and belly were happy. She jumped up to put her plate and glass in the dishwasher.

Ethan stopped her. "I'll do that. Now go and brush your teeth and then bugger off and enjoy yourself, for God's sake!"

Alice was back within minutes, having brushed her teeth and rinsed with mouthwash. She grabbed her bag, then flashed them a smile. "Thank you so much. I really appreciate the effort you've gone to for me today. I'm going to make some new memories, okay?"

They slid from their stools and moved over to her, then enfolded her in a three-way hug. Then, as if they'd choreographed it, they each kissed one of her cheeks at the same time and wished her a happy birthday.

"We'll see you later," Jeremy said as they disentangled. "Your lift will be waiting outside the main doors of the spa at six. Don't eat too much at lunchtime, because we're doing something special for dinner. Leave room for that, okay?"

She nodded, stood on tiptoes, and gave them both a quick kiss, then left the room before she started crying again. *No more tears. They've gone to a lot of trouble to give you a good day. So that's exactly what you'll have.*

When she stepped out of the manor's side door and saw the white limousine waiting for her, her jaw almost dropped into the gravel beneath her feet.

Immediately, the chauffeur got out and opened the back door for her. "Madam," he said, indicating she should get in.

Still gobsmacked, she turned back to the house and looked up. As she'd expected, Jeremy and Ethan stood at one of the windows that overlooked the staff and residents' car park, grinning inanely. They waved. She waved back, then blew them a kiss. She got into the limousine before she was tempted to rush back inside and snog their faces off.

As she settled onto the cool leather of the seat, she felt like an utter tramp. She was dressed in such scruffy clothes, yet was about to be driven to a spa in the lap of luxury. Though the car's blacked-out windows meant nobody could see her, anyway. People would probably look at the vehicle as it passed them on the streets and think she was some kind of celebrity, swigging champagne and generally being fabulous. She could dream, anyway. There *was* champagne, she realised as she spotted the cooler. But it was barely nine o'clock in the morning, so she wasn't going to partake now. Maybe on the way home. It *was* her birthday, after all. And so far, it was shaping up to be the best one she'd had for a long, long time.

***

Alice climbed back into the limousine, not giving a shit who might be looking at her in her crappy clothes and wondering who the hell she was. She was chilled out beyond belief and felt like she was floating. She'd totally splurged the voucher Jeremy and Ethan had given her, managing to squeeze in four treatments, as well as some time in the pool, hot tub, sauna and steam room. She hadn't read any of her book, she'd been so busy. But the good kind of busy that meant she would be lucky to stay awake on the return journey to Davenport Manor. The ride in the limo was really smooth, which didn't help.

She remembered she'd promised herself a glass of champagne to celebrate her birthday. Pouring and drinking it ought to help her stay awake. She dropped to her knees on the thickly-carpeted floor of the car and shuffled over to the sideboard where the bottle of champagne nestled in a bucket of fresh ice. She slid a glass from the hook it was on and put it down, before wrestling with the bottle's foil-covered cork. Eventually, she opened it with a loud and satisfying pop and did her best to get as much of the gushing liquid in the glass as she could. Inevitably, some of it bubbled over her hands and onto the carpet, but she guessed that happened a lot. It was virtually impossible to open champagne without spillage. The cork had disappeared altogether.

Soon, she was perched on the leather seat with her feet tucked beneath her, sipping the champagne. She felt like royalty. Lady of the manor, perhaps. She giggled. It wasn't the first time she'd had that fantasy, after all. After another sip of the champagne, her giggles turned into peals of laughter. She hoped the partition between her and the driver was soundproof; otherwise he'd think his passenger was an insane person, travelling alone in a limousine and yet finding something incredibly funny. She wasn't interrupted, however, so she carried on enjoying her sudden bout of mirth, and wondering exactly where it had come from. She suspected it was something to do with the fact she was having the best birthday of her life. And she still had a special meal and an evening with two sexy men to look forward to.

Her laughs turned into full-on guffaws. She was still grinning like the Cheshire cat when they approached Davenport Manor. Tears streamed down her cheeks, and she couldn't wait to get inside and tell Jeremy and Ethan what a wonderful day she'd had.

The car pulled to a stop, and she resisted the urge to let herself out. Instead, she snagged her bag and the bottle of champagne, figuring Jeremy had already paid for it, and climbed out as gracefully as possible when the chauffeur opened the door. She thanked him and made her way to the manor's side door. It flew open to reveal Ethan. He nodded to the driver, who got back into his car and left the premises. Alice guessed Jeremy had settled up his bill beforehand. Or maybe he had an account with the limo firm. It didn't matter either way—she'd had a delightful journey, thanks to her two favourite men.

Ethan took her free hand and pulled her inside, then closed and locked the door behind them before wrapping his arms around her and holding her tight. After a minute, he leant down and kissed her—a long, deep kiss which left her heart pounding and her skin tingling. When they parted, she was wide-eyed. "Wow. What was that for?"

"I missed you," he said simply. "Plus I remembered I hadn't given you a proper birthday kiss. Did you have a good day?"

"Better than good. I'll tell you and Jeremy all about it. Where is he?"

"Where do you think, sweetheart? In the kitchen, of course."

"Really? What do you two have planned? Do I need to go and shower, or get changed first?"

Ethan looked her up and down, and she tried not to cringe under his scrutiny. She knew she looked a mess. A relaxed mess, but a state nonetheless. Her hair was all greasy from her Indian head massage, and her face was probably as shiny as a mirror due to all the lotions and potions they'd used during her facial. At least her nails looked good. She'd had a manicure and pedicure and her hands and feet were almost model worthy.

"Nope. You're perfect as you are. Come on."

Luckily he didn't see her blush as he'd already turned his

back and was leading the way to their living quarters. As they drew closer to the kitchen, Alice picked up a delightful scent. It seemed the men really were cooking up a storm. And it was all for her.

Just before they got to the kitchen door, Ethan stopped and turned around. “Close your eyes.”

She did as he asked, then sensed him moving around her. He put his hands over her eyes and led her slowly forward, opened the door and helped her into the room. The food smells, now they were close up, were mouth-watering. She suspected the two of them had made her favourite—lasagne with garlic bread and chips. She knew chips didn’t really go with the meal, but she didn’t care; she loved them. And as for the garlic, well, at least the three of them would stink and keep the vampires away together.

She smiled as Ethan guided her further into the room, wondering what would be revealed when her vision was restored.

Seconds later, Ethan said, “Are you ready, Alice?”

“Of course,” she replied excitedly. “Please don’t keep me in suspense any longer.”

The two men laughed, then Ethan removed his hands. Instantly, she opened her eyes and let out a little squeal at the sight before her. They’d only gone and decorated the place! They’d put up a banner, balloons, streamers, and there were even some party poppers on the breakfast bar, just begging to be used.

“We thought you’d prefer a nice, home-cooked meal, rather than going to a restaurant. If we got it wrong, though, please say and we’ll take you out. But it’ll have to be tomorrow—I’m not letting this food go to waste,” Jeremy said with a wink.

She put her bag and the bottle of champagne down on the side and looked at each man in turn. When she curbed her excitement enough to speak, she said, “You know it’s not my thirtieth, don’t you?”

Jeremy frowned. “Of course, why?”

“Because you’ve gone to an awful lot of trouble for a thirty-first birthday.”

Ethan grabbed her from behind and pulled her into a hug. “Alice, numbers don’t matter. You should have a fuss like this made of you every year.” He pressed a kiss to her hair, and she tried to wriggle from his grasp. “What’s the matter?”

“My hair’s all gross from my Indian head massage. It’s full of oils and stuff.”

He buried his nose in the brunette mass. “Mmm, whatever oils they used, they smell yum.”

Alice struggled harder to free herself. “Eww, don’t do that. You’ll get gunk all over your face.”

“I don’t care. Though to be fair, I’d rather have your pussy juices all over my face.”

She gasped, then elbowed him. He relented and let her go, then held his hands up in supplication. “Okay, I get it. No sniffing or hugging. It’s your birthday.”

“Yes,” she said decisively. “It is. Now, do I have time for a shower?” She looked at Jeremy, guessing he was in charge of cooking times. Ethan might have said she was fine as she was, but she just didn’t feel comfortable. She wanted to be clean and hug- and sniff-worthy.

He nodded. "Don't be too long, though. You have about half an hour, otherwise we'll be eating a blackened lump."

She flashed him a grateful smile and scampered back to her room, then stripped off and jumped into the shower. She hadn't meant to be so mean to Ethan, especially after the effort he and Jeremy had gone to, but her head massage had been the last of her treatments and she'd only just had time to grab her stuff and get to the front of the building before the limo was due. She didn't want to be late, and as a result, she'd arrived home feeling a tad unwashed. She'd make it up to Ethan later.

As she scrubbed her scalp, she ruminated on just what a wonderful day she'd had. Her packed timetable meant she hadn't had time to linger on her crappy memories. Even when she was chilling out in the sauna and hot tub, she'd been so relaxed she hadn't thought about much at all. Apparently, Jeremy and Ethan's present to her had been exactly what she needed. Some time off, and a lovely day. And the best part was that the day wasn't over yet.

She finished showering as quickly as possible, then dried off and headed back into her bedroom. After dressing speedily, she popped on some light makeup, then brushed her hair and left it loose. It would soon dry.

Alice returned to the kitchen well within her allotted half an hour, so she sat down at the breakfast bar and watched Jeremy and Ethan as they buzzed around putting things away, loading the dishwasher, and so on.

After a minute or two, her gaze landed on the pile of cards which still sat on the table. She slid the stack in front of her and began opening them. There weren't many—most of her friends had sent text messages or emails instead—so it didn't take long. But the ones from Jeremy and Ethan more than made up for the lack of numbers. They'd obviously chosen carefully, as they both said *To Someone Special* rather than something bland like *To My Friend.* They couldn't have gone with *To My Girlfriend*, because she wasn't, was she? Maybe they did cards these days that read *To My Friend with Benefits*, but Jeremy and Ethan had decided to play it safe. She bit back a giggle, then picked up all the cards and headed into the living room to arrange them on the mantelpiece.

That done, she slipped back into the kitchen and crept up behind the nearest man, who happened to be Ethan. She put her arms around his broad body and gave him a hug. "Thank you for my card. And everything else."

She was squeezing him so tight that he couldn't turn around. Instead, he looked over his shoulder. "You're welcome, sweetheart. But you've got another present to come later."

"Really?" she squeaked. "You two have seriously spoiled me today."

"Well," Jeremy said, glancing over from where he stood wiping down the worktops, "you're worth it. We've had all this planned for weeks because we wanted you to have an incredible day. And," he hesitated for a moment, the tiniest of frown lines marring his handsome face, "be left with nice memories of us when you leave."

She cleared her throat loudly and released Ethan. "Well, let's not think about that, shall we?" She crossed the room, then all but launched herself at Jeremy and kissed his cheek. "Thank you, for everything." Eager to move the subject well and truly on from her leaving, she asked, "So, is dinner nearly ready, then?"

Jeremy laughed, and aimed a light slap at her arse. "Go and sit down. It should be almost done. I'll check on it while Ethan gets you a drink."

"I can get my own drink, you know, if Ethan's busy."

"He's not," Jeremy replied smoothly. "He's done his bit now, so he's on drinks duty. Now do as you're told and get your glorious backside in a chair."

Suitably chastised, Alice moved to the breakfast bar. Just as she was about to clamber up onto a stool, Jeremy stopped her. "Uh-uh, not there. In the dining room."

"Um, okay." She raised her eyebrows. They'd never eaten a meal in the dining room before. They really *were* going to town for her birthday.

"Before you go," Ethan said. "What would you like to drink? We've got… well, the usual."

"Wine, please. Whatever's open. Oh, no, wait! I've got the champagne from the limo. Let's finish that first, before it goes flat. That would be a terrible waste."

Ethan smirked. "That it would. Right, champagne it is. Now, off you go." He wafted his fingers at her, encouraging her to leave and go into the dining room.

Alice went into the little-used room and let out a strangled noise when she saw they'd decorated in there too. There were helium balloons tied to the backs of three chairs—the ones they'd be using, she assumed—candles, napkins folded origami-style, and a banner hanging from the wall behind the chair at the end of the table. It read *Birthday Girl*. She didn't know whether to laugh or cry, so she opted for the former. All this and she still had another present to go—she could hardly believe it.

Settling into the chair that had been reserved for her, she sighed contentedly and waited for the men to join her. Soon, Ethan came in with the remainder of the bottle of champagne and poured it into the three glasses that were already part of their place settings, then sat down next to her. She grinned at him.

He reached for her hand and pressed a kiss above her knuckles. "Happy birthday, Alice."

She blushed. "You already said that."

"I know." He gave a casual shrug. "But I felt like saying it again."

Jeremy entered the room then, skilfully carrying three plates. Anyone would think he was a fully-trained waiter, not a ridiculously wealthy lord. But was he *actually* a lord? She'd joked to herself about it many times, but she knew money didn't necessarily equal a title. She decided to ask him about it tomorrow. For now, she just wanted to get her teeth into her dinner. Then Jeremy and Ethan, hopefully. She covered up her smirk by grabbing her glass of champagne and holding it in front of her mouth for a second, before taking a healthy gulp. It was then she remembered she hadn't eaten since lunchtime, so she'd better get some food inside her before she drank any more. Otherwise she'd be having an early night—by herself! She hurriedly put the glass back down.

Jeremy approached the table and put her plate in front of her, then did the same for Ethan and finally himself. He sat down. Alice flashed him a grateful smile. "Thank you. Both of you. It looks, and smells, absolutely delicious."

"You're welcome," they said in unison.

Jeremy picked up his glass of champagne and raised it high. "To Alice. Happy birthday, sweetheart."

Alice and Ethan lifted their glasses, and the three of them chinked them together. They voiced the obligatory "cheers", then Jeremy said, "Now let's dig in before it goes cold. Enjoy!"

They fell silent, except for the soft clinking and scraping of cutlery against their plates, chewing and swallowing sounds, and occasional moans of utter gastronomic delight. They shared glances and smiles as they ate, but nobody spoke until all three were finished.

Only then did Jeremy break the silence. "Well, I guess by your empty plates that the food was good?" He looked over at Alice, who nodded profusely and rubbed her tummy. "I hope you're not too full. There's dessert yet. Think you can manage some? Ethan?"

"I'd love some," Alice replied. "But can we just have five minutes, first? I promised Ethan I'd tell you two all about my day."

"Of course," Jeremy agreed with a nod. "Come on, dish the dirt. I take it you enjoyed yourself?"

With that, Alice launched into her story, telling them about everything from her limousine journey to her treatments, her downtime, and the ride home. She conveniently didn't mention her giggling fit.

When she was done, the two men commented on how happy they were that she'd had a good time. Then Jeremy spoke. "Ready for dessert now?"

Alice and Ethan nodded enthusiastically. "Yes, please!"

Jeremy piled up their plates and took them away. Alice and Ethan took sips from their champagne, then their gazes met. He smirked, a wicked twinkle in his eye. Was he thinking what she was thinking—that they'd be able to go to bed when they'd finished dessert? And not to sleep.

She didn't get chance to make a cheeky comment because Jeremy had returned, and this time he was carrying something with… candles. Birthday candles. She let out an excited yelp as she realised it was a cheesecake—her favourite—which had not nearly enough candles for her age pushed into its surface. She watched, wide-eyed, as Jeremy placed it down on the table between the three of them, then turned to her with a triumphant smile. "You like?"

Her pulse raced, and she grinned from ear to ear. "Do I *like*? What do you think? You know I love cheesecake. Is it—?"

"Vanilla? It sure is. Your favourite. And it's even homemade."

Alice looked at the dessert, noticing that it wasn't quite picture-perfect. He was telling the truth—they had indeed made it from scratch. "Wow, you two *have* been busy today. Have you done any work at all?"

"Not really," Jeremy said. "But that's just one of the perks of being the boss, isn't it?"

"I guess so," she replied. "Well, I'm very glad you both

bunked off for this—all of it, I mean, not just the cheesecake."

"You'd better blow out the candles, before they drip onto it," Ethan put in. "We promise we won't sing."

"I'm glad to hear it." She laughed, then bent and blew out all the candles in one go—not such a tough task, given there were only nine. "Why nine?" she couldn't help asking. "Is that how many were left in the packet?"

"No," Jeremy said sternly. "It's how many months you've been at Davenport Manor. Well, nearly."

"Oh." She had no idea how to respond to that, so she just smiled and began to gently ease the candles out from their sticky prison. Once they had all been removed, she grabbed her knife and looked at each man in turn. "Three ways, yes?"

"Sounds like a good plan to me," Ethan said. "I can't wait to taste it. It's the first cheesecake I've ever made—or *assisted* with making, anyway." He'd corrected himself when Jeremy gave him a pointed look.

The room grew quiet again as Alice cut up the cheesecake and served it onto the three plates Jeremy had supplied. Then they tucked in. Despite thinking she was full after her dinner, Alice still managed to polish off the large slice of delicious cheesecake without feeling stuffed. Besides, she'd be working off some of those calories soon enough.

Ethan saw her grin. "What are you smiling at?"

"Oh, nothing," she said casually. "Just happy, that's all."

"I'm very glad to hear that," he replied. "Now, we have one more present for you."

Of course. She'd almost forgotten. Still grinning, she glanced from Jeremy to Ethan and back again. They kept her waiting for a few seconds—which felt more like weeks—until her raised eyebrows disappeared almost into her hairline. Then, finally, Jeremy spoke. "It's not a physical gift, Alice. At least, not in the usual way, anyway."

"Oh?" she prompted. God, would he spit it out already? The suspense was driving her crazy.

"Well," he said, twisting his fingers together and staring at them. Alice frowned. He was *nervous*? Then he looked up and fixed her with an intense stare that made her want to fidget in her seat. What the hell was he going to say? "Ethan and I talked, and because we've really tested you these last few months, we've decided it's time for you to get your own back."

"G-get my own back?" What on earth was he talking about? Unless… She snapped her head from side to side, gaping at each of them in turn.

"Yes," Ethan said decisively, folding his arms across his broad chest. "Now it's time for you to give *us* a task. We'll do whatever you want. Within reason."

"That last bit is very important," Jeremy chipped in. "We'll do anything, but not with each other. We just don't swing that way, okay?"

Alice chuckled. She hadn't even thought of that. Watching them fuck would be hotter than the fires of hell, but honestly, she'd really rather they were focusing on—and fucking—her. "All right," she said, nodding. "I like the sound of that, very much. So, how about I go to your room, Jeremy? I'm guessing that's where the majority of the props are? You two can do some clearing up and give me a few minutes to think."

With that, she grabbed her glass and drained it, before leaving the room as fast as she could without looking too eager.

Chapter Twenty-one

Alice all but fell into Jeremy's room in her haste to get through the door. She had a scant few minutes to decide what task she would give the two of them. Damn, it was hard. Jeremy had had God knows how long to put together his smutty little list, and she had… not very long at all.

She decided to check out Jeremy's toys. Maybe they would give her some inspiration. She knew from the anal sex day, as she'd come to think of it, that he had some stuff in his bedside cabinet.

A thorough examination of the cabinet didn't yield very exciting results, unfortunately. The condoms and bottle of lube were still there, but everything else was non-sexual paraphernalia. Bollocks.

The next most obvious choice was under the bed. She got down on the floor and peered under the four-poster. There was a large plastic box, and Alice found herself hoping it didn't contain shoes or magazines. The dirty kind of magazine would be okay, but not really what she was looking for. She pulled at the box, surprised to find it heavier than she'd expected.

Eventually, she freed the box from its dark hiding place and yanked off the lid, keen to see what kinky delights it housed. She wasn't disappointed, but *was* surprised Jeremy and Ethan hadn't used any of this stuff on her before. The props they'd made use of in her tasks had been mostly household paraphernalia—but then she supposed that was the whole point. Not every home contained an old-fashioned carpet beater. And the ones that did used it to beat carpets, not arses.

After poking around in the box for a little longer, she spotted something that gave her one hell of an idea.

Just then a knock came at the door, and Jeremy called out, "Are you ready for us, Alice?"

"Hang on!" She removed her chosen item from the box and put it on the floor. Then she closed the box and shoved it back under the bed before tucking her secret weapon away next to it, so the men wouldn't see it until she was ready.

She stood and smoothed down her almost-dry hair, then realised just how much it would get in the way, given what she had planned next. She moved over to the door and opened it a crack. "Could one of you go to my room and grab a hair tie for me, please? I'd like to put it up out of the way."

Without replying, Jeremy turned and headed quickly down the corridor. Ethan continued to wait outside the door until his friend came back, bearing the goods. Alice took the tie from him, voicing her thanks, then quickly manoeuvred her hair into a style that would keep it out of the way. "All right," she said, opening the door wider, "you can come in now."

Jeremy and Ethan entered the room. Alice smirked as they glanced around, clearly expecting to see something that would indicate what she had planned. She closed the door loudly, making the two of them jump and spin around to face her, looking puzzled.

She gave a beatific smile. "I didn't have much time to think about this, but you'll be pleased to discover I have indeed come up with a task for the two of you. And it won't involve you touching each other. Not much, anyway."

Their alarmed expressions made her want to laugh, but she managed to hold it in—just. There'd be plenty of time for that when she had them where she wanted them. "Don't worry, it's nothing like that."

She pressed her lips firmly together as the men heaved a sigh of relief. She couldn't, *wouldn't* laugh now. This would be impossible to go through with if she had the giggles. Tapping into her bossy side, she said, "Right, clothes off, the pair of you. Then get on the bed, side by side."

Jeremy and Ethan exchanged a glance, before scrambling to do as she said. Alice leant on the door, arms folded, and enjoyed the show. When they were in position, she crossed the room and stood by the side of the bed. Which happened to be the side Ethan occupied. The two of them looked at her expectantly as she casually raked her gaze across their naked bodies. She was pleased—though not at all surprised—to note that although they had no idea what was going to happen next, their cocks were already stiffening. She hoped their stamina matched up to their eagerness.

"Right," she said, clapping her hands. "When I first started digging through Jeremy's toy box, I had no idea what I should make you randy buggers do. But then I found something *very* interesting, which inspired the perfect plan, not to mention the perfect antidote to the challenges *I've* completed."

The men said nothing, so she continued. "If you're ready, we'll begin."

She didn't wait for an answer. Instead, she retrieved the coils of rope from under the bed and tossed them onto the mattress beside

Ethan. Then she climbed up onto the mattress and crawled up Ethan's body, tugging one of the ropes along with her. She straddled his head before securing his left wrist to the nearest bedpost. It took a considerable amount of concentration—she was certainly no bondage expert, but she'd experienced enough of it first-hand in the last eight and a half months to give her a good idea of what to do. She checked he couldn't escape, but also that his circulation wasn't restricted. Satisfied, she bade Jeremy stretch his left arm out. Once he did, she quickly secured his wrist to the same bedpost.

Next, she tied each man's left ankle to the bedpost, then moved to the other side and did the same in reverse. The result was Jeremy and Ethan were both spread-eagled on the bed, like slightly overlapping Xs. That was what she'd meant by touching—and although it wasn't ideal, it was the only way she'd been able to think of to have them bound next to one another and completely at her mercy.

Alice moved to the foot of the four-poster to examine her handiwork. It was very impressive indeed—especially when factoring in the now fully-erect cocks jutting eagerly up towards their owners' bellybuttons. The two men had remained silent throughout the process of being tied up, but had watched her every move. They still watched her now, even as she admired them. She decided to give them something to *really* look at. She stripped quickly but effectively, and stood naked, grinning widely as their shafts bobbed in response.

"Right," she said, making her way to the side of the bed and climbing up onto the mattress once more. "Your task is… stay hard.

I'll do the rest."

Looking at the prone male bodies in front of her, Alice hardly knew where to start. She'd placed them at her mercy simply because they'd never been that way before. During every challenge, the focus had been on her. On touching her, pleasuring her. That wasn't a bad thing, of course, but what she really wanted to do was lick, nibble, suck, kiss, and many other things to Jeremy and Ethan while they laid back and enjoyed it. An added bonus was that, while they couldn't touch her, they couldn't turn the tables, either. She'd give to them, but she'd also take. Take exactly what she wanted.

This time, she was in charge. And she was going to make the most of it.

She knelt in between them, next to their bare, muscular thighs. Their gazes remained on her as she reached out and grasped a hot, velvety cock in each hand. She pumped them very slowly and gently—she didn't want them to come just yet, after all—smirking as they groaned and jerked their hips, forcing their shafts roughly into her grip.

"Hey," she snapped, releasing them immediately. "We'll have none of that. The whole point of this is that *I'm* calling the shots. So keep still, unless I say otherwise. Understood?"

She usually found it difficult to be so bossy and commanding, but something about this situation made her *want* to take charge. Perhaps because she really did want to explore Jeremy and Ethan's bodies uninterrupted. She was no dominatrix. But on this occasion, she figured she could be just dominant enough to get what she wanted. And even if she couldn't, they'd have to do what she said anyway, or they'd be tied to Jeremy's bed for quite some time.

Jeremy and Ethan nodded frantically at her words, so she began to stroke their cocks again. She enjoyed the feeling of their flesh hardening further beneath her fingers, and hearing the men breathe heavier, and faster. She was doing that to them. Alice Brown, long-time singleton and super-shy girl, had two smoking hot men tied to a bed—willingly—and was subjecting them to erotic torment. It was a struggle not to let the power go to her head. Instead, she forced herself to keep calm and stick to the plan—tease the hell out of them, like they'd done to her on countless occasions.

She tormented them for a while longer, then removed her hands—smiling as they groaned their disappointment—and crawled up the bed. Having decided that because she'd used her left hand on Jeremy, he hadn't had such a skilful stroke, she leant down and kissed him first. She pressed her lips softly against his, then slipped her tongue into his mouth and gave it everything she had. She possessed his mouth the way he had hers so many times, tangling her tongue with his; fighting, loving, enjoying.

Cupping his face, she deepened the kiss, her jaw working faster, tongue moving more excitedly until she could hardly breathe. She pulled away with a gasp, gratified to see that Jeremy looked as lust-drunk as she felt. They stared at each other, shell-shocked, and Alice had to swallow the three words on the tip of her tongue that were threatening to be voiced. Quickly, she pressed an altogether more chaste kiss to his swollen lips before moving over to Ethan.

She grinned at him, her heart leaping when he returned the

smile and his dimples appeared. He really was the most adorable, giving, sexy man. But then so was Jeremy. She was still finding it hard to come to terms with the fact she was in love with them both. She'd done some research on three-way relationships and discovered, although they were relatively rare, they did exist. She was most definitely not alone, and knowing that had made her feel much better. It would see her through the next fortnight, at least.

Turning her attentions back to Ethan, she bent and kissed each of his dimples before pressing her mouth to his. He tensed, and she suspected he was struggling not to respond to her; to wrap his arms around her, to kiss her back. He *couldn't* wrap his arms around her, of course, the ropes would see to that, but he managed to resist deepening the kiss.

She slotted her fingers into his thick hair and tugged it lightly. His lips were soft and warm against hers, and she experienced an odd combination of feelings—contentment and extreme arousal. She had two hot men at her mercy, and she was guaranteed a good time. What could be better?

Unable to hold back any longer, she pushed her tongue between Ethan's lips and enjoyed a long, delicious, and incredibly sensuous kiss. She had no doubt his cock was rock hard, and was glad she wasn't astride him at that moment in time, because she'd have found it very difficult not to take advantage. She would at some point in the course of the evening, naturally, but not just yet. There was much more to indulge in before that happened.

After a while, she felt like she'd fallen into some kind of erotic trance, and ended their kiss before her brain turned to mush, leaving her incapable of anything else.

She shared a look with Ethan, similar to the one with Jeremy—but somehow more intense. It wasn't that she felt more for Ethan; it was just that he seemed to say more with a look than should be possible. And right now, he was making her feel like the most desirable woman in the world. She quickly moved away before her resolve crumbled and she rode him until his teeth rattled.

Hmm... what to do next? The possibilities were endless. Eventually, figuring Jeremy probably felt a little neglected by now, she kissed him again, then began working her mouth down his body. She swirled her tongue around each of his nipples, then dipped it into his bellybutton, before trailing it along the line of hair which led to his groin. As she moved to kneel between his legs, his thigh muscles flexed with the effort of keeping still. Smirking, she slowly lowered herself so her mouth hovered over the tip of his cock. He could probably feel every warmth breath caressing his skin. She held still for a few seconds longer, prolonging his erotic torture, then sunk down on his shaft, taking half of it into her mouth before stopping. Jeremy's strangled yelp amused her mightily—ah, what sweet revenge! She couldn't get nine months' worth of teasing into one night, but she'd do her best.

She pulled in a deep breath through her nostrils, then sucked more of his cock into her mouth, further and further, until the tip hit her gag reflex. She'd never attempted deep-throating before, but she decided now was the time. Resting her forearms on his thighs had the added benefit of preventing him from moving. The last thing she wanted was him bucking into her throat. If she was going to do this, she was going to do it at her own speed. And if it turned out she couldn't, well that was fine too.

Taking it slowly and calmly, Alice inched her lips down Jeremy's shaft. Since her eyes were closed, she couldn't see his facial expression, but heard his increasingly laboured breathing as her throat enclosed him. Suddenly, she became aware that she'd done it—she'd managed to get his glans past her gag reflex! Unwilling to push her luck by trying to get it deeper, she swallowed, and flicked her tongue over the skin she could reach.

The sensation was obviously too much for Jeremy. He let out a string of expletives, his cock throbbed, then his balls emptied directly into her throat.

Alice remained frozen in place, waiting until he'd finished before pulling back and wiping her mouth on the back of her hand. She could hardly believe she'd just done that. A glance at Jeremy's thunderstruck expression told her he couldn't either.

Ethan, on the other hand, looked massively turned on—his cock fit to burst and his hooded eyes full of lust.

"Oh, you'll get yours soon enough, gorgeous." She gave him a saucy wink. "But I think one deep-throating exercise is enough for today."

She stretched up and pressed a kiss to Jeremy's lips, then moved to kneel between Ethan's thighs once more. For a moment, she drank in the delicious sight of him, naked and erect. Then she straddled his stomach and leant down, engaging him in a kiss so hot it made her toes curl. Up until now, she'd been so focused on Jeremy and Ethan that she had hardly noticed how *her* body was reacting.

But it was impossible *not* to notice the slick of liquid that trickled from her pussy and pooled on Ethan's toned torso. She sat up, and immediately Ethan's gaze flicked to the place where their bodies met. He met her eyes, then quirked an eyebrow at her, his dimples threatening to appear.

Before he had chance to say anything, though, Alice manoeuvred so her knees were either side of his head. She walked her hands back down the bed, then, when her face grew level with the wet patch she'd just left, she bent and sucked it off him.

Ethan let out a growl. "You are such a dirty girl, Alice."

"What can I say?" she shot back. "I've had good teachers."

Both men laughed. She turned to look at Jeremy over her shoulder, then winked at him before continuing down Ethan's body. On reaching his cock—which was ready and raring to go—she circled it with her fingers and stroked up and down a couple of times. He groaned, and a bead of pre-cum gathered at its tip. Immediately, she licked it up, then poked her tongue into the slit to try to taste more of him. There was another groan, then, "Alice…"

Only then did she realise she was still kneeling over his face, but because he was tied down, he couldn't move up enough to reach her, or grab her arse and pull her on to him. She lowered herself carefully, so she didn't go too far and end up smothering him, and continued to stimulate his cock with her hand, while flicking her tongue around its tip. Once she was in the right place and Ethan began to lick and suck at her pussy, she closed her lips around his prick.

He moaned against her folds, and the vibrations caused a

fresh gush of her juices to run into Ethan's waiting mouth. Alice reached down and lightly scratched her fingernails against his ball sac. He bucked his hips in response, forcing his throbbing shaft deeper into her mouth. She landed a light, admonishing slap on his inner thigh, before gently cupping and caressing his balls as she danced her tongue and lips around him.

Suddenly, Ethan focused his efforts on the tiny spot next to her clit which always sent her skyrocketing towards climax, making it increasingly difficult for her to concentrate on what she was doing to him. This was the reason she both loved and loathed doing a sixty-nine. Double the pleasure, but also quite taxing for the brain.

Remembering she was in charge and could do whatever the hell she liked, she stopped what she was doing and pushed herself up on her hands. The movement shoved her pussy harder into Ethan's face and she simply knelt and enjoyed herself as his talented tongue thrust her closer and closer to orgasm.

It wasn't long before she was gripping the duvet until her fingers ached. She trembled as she creamed over Ethan's face for the umpteenth time, her internal muscles clenching as she grew closer to the precipice. Seconds later, she teetered at the very edge, her entire body feeling like it was fit to burst—and then it did. She screamed so loudly her throat would hurt later, but she didn't care. Her pussy spasmed wildly; every cell of her being tingled with immense pleasure. Her arms could barely hold her up, but since neither of the men was in a position to help her, she held on until she felt able to move, then rolled into the gap between them and waited until her climax waned.

After a minute or so she sat up, a goofy, post-orgasmic grin on her face. Both men were staring at her intently, awestruck. Ethan's cock was still rock hard, and Jeremy's had clearly recovered from its previous release. Her grin widened. She knew *exactly* what she was going to do next.

She knelt between the two of them yet again, then grabbed an erection in each hand. Despite knowing full well she would pay for this utterly insane idea later, she chanted, "Eeny, meeny, miny, moe," giving each cock an indicative squeeze as she landed on it in the silly rhyme. As she reached the final "moe", she abruptly released Ethan and straddled Jeremy's hips before guiding the tip of his prick inside her pussy and lowering herself onto it.

The air filled with their blissful moans as her cunt devoured Jeremy's cock. Soon he was buried inside her to the hilt, and she flopped forward onto his torso, savouring the sensation of his warm skin against hers. She stretched up to capture his mouth in a searing kiss as she rolled her hips, starting both their journeys towards another climax.

Jeremy pulled her bottom lip into his mouth and sucked on it—an action that had always driven her crazy and did so even more now, because he couldn't touch her any other way. Except with his cock. But then, whose fault was that? She'd tied them up with the intention of teasing and touching them, then using them for her own pleasure. Right now, though, she'd much rather they were touching her than bound and pretty much helpless. She wanted both of them fucking her. At the same time.

Alice rocked slowly on Jeremy's shaft for a while longer as

they kissed, then sat up. Her mind made up, she got off both Jeremy and the bed in one continuous movement, then moved to untie the men. She removed the ropes from the bedposts, and when Jeremy and Ethan realised what was happening, they freed their own wrists and ankles. That done, they looked at her questioningly.

She grinned. "I enjoyed that immensely, and I hope you did too. But it's time to play a new game now. Ethan, could you grab the lube and a condom, please?"

Her words were a dead giveaway as to what she had in mind, but Jeremy and Ethan still stared at her incredulously. "Come on!" she barked, channelling what was left of her assumed bossiness in order to get what she really wanted.

Ethan moved at once, and seconds later he was back on the bed, clutching the requested items.

"You," she pointed at him, "are going to need those. So get rubbered and lubed up, and I'm going to screw your friend here while you do it. Okay?"

Ethan nodded his assent. Alice turned her attention to Jeremy. "Right," she said, climbing onto the bed at its foot and shuffling halfway across it. "You, on your back. I'm going on top of you, then Ethan's going on top of me."

Jeremy did as she asked without uttering a word. He held his arms out and Alice quickly went into them. Before long, they'd resumed the position they'd been in before, except now he could move his arms and legs—something he clearly intended to make the most of. He roamed his hands over her body, cupping and squeezing her voluptuous arse, sweeping up her sides and touching as much of her breasts as he could—which wasn't too much, as they were crushed against his chest. He moved his hands to her face and held it tightly as they kissed like there was no tomorrow. All the while, Alice rocked on his shaft.

Despite being busy with Jeremy, Alice was still hyper-aware of Ethan. She heard the noises she'd expected; the tearing of the condom wrapper, the snap as he secured the rubber in place and finally, the slick sounds as he slathered lube over his sheathed cock. The mattress dipped as Ethan moved behind her. There was some commotion, presumably as he insinuated himself between his friend's legs, then after a brief pause, a lubricated finger pressed against her back entrance.

Alice was so relaxed and turned on that the invasion didn't worry her one little bit. She might feel differently when it was Ethan's cock as opposed to his finger, but she'd cross that bridge when she came to it. Her pussy fluttered involuntarily as Ethan's digit penetrated her, wringing a yelp from Jeremy. She grinned at him, then rolled her eyes back in her head and let out a moan when one finger was replaced with two. God, it felt good. She pushed herself up on her hands and tucked her knees either side of Jeremy's abdomen, giving Ethan easier access.

He finger-fucked her arse, gently stretching her. Getting her ready. She temporarily stopped moving on top of Jeremy, until she felt more comfortable. Ethan pulled his fingers out and prepared to replace them with his cock. He pressed it against the tight bud of her anus for a second, then pushed slowly until she admitted him. Alice let out a strangled noise as the mixture of pleasure and pain washed over her. Jeremy quickly palmed her tits then pinched her nipples to distract her. She gave him a grateful smile, then closed her eyes. Breathing in through her nose and out through her mouth, she forced herself to be calm as she was penetrated by two men. Her tactic worked, and Ethan was soon balls-deep inside her arse. He spouted some unintelligible rubbish, followed by something she understood. "So. Fucking. Tight."

The words sent a shiver of arousal through her, and she flexed her internal muscles as best she could, then giggled as both men swore at her. The action highlighted just how full she was, and she idly wondered if Jeremy and Ethan could feel each other's cocks through the wall between her pussy and her arse. She'd ask later—right now, she didn't want to ruin the mood. She wanted the fucking of her life, and was confident she was going to get it.

"Okay," she said, "I'm ready when you two are. I've no idea how this is going to work, though. Perhaps Ethan should start moving first, and see how it goes?"

Ethan leant down and landed a series of kisses across the back of her neck and shoulders before murmuring in her ear, "That sounds like a good plan, Alice. I'll be as careful as I can, but please remember your safe word and don't hesitate to use it if you want me to stop."

"Will do." She dredged the word from the depths of her brain, just in case, but she doubted she'd need to use it.

With that, Ethan began to fuck her arse, while Jeremy resumed playing with her tits. The combination sent so much pleasure coursing through her veins she was convinced someone could smack her over the head with a frying pan and she wouldn't notice. A girl could get addicted to this feeling. She also had the answer to her earlier question—she could feel both hard cocks rubbing against one another through her internal wall, so she knew they could, too. Neither of them seemed bothered about it—but since they'd shared women before they were probably used to it. She didn't want to think about that, though.

She glanced down at Jeremy. He raised a querying eyebrow. "Shall I try and move now?"

So overwhelmed she couldn't speak, Alice nodded hurriedly.

Jeremy gripped her waist, then spoke to his friend. "I'm going to start thrusting too, Ethan, so we'll have to try to work out some kind of rhythm, okay?"

"Yep. Go for it," came the reply.

There were a couple of clumsy, awkward movements to start with, but Jeremy and Ethan soon got into a pattern where they rocked Alice back and forth between them. It worked well—when she was full of one cock, the other was almost out, and vice versa. It felt so good she could barely think—especially since now the men had figured out their rhythm and grown comfortable with it, they'd let their hands roam too. Jeremy toyed with her clit, while Ethan teased her breasts.

Suddenly, the pleasure became too intense. She felt like one big erogenous zone, as though a mere breath on a strand of her hair would set her off catapulting towards climax. But the stimulation was much more powerful than that, and her orgasm hit like she'd crashed into a brick wall—no build-up, no tingles, just an incredibly potent sensation that thundered through every cell of her being and left her feeling like she'd gone through a washing machine spin cycle. She didn't even know she'd made a noise until she stopped, her throat burning.

She swayed, and Ethan grabbed her around the waist to stop her flopping forward. Which was lucky, really, because she was so wrung out she'd probably have ended up head-butting Jeremy if he hadn't. The men carried on fucking her as her orgasm waned, and delicious sensation continued to flicker through her body even as her eyelids grew heavy.

She just managed to stay awake until Jeremy and Ethan climaxed. When they were done, they gently disentangled themselves and bundled her under the bedcovers. The last thing she was aware of before she drifted off to sleep was the two of them cuddling up on either side of her, stroking her hair, and whispering words of endearment into her ears.

Chapter Twenty-two

Alice woke up feeling all warm and fuzzy inside. Not to mention achy in the good way, the way that reminded her she'd had sex recently. Damn good sex. Her happiness bubbled up as memories of the previous day and night came back to her. It had been *brilliant.* A wonderful day out, a delicious meal, an extra surprise from Jeremy and Ethan, and some smoking hot bedroom action. Followed by the three of them falling asleep together in Jeremy's beautiful four-poster bed.

Alice stretched her arms out to either side in the hope she might discover some morning wood she could take advantage of. Almost immediately, her mood took a dive. She opened her eyes and looked blearily to the left, then the right. She was all alone in Jeremy's big bed. *Well, this sucks. Two men, and they've both buggered off!*

She lay, getting increasingly grumpy, beneath the thick duvet and sent unpleasant vibes to Jeremy and Ethan, wherever they might be.

It wasn't until she rolled over and looked at the clock on the bedside table that she realised why they weren't still in bed with her. It was ten o'clock. On a work day. *Shit!*

In her haste to get out of bed, she became horrendously tangled in the duvet and bedsheets and ended up in a pile on the floor. Thanks to the soft, thick bedding, only her pride was damaged. At least Jeremy and Ethan hadn't seen her mishap.

When she finally extricated herself, she huffily dumped the offending items on the bed before pulling on enough of her clothes to render herself decent, then scurried down the corridor to her room.

She showered and dressed in record time, downed a glass of juice, then stuffed a cereal bar into her pocket to eat when she got to her office. But first, she intended to pay a visit to Jeremy and Ethan and find out what on earth had possessed them to let her sleep in so late. Especially after a day off—she dreaded to think how many emails she had waiting in her inbox. And the other staff probably thought she was a total slacker.

Alice smiled as she walked up the corridor and saw Jeremy's office door was ajar. Was it really only just under nine months ago that she'd caught him up to… Actually, she never *had* discovered exactly what he'd been doing, and with whom. Not that it mattered now. *She'd* been the one in his bed for the past few months. And in a couple of weeks she'd move on, and so would he and Ethan.

Determined not to dwell on that particular thought, she moved closer to the door, ready to storm in and tear the two guys a new one. If they were in there, that was. She listened carefully on the other side of the door—firstly to make sure at least one of them was in the room, and secondly, to ensure they weren't on a conference call or something.

She quickly ascertained that both Jeremy and Ethan were in the office, and they weren't talking on the telephone. They were, however, having a discussion that sounded somewhat heated.

"Mate, come on. I know it's a shit situation, but if we don't tell her, she'll never know," Ethan said.

"Talk about stating the bloody obvious," Jeremy replied flatly.

Ethan sighed. "You know what I mean. If she never knows, how will *we* know if she feels the same? If things can continue?"

"She could end up working hundreds of miles away. I can easily afford for us—and her—to travel to see each other, but it's not the same as seeing her every day, spending quality time with her, is it? Even if she does feel that way, how could we possibly make it work? She might not want a long-distance relationship. Or any relationship, for that matter."

Alice didn't hear Ethan's response. She was too busy gaping. They were talking about her! Specifically, the possibility of the three of them having a long-distance relationship once she'd left the manor. And they didn't just mean sex. Not simply friends with benefits, but a proper relationship.

It sounded as though Jeremy and Ethan had just as many what-ifs going through their minds as she did hers. But that wasn't the main part of the conversation her brain had latched on to. No, the element now bouncing around in the front of her mind was that, although neither of the men had spoken the actual words, they clearly felt the same way about her as she did about them. The startling realisation made her nauseous. Then angry. Her cheeks flushed. Why the fuck hadn't they told her?

If she thought about it, though, they had. Not in so many words, but in their actions. For the past eight and a bit months they'd put her through some pretty hair-raising tasks, but not once had they actually been horrible to her. Quite the opposite, in fact. They'd been caring, considerate, and when it came to her birthday, extravagant. Yes, they were nice guys, but why would they have gone to all that trouble if she was just a friend with benefits? There had to be more to it than that. Yet they hadn't said the words out loud. And if Jeremy got his way, she'd leave Davenport Manor for good without them ever saying them. If she hadn't been listening to their conversation, she'd never, ever know. She'd go through life thinking her feelings were one-sided. That she was just a bit of fun.

What a bastard! Her anger turned to fury, rushed through her body and took over her rational mind. She crashed through the office door so forcibly that it whacked into the side of the filing cabinet next to it—but she didn't care. She was livid. So livid it was a struggle to speak. Only when she saw the surprised looks on their faces was she spurred into speech.

"What the fuck?" she yelled. So it wasn't the most articulate or intelligent start to her rant, but it *was* a start. And she had no intention of stopping. "Oh, don't look so surprised. I heard what you were saying. About me. About long-distance relationships. Were you *ever* going to tell me?" She aimed the last part at Jeremy—as she knew Ethan was all for it.

Jeremy stepped out from behind his desk, hands held up in surrender. "Hey, Alice, calm down."

Her nostrils flared. "Calm down? So you think I'm wrong to be upset, do you? Upset that the two of you have been keeping this from me for God knows how long?"

Ethan moved to stand next to his friend, and put a hand on his shoulder. They exchanged a look, and Jeremy gave a small nod. With that, Ethan walked over and took Alice's hands. "Look, Alice. If you're angrier at Jeremy than you are at me, you obviously heard the part about me wanting to tell you. I've always wanted to tell you—ever since we started feeling this way. But," he held her hands tighter, "to be fair, you've been keeping your own feelings quiet too, haven't you?"

Alice opened her mouth, but nothing came out. She didn't know what to say. He was right, of course. She'd been so pissed off to discover that they loved her like she loved them, that she'd forgotten what a hypocrite she was being. She could have told them first, and she hadn't. But she had a good reason. "Y-yes," she finally said. "But to be fair, I was just protecting myself. I thought you two would laugh me into the middle of next week if I told you how I felt. I mean, come on—look at me. And then look at the pair of you. There's no comparison, is there?" Suddenly overwhelmed by emotion, she bowed her head so they couldn't see her face when the inevitable tears began to fall.

Jeremy stepped forward so fast Alice could have sworn he flew. He pulled her hands from Ethan's and yanked her to stand in front of him, then put a finger beneath her chin and lifted her head. "Alice!" He eyes blazed, and she was suddenly very glad Ethan was there, because Jeremy was scaring her. "What the fuck are you talking about? There's no comparison? Between us and you?" He sighed heavily and wiped away the tears that streamed down Alice's face. "God, I don't know who battered your self-esteem so badly, but I'd like to have words with them. Seriously, believe me. Believe *us*. No matter what you think about yourself—and we'll do everything in our power to help you change that—there is absolutely nothing wrong with you. Nothing. You're beautiful, intelligent, funny, fun to be around. And sexy. God, are you sexy. Ah-ah," he held up a finger, "no arguments. That's *our* opinion, and we're entitled to it, okay?"

He didn't look scary any more, thankfully. But he didn't look happy, either, so she nodded. Then she nodded harder as the meaning of his words truly sunk in. It didn't matter whether she thought she was good enough for them or not—they wanted her anyway. She glanced over to see Ethan bobbing his head earnestly—apparently agreeing with every word Jeremy had just said.

"Just to clarify, Alice. To be absolutely sure we're on the same page… we love you," Ethan said.

As heat burned her cheeks, she swiped the remaining tears from her face and opened her mouth before she lost her nerve. "I love you too. Both of you. At first I didn't understand *how* I could love both of you. Then I came to terms with it—but I was still too scared to tell you. And the closer to me leaving it got, the harder it became. I think… I was going to leave without telling you."

Jeremy squeezed her hands and fixed her with a meaningful stare. "See? You're just as bad as us. Well, me, anyway. Ethan's a braver man than me. He was trying to make me understand that distance didn't matter—that we'd make it work, somehow. If you felt the same, of course." He took a shaky breath. "Well, I guess we have that question answered, at least. But there are many more we'll have to figure out to be together. We know you won't give up your career to stay here, and we wouldn't dream of asking you to. Have you got another job lined up yet? I haven't had any requests for references."

"You're right—I've worked my arse off to get here, and I'm not going to stop now. Plus, can you actually see me as the housewife type? I'd be bored stiff. Anyway, I have applications out there, but no interviews yet. It seems people don't leave these kinds of jobs once they have them. I may have to wait for someone to retire, or die. You'll have to start pulling some strings with those contacts of yours, Jeremy, otherwise I'm going to end up destitute."

The three of them laughed. Seconds later, Alice was immersed in the delicious scent of male as Jeremy and Ethan enveloped her in a hug. She sighed happily, almost delirious in the knowledge that they loved her too. Finally, they were all on the same page. But they had a lot to work out. She'd applied for positions at two properties within an hour's drive of Davenport Manor, but they couldn't pin all their hopes on her getting one of those roles. They had to prepare for the worst.

The phone on Jeremy's desk rang, startling them. Jeremy pressed a kiss to Alice's hair before disentangling himself from their embrace. He cleared his throat, then reached over and picked up the handset. "Jeremy Davenport speaking. How may I help you?"

Alice stifled a giggle. It was amazing how he'd gone from being so… well, human, to a consummate professional almost in the blink of an eye. She looked at Ethan, who also sported an amused expression. He ruffled her hair and let her go, and they waited for Jeremy to finish his phone call so they could continue their conversation. Alice shuffled her feet impatiently—she wished the caller would bugger off so the three of them could get things sorted. It had been difficult enough to get to this stage; it was going to take lots more effort to work out what the hell happened next.

Alice didn't even pretend not to listen to Jeremy's end of the telephone call. Though he wasn't saying very much. He nodded a great deal, and muttered lots of "okay"s and "I understand"s—but whatever the caller was telling him was obviously pretty shocking, as his face had lost all its colour. His eyes grew wider and wider, until Alice began to worry they'd pop right out of his head.

Finally, there came a break where Jeremy could get a word in. "It's fine, honestly, Erin. Of course, we'll miss you desperately, but there are certainly no hard feelings from my perspective. Just don't be a stranger, okay? I'll make a start on the paperwork as soon as I get a moment."

Alice's heart pounded. She tried hard not to jump to conclusions, but it was impossible. It sounded like Erin had exercised her right to extend her maternity leave to the maximum twelve months. Which meant… Alice had another three months at Davenport Manor!

Jeremy concluded his phone call, his hand trembling as he lowered the handset back into its cradle. God, if she hadn't heard his half of the conversation, she'd have thought someone had died. Why was he so shocked? It wasn't as if he was going to be left without a property manager for three months. He had a fully-trained back up right there in the room.

Jeremy leant against the edge of his desk and rubbed his hands over his face, then raked his fingers through his hair. Alice's own fingers ached to smooth the mussed locks back into place.

The silence was deafening. She glanced across at Ethan, who

stared expectantly at his friend. She knew he'd have realised what was going on—he was a bright guy, and if she'd worked it out, he would have too.

Eventually, Jeremy spoke. It was clearly an effort for him to get the words out. "That was Erin. She's, uh… she's not coming back."

Ethan's face brightened. "What, she's going for the full twelve months' leave? That's great! It means we get to keep Alice for longer." He grabbed Alice and swung her round, laughing and pressing kisses to her face and hair.

"N-no," Jeremy replied. He cleared his throat. "I mean *no,* she's not staying away another three months. She's not coming back at all. She's decided she wants to be a stay-at-home mum. There will be some paperwork to do before it's official, but it seems we're in the market for a new property manager."

Not for the first time that day, Alice gaped. *Not just three extra months—possibly forever.* "God, I can't believe it. I thought she loved her job."

"Well," Jeremy replied, a smile tugging at his lips, "it seems she loves motherhood more. And although I shall miss her, I respect her decision." He turned to Ethan. "Since we're on the lookout for a replacement, do you know anyone who might be suitable for the role?"

Ethan rubbed his chin thoughtfully. "There were a couple of hopefuls when we interviewed for the maternity cover. Perhaps we could give them a call and find out if they're interested."

Despite knowing perfectly well that they were winding her

up, Alice exploded. “Hey! You’ll do no such fucking thing. I’m right here. And now I know you need a permanent property manager, you’re never getting rid of me.”

Jeremy and Ethan laughed at her outburst.

“We’re just teasing you, Alice. Are you mad? Did you really think we’d send you away now? Knowing how we feel about you, and with Erin not coming back?” Jeremy said, flashing her a smile. “You’re not going anywhere, missy. It seems we have a lot to sort out. Both professionally and personally.”

“P-personally?” She gulped. She knew work-wise he meant dull paperwork and stuff, but personally? What did he want to change in their private life? Weren’t things good as they were?

“Yes, Alice, personally. What are your thoughts on doing some renovation?”

She frowned. What the hell did any kind of work on the house have to do with her? Unless he wanted her to help him sort out the planning permission. But that made no sense…

“Oh for God’s sake, Alice! What do you think I’m on about? I mean knocking our three bedrooms into one! Walk-in wardrobes, a bigger en suite and, most importantly, a bigger bed.” He wiggled his eyebrows saucily. “We might even use it to sleep, sometimes.”

Alice walked over to give him a playful swipe. She never got the chance. He grabbed her wrist and pulled her up against him. With his free hand he gripped her chin and captured her lips in a smouldering kiss that turned her pussy molten within seconds. She succumbed, returning his kiss for a minute or so before pulling away and murmuring, “That sounds like a perfect plan to me. In fact, I can't think of anything better."

"I'm glad to hear it," Jeremy said. "We've waited for you for a very long time, and we hated the thought of having to let you go. Now we don't have to, I'm a very, very happy man."

"That makes two of us," Ethan said from close behind her. She turned in Jeremy's arms to face her other lover, then reached up and slipped her arms around his neck. He bent and kissed her, his skilful lips and tongue sending her pussy into a complete meltdown.

Sandwiched between the two sweetest, kindest, most attractive men she'd ever met, Alice sent her heartfelt thanks to whatever deity might be listening. She was the luckiest girl in the damn world.

"Hey, Alice," Jeremy murmured into her ear.

She didn't pull away from Ethan. Instead she made a "mmm?" sound, knowing Jeremy would hear it.

"I love you."

That stopped her in her tracks. She broke their kiss and looked over her shoulder at Jeremy. Grinning, she said, "I love you too." Then she turned back to Ethan.

"And I love you."

Ethan's dimples appeared, more pronounced than ever. "I love you too."

"Wow." Jeremy trailed his hands up and down the fabric that covered Alice's stomach. "That wasn't so hard, was it? Why on earth didn't we say it before?"

Ethan landed a playful punch on his friend's arm. "For fuck's sake, mate, that's what I've been telling you! It all worked out perfectly, and then good old Erin went and put the cherry on top of our perfect threesome cake, didn't she?"

"She sure did," Alice said. "And you know what? I couldn't be happier. I am deliriously, sickeningly happy." She sighed and eased herself out of their grasp. "And now I have to go and work through the emails in my inbox. I can't just leave them for Erin now, can I?"

"You'll do no such thing," Jeremy said, pulling her back onto him and pressing his erection into her arse crack. "We've just had something seriously important happen, and I think we should mark the occasion."

"I second that motion," Ethan agreed, leaning in for another kiss.

Alice closed her eyes and let the moment take her. They were right: something major *had* just happened. Her emails could wait—she had forever to take care of them.

Forever. The thought both thrilled and terrified her. She'd never thought about forever with a man before, much less two of them. And with the perfect job and a beautiful home thrown in, too. She was indeed blessed.

She abandoned all thought and reason as Ethan's lips met hers, and just concentrated on the physical sensations. And they were plentiful. When his tongue sought hers, she poured every iota of passion she had into kissing him back.

Jeremy nibbled the side of her neck, multiplying her arousal, and she moaned loudly.

Ethan pulled away. "Fuck, Alice. You drive me crazy." He

grabbed her wrist and pressed her hand to his crotch.

She couldn't help the blush that came to her cheeks at his words. Ignoring it, she cupped and squeezed his growing bulge. She shoved her arse back and rolled her hips, effectively stimulating two delicious and eager pricks at the same time.

Jeremy growled and reached up to cup her ample breasts. "You sexy little wench. It's hardly surprising we're under your spell, is it?" He pinched her nipples almost brutally, and she squealed and writhed beneath his touch. Then she clamped a hand to her mouth, suddenly remembering the door was open, and that anyone could hear them.

"We'd better shut the door," she said, her voice muffled beneath her fingers. "Someone might come up the corridor, and we won't hear them."

"What, like you did, you mean? All those months ago?" Jeremy asked.

She removed her hand from her mouth. "Yes," she whispered, feeling a lurch in her chest at the thought of him with another woman. It was ridiculous, because he was with her now, but it still wasn't a pleasant thought. She found her voice. "But I didn't do it on purpose. I got so far and I could hear you and *her* in here, and I just froze. Part of me wanted to run away, but then you would have thought I was late for our meeting, and I was desperate to make a good impression. The other part of me couldn't interrupt—it would have been horribly embarrassing for everyone. Then Ethan caught me, and well, you know the rest."

"I *do* know the rest." He smirked. "But actually, *you* don't know the whole story. In fact, I have a little confession to make."

Alice raised her eyebrows. What the hell could he possibly have to confess? "Go on."

"Well. How can I put this?" He paused for a couple of seconds. "I guess *simply* is the best way. So just hear me out, okay?"

She nodded eagerly, desperate to hear what he had to say.

"Ever since I met you in that first interview, I was attracted to you. I thought you were sexy, sweet, and very intelligent, if not a little shy. You were also perfect for the job. But I had to continue with the other scheduled interviews, knowing all along that you were the one. In the meantime, I'd spoken to Ethan about you—about your wit, your personality, and your delectable figure. He was very eager to meet you.

"Over the few days following your interview, I couldn't stop thinking about you, and the more I thought about you, the more I thought you'd be perfect."

"Perfect for what?" she interrupted.

"Isn't it obvious? To help Ethan and I complete all the tasks on my list. Ethan hadn't met you by that point, of course, but we have very similar taste in women, so he trusted my judgment. Don't ask me how, but I suspected you had a latent desire to experiment sexually, but that you would need a good shove to act on it. And so, when you started working here, I tried to figure out a way of finding out if I was right. Preferably without being sued for sexual harassment."

He and Ethan grinned at each other, then Jeremy spoke again. "It was Ethan who had the idea to set you up. Test you. I'd call you to my office, and there'd be some dubious sounds coming from inside. If you turned tail and ran, then I'd definitely get sued for sexual harassment—and probably more—if I presented you with the list. But if you stayed, listened to what was happening inside my office, then there was a good chance you'd be up for it. The blackmail thing was just another prod in the right direction. I'd never have ruined your career if you'd said no—but the way you acted when you thought you had no choice…" His eyes gleamed. "It was electric, Alice. God, watching your face as you went from disbelief, to acceptance, to determination was just incredible. All along, that undercurrent of desire was apparent, which reassured Ethan and I that we were doing the right thing. That although we were coercing you, we weren't truly forcing you."

Alice gulped in an attempt to dampen her dry mouth. "So, who was she, then?"

Jeremy frowned. "Who was who?"

"The woman in your office."

"Oh!" He laughed. "I see. Alice, there wasn't a woman in my office. I was in there by myself, playing a clip from a porno film on my laptop with the sound turned up."

A whoosh of breath escaped Alice's mouth. *What the hell?* She hadn't expected that. Any of it. Jeremy being attracted to her from the very start; thinking she'd be perfect for the tasks; blackmailing her…

And to think if she'd walked away from that office door, things could have been very different.

She nodded slowly as all the pieces slid into place. "Well, it was a bloody elaborate scheme, but I'm very happy the two of you cooked it up." She gestured between them. "Look at us now."

"Yes," Ethan said, "look at us now indeed. So, since everything's out in the open, shall we continue where we left off before Jeremy's confession?"

Alice licked her lips and grinned wickedly. "I can't think of anything I'd like more." Her face fell. "Though we might have to wait until later. What about the staff and volunteers? What if they need us?"

"Fuck 'em," Ethan said, moving across the room and locking the door. "Fuck the lot of 'em. They can cope without us for a little while. We've got some celebrating to do."

When he returned, Jeremy clapped him on the shoulder. "Couldn't have put it better myself, old chap. Let's celebrate Alice and her new *permanent* job. Or should I say *jobs*? Property manager, sex goddess, and one third of a seriously sexy three-way."

Alice's laughter filled the room. That was until Jeremy and Ethan did a superb job of silencing her—for a while, at least.

***

A note from the author: Thank you so much for reading *Stately Pleasures*. If you enjoyed it, please do tell your friends, family, colleagues, book clubs, and so on. Also, posting a short review on the retailer site you bought the book from would be incredibly helpful and very much appreciated. There are lots of books out there, which makes word of mouth an author's best friend, and also allows us to keep doing what we love doing—writing.

About the Author

Lucy Felthouse is the award-winning author of erotic romance novels *Stately Pleasures* (named in the top 5 of Cliterati.co.uk's 100 Modern Erotic Classics That You've Never Heard Of, and an Amazon bestseller), *Eyes Wide Open* (winner of the Love Romances Café's Best Ménage Book 2015 award, and an Amazon bestseller), *The Persecution of the Wolves, Hiding in Plain Sight* and *The Heiress's Harem* series. Including novels, short stories and novellas, she has over 170 publications to her name. Find out more about her writing at **http://lucyfelthouse.co.uk**, or on **Twitter** or **Facebook**. Join her **Facebook group** (**http://www.facebook.com/groups/lucyfelthousereadergroup**) for exclusive cover reveals, sneak peeks and more! Subscribe to her newsletter here: **http://www.subscribepage.com/lfnewsletter**

If You Enjoyed Stately Pleasures

If you enjoyed this sexy story with BDSM and multiple partners, you may enjoy the books I've listed below. My full backlist is on my website **(http://lucyfelthouse.co.uk)**.

Eyes Wide Open

A chance meeting opens Fiona's eyes to some very sexy possibilities.

Recent graduate Fiona Gillespie is stuck working in a grimy pub in London's East End, and living in a horrid flat. It's only while she figures out what she wants to do career-wise, but that's easier said than done.

When she sees an advertisement for a job at a plush Mayfair hotel, she jumps at the chance. Determination and a spot of luck land Fiona her dream role—and it comes with accommodation included.

Her job and living situation sorted, things are on the up. Unfortunately, her personal life is lacklustre. It doesn't bother her, though—not until she meets businessmen James and Logan, and her head is well and truly turned.

When a misunderstanding leads Fiona to James and Logan's sumptuous top-floor hotel suite, she has no idea what she's about to uncover. Her imagination runs wild, but not wild enough to get to the truth—James and Logan are a couple, and they're into some seriously intriguing activities.

Fascinated, she launches herself into a whole new world with the two men. But is this just physical, or is their arrangement set to become something more?

More information and buy links: **https://lucyfelthouse.co.uk/published-works/eyes-wide-open/**

Mia's Men (The Heiress's Harem Book One)

Mia's world has fallen apart. Then, just when she thinks it can't possibly get any worse, it does.

Mia Harrington's father just lost his brave battle with cancer. Naturally, she's devastated. With her mother long-since dead, and no siblings, Mia has a great deal of responsibility to shoulder. She's also the sole beneficiary of her father's estate. Or so she thinks.

Unbeknownst to Mia, her father made a change to his will. She can still inherit, but only if she marries a suitable man within twelve months. If she doesn't, her vile cousin will get everything. Determined not to lose her beloved childhood home, she resolves to find someone that fits the bill. What she isn't expecting, however, is for that someone to be into sharing women with his best friend. In the meantime, Mia's friendship with the estate gardener has blossomed into so much more.

She can't possibly plan to marry one man, while also being involved with two others …or can she?

More information and buy links (books two and three are also available): **https://lucyfelthouse.co.uk/published-works/mias-men/**

Made in the USA
Middletown, DE
20 July 2021